SIREN BURN

THE SIREN SERIES BOOK TWO

THE SIREN SERIES
BOOK 2

HANNAH WEST

Tethered Press

INFORMATION FOR READERS

This title was previously published in 2016. It has undergone an extensive rewrite and contains new content but the story is the same.

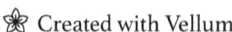 Created with Vellum

For Katie and the woodland cottage we've been building.

ACKNOWLEDGMENTS

There are so many amazing people I need to thank for supporting me in the rewrite of this book. First, I'd like to thank my manager — Oh wait, that's my speech for the Oscars, hang on...

Okay, here we go. I'd like to thank my husband Mark and Son Ethan, for their unwavering support. Neil J Hart for the stunning cover designs. Anne Loshuk for all the work you've put into my books over the years. Katie Longdon for reading and supporting me with all of my stories. Shaun Arrowsmith for consistently championing my books. Luke Fisher for the fantasy book recommendations and for beta reading for me, and Beth Torrington for taking the time to be an amazing beta reader.

And to my other betas, who know who they are but hate being in acknowledgments.

And to all of my readers for supporting my journey and helping make my modest dreams a reality.

1

Creatures shine like freckles along the seabed; little stars amid sand and rock. Not that I truly remember stars after so many years. The palace rises into view: pillars of light from the fathomless deep. The shine is brighter than before I left, meaning Father has returned early. I mentally groan at the argument my absence will cause and speed up.

I reach the transparent dome separating the palace grounds from the rest of the ocean and slip through the barrier, taking a breath of air as my skin and hair dry. I dress in the clothes I stashed earlier and run towards the palace.

'There you are,' Milos says meeting me at the top of the marble steps.

The armour he's wearing suggests he's just returned from the surface and I push my envy away at the simple freedoms he takes for granted. I've only been to the surface twice in my whole life and I'll never be allowed to compete in the Guardian Isle Games.

'Did you win?' I ask.

His smile fades. 'Nobody won this year, the Games were...interrupted.'

'Interrupted?'

'Your father will know you've been outside the dome, Dante,' he says avoiding my question. 'Even *I* can smell the ocean on you.'

I huff, 'What's the weather like up top?'

'Stormy.'

The weather is affected by my father's temperament. If the weather is bad, Father's mood is still foul. That, or Zeus is angry and that too will lead to Father's anger. Either way, I lose.

'Do you know why he's so angry?'

'If he won't tell his son what's going on, he's hardly going to tell me,' Milos says. 'I'm a distant, distant, distant relative through marriage, Dante. Your father tolerates me at best.'

'He *tolerates* everyone lately,' I say.

Milos grimaces. 'He sent me to find you.'

I take a longing look at the ocean beyond the dome and sigh, 'Let's get this over with then.'

Tremors shake the marble as we approach my father's chambers. I wince at the sound of objects crashing within. An attendant hurries out, flowing garments rustling as she sprints past us.

The doors blast open when I reach for the handle, Father's roar stilling my feet, 'Where have you been?'

Milo bows his blond head and escapes back down the hallway.

'*Coward*,' I hiss into his mind. He mentally snickers in response, before disappearing around the corner. 'Swimming,' I say aloud.

Father's nostrils flare as he inhales the smell of salt on my skin then snarls, 'Outside of the dome.'

'I didn't go to the surface.'

He hurls his trident across the room, spearing the marble with the glowing tines. 'You're hereby forbidden from leaving the dome, Dante.'

I resist the urge to roll my eyes, since I'm already forbidden to leave the dome. We both know I still do it. Like my father, I'm an aqueous creature. It would be cruel to enforce such a thing and he knows it.

He flings himself into an ornate armchair, too small for his muscular frame and rubs his temples, before reaching for a folded parchment. Gold light glitters from the broken Apollyon seal along the edge, something fluttering from between the pages as he unfolds the missive. I meet his green gaze, curious as to what the sun god wants.

He retrieves the object that fell and holds the long, golden feather up for me to see. My breath hitches because I've seen feathers like it before, only black instead of gold.

'It belongs to a god-sired Siren,' he says confirming my suspicion.

'There's another?'

'Yes.'

I lick my bottom lip before asking, 'Is he yours?'

'You're the only Siren I've sired, Dante.'

I glance at the missive with the Apollyon seal. 'Apollo's then?' At Father's nod I ask, 'Is he free from Anthemusa, like me?'

'He is.'

'When can I meet him?'

'Olympus knows the other Halfling inherited Siren abilities on their seventeenth birthday and they've been hunted for it since. I won't risk them discovering you, Dante.'

'This is why you've been so angry,' I say feeling betrayed. 'You've known for a while and haven't told me.'

'For your safety.'

'But this boy and I are the same,' I say plucking the feather from his fingers. Siren energy, prickles my fingers on contact and my insides light with ice. 'He has wings like me,' I say staring at the feather. 'Does he have Siren song like me too? Can he—'

'Apollo's child is his concern, not yours or mine,' Father says.

'But if I could just meet him—'

'No.'

'Father!'

'A god has freed two Sirens to hunt the Halfling, Dante. I won't risk them learning of your existence too.'

'I'll be careful,' I say, desperate. 'Nobody will discover what I am.'

Father's eyes glow neon with anger. 'You are confined to the palace grounds. If you want to swim, use one of the many pools within the dome.'

'But—'

'If I catch you outside the dome, I'll confine you to your rooms.'

The ground trembles against my anger as I match his glare. He glares back and I know he won't yield. The acid of my song, coats my throat and each inhale becomes torture. Darkness hazes my vision and I know it's my cue to leave.

I lock myself in my suite of rooms and take the golden feather from my pocket. Pain slices my shoulders as my wings unfurl, showering jet feathers across the floor. I hold one against the golden feather for comparison and find mine much longer, meaning Apollo's son must be smaller than me.

I try to picture him: seventeen with golden hair the same shade as his wings. His eyes might be black like the Sirens on Anthemusa or maybe, like me, they're the same shade as his father's. Just the thought fills me with desperation to meet him.

I place the feather on my nightstand before dropping into the sunken pool in the centre of my bedroom. I wait for my wings to dissolve then climb out and tear off the remains of my ruined shirt. I pull on fresh clothing, tuck the feather into my pocket then leave to see my mother.

I stand in the little room and stare at my mother's beautiful face. Her expression is serene and inviting, making it difficult to believe she was the monster everyone claims she was. I touch her cheek, cold and unyielding beneath my fingers; forever set in stone by the gorgon's gaze. It seems a cruel way of keeping my existence secret and I spent hours as a child in this room, wondering what she was like when alive.

'You still come here,' Father says from the doorway.

'So do you, it seems.'

'I loved her.'

'I could've loved her too, if you'd let her live long enough for me to know her.'

'She would've killed you,' he says. 'I've told you many times, they lack the capacity to love back, Dante.'

I've lost count of how many times he's warned me of how vicious Sirens are. I was raised with stories of how ruthless my mother had been: of how she'd have killed me the moment I was born, had she been given the chance.

'Are you talking about Sirens, or women in general?' I scoff.

'Any female that discovers what you are, will fear you, Dante.' He sighs, 'I know you think me unfeeling but I'm trying to save you pain.'

He believes what he's saying but I've spent my life in a luxurious prison, cut off from the world and its wonders. All because my mother was a monster. Father sired me with her though, so surely there was at least a sliver of good in her.

'Maybe I should just go to Anthemusa,' I say. 'At least there, I'll be surrounded by beautiful females for the rest of my pathetic existence.' I'd be exchanging one prison for another but at least my misery would have company. The beings around me wouldn't fear me for simply being what I am.

'A Siren's beauty is skin deep, Dante. Inside they are all monsters; something I found out the hard way.'

I wonder if he realises, he just called me a monster? It isn't the first time and it won't be the last. I'm sure he thinks I'm immune to derogatory comments about Sirens by now and I know he doesn't include me when he says such things, but it still needles.

I turn and eye the blue-green silk of his formal tunic. 'You're leaving for Olympus again?'

'I'm leading the ocean-bound search for the escaped Sirens,' he says then gives me a pointed look. 'I've told Milos to keep you company.'

'To babysit me, you mean.'

He rests his hands on my shoulders. 'I love you, Dante.'

I sigh, 'I love you.'

He smiles then disappears in a flare of blue light, and I retrieve the feather from my shirt. I stroke the silky gold between my thumb and forefinger. A ghost of Siren energy remains within, making me shiver as it sinks into my skin like an icy splinter. The need to find the other god-sired Siren, grows.

2

INARA

I sit in the corner of the dark attic, knees pulled to my chest as Aaron calls from somewhere below. I wallow in self-hatred, the look he'd given me forever seared into my brain. I bury my face in my hands, icing sugar from the cake I baked him making them smell sweet.

'Inara,' Logan calls, adding to a cacophony of voices now joining Aaron's, letting me know the others have woken from my song.

I'm such an idiot.

Aaron insisted it wasn't a big deal but the look he gave me... I cringe. He claims I'm different from the other Sirens but I'm not so sure. That side of me grows stronger each day, its dark ice crusting my insides. I want to tell him about it but he might think releasing me from Anthemusa was a mistake.

There's nobody else to confide in. Even if it weren't too dangerous for Helen to come here, I don't want her to worry. She's living her life and I won't risk her dropping it all for me. I can't confide in the others either because they were raised on stories of the monsters populating Anthemusa. Feeding that fear could make them see me as a threat and put a target on my back. Just thinking of them looking at me the way Aaron did earlier, makes me nauseous.

My wings push for freedom at the thought, making me wince. I've been stuck in this house for months, hiding from my mother and sister while my insides twist with ice and fire. It's a constant struggle between the two halves of my nature, each clawing for supremacy and I'm getting less and less sure of which side will win.

Today was supposed to be a good day, but my Siren side always ruins the bright spots in my existence. I've been shying away from civilisation because of it but I'd do anything to get lost in it right now.

The attic door opens, dust sparkling in the shaft of light it creates. 'Goddess?' Aaron asks then sniffs when I don't answer. 'I smell you in here.'

I sigh, 'Go away.'

He ignores me and steps inside. 'Where are you? I can't see a thing with the light off.'

'That's the idea, Aaron.'

He sighs, 'It was an accident, Inara. If I'd known the others were planning on surprising us, I never would've asked you to sing to me.'

'It was a stupid idea and I never should've let you talk me into it,' I agree.

He makes his way over and kneels in front of me. 'Everyone's fine, though.'

'Good. You can go now.'

'The others want to see you.'

'They're here to see you, not me.'

'Are you really going to sit up here all day, on my birthday?'

I suppress a growl and ask, 'Do you want any cream with that slice of guilt pie?'

'You know, this is the best birthday I've ever had,' he says.

'What happened on the other eighty-one: asteroid? Tsunami?'

'So you surprised a few people with your voice. They'll get over it.'

'You looked at me the way you did back then, Aaron—back when you hated me. Maybe they'll get over it, but I won't.'

He releases a heavy sigh, then drags me from the corner. I find myself in his lap, lips against mine, kissing the heck out of me. I grip his shoulders, toes curling against the delicious sting of his lightning. He's playing dirty and knows it.

He rests his forehead against mine, heavy breaths filling the sliver of space between us. 'What do you see when I look at you now?'

I sigh, 'The way I feel for you, staring back at me.' *But is it enough for you to look past what I'm becoming?*

I open my mouth to tell him but the words get lodged in my throat, the look he gave me still vivid in my mind's eye. The first days we met, play like a sick movie in my head and I want to cry. We're so close right now but he feels a million miles away.

'And what *do* you feel for me?' he asks.

'Can you really not tell?' I rasp, desperate for him to take my fear away. I need him to know what he means to me, so he'll know I'll never hurt him when I eventually find the courage to tell him the truth.

He sears me with another kiss in answer and I cling to him in the darkness of the attic.

Aaron coaxes me back downstairs and we find everyone in the kitchen, nobody showing the least concern over what happened. If only they knew the insidious thirst, seeing them frozen by my voice created. Saliva floods my mouth at the thought but I swallow it back, shoving the icy need deep.

'I'll cut the cake,' Talia says drawing her short sword.

I step protectively in front of my baked creation. 'I've witnessed that blade covered in blood, Talia. Besides, Aaron hasn't made a wish yet.'

Five pairs of eyes stare blankly at me, before Logan asks, 'What?'

I point to the cake. 'Aaron blows out the candles and makes a birthday wish.'

'That's ridiculous,' Logan scoffs.

'*You're* ridiculous,' I scoff back then look between the incredulous faces around me. They're from a land of mythical creatures and *this* surprises them? 'Where the heck is Helen when I need her to back me up on stuff like this?' I huff.

'Viewing another university with her parents,' Alexander answers.

Envy snakes through me at the reminder and my chest tightens with panic. She's living the life we mapped for ourselves but is leaving me behind. The dreams I made are being erased and there's nothing I can do to stop it. I'm stuck here, a monster in a cage, surrounded by warriors that might turn on me one day for what I am. Sometimes I wonder if they know it and that's why they're here, to protect everyone else from me.

'How does this work again?' Aaron asks.

I school my features but the worry line between his eyebrows doesn't disappear. He knows I'm struggling with the isolation of hiding but doesn't know how to fix it. I won't tell him what's wrong, other than the PTSD from everything that's happened since the Games last year. I've begged him for a phone, so I can at least scroll social media or get lost down a rabbit hole of vlogs but he says it's too dangerous. Anything that might lead to my location is vetoed in seconds and, honestly, I think I'm going insane.

This day is about Aaron though, and it's like I'm actively trying to spoil it. I force a smile and light the candles then pick up the cake.

'Make a wish then blow out the candles,' I explain. 'But don't tell anyone what you wish for or it won't come true.'

I shoot Logan a withering glare when he snorts but Aaron grins and blows out the candles. He looks so pleased with himself, that I smile for real. He finds joy in things I'd started to take for granted and experiencing them with him is like experiencing them for the first time.

'Now we cut it?' Talia asks, brandishing a knife from the kitchen drawer.

I surrender the cake and she tells me my slice will be biggest, since I'm so thin now. My smile falters as she turns away because I wish everyone would get off my back about the weight I've lost. It's the stress of worrying about Callista and Mila finding us, combined with being stuck in this house with secrets I'm afraid to share. The itch to escape cramps my shoulders all over again and I wince. I haven't released my wings since the day I woke up here and it's getting more and more painful to hold them back.

Adonia hands Aaron a gift and an approving smile lights his face, as he grips the hilt of the sword to test its weight.

'It has good balance,' he says.

'It's made from adamant, like the sickle used to castrate Cronus,' she answers.

His eyebrows reach for his hairline. 'Where'd you get it?'

Her smile turns coy, blue eyes glowing under her dark fringe. 'Talia and I went to great lengths to retrieve it, so don't lose it,' she says cryptically.

Aaron grins at the blade with appreciation. 'How would I lose an unbreakable blade?'

'You could die,' Logan says.

Aaron gives him a narrow-eyed stare. 'Thanks.'

'You asked.'

Alexander passes over another gift. 'Helen and I coordinated.'

Aaron accepts the scabbard from Alexander and sheaths his new weapon. He slings the leather harness over his shoulders and secures the swords to his back.

'Want to test it out?' Logan asks, challenge glinting in his dark gaze. 'If you best me, I'll surrender the gift you asked for.'

Aaron walks outside in answer and Alexander, Adonia and Talia follow them into the valley. I stay back, since watching them fight triggers the wintry instincts I'm struggling to hide. I won't let the dark side of my nature ruin Aaron's birthday more than it already has.

As if listening, my Siren voice flares, cold and searing up my throat. Just thinking about it is enticing enough to lure it out and I hiss at the acid burn of forcing it back. The sound reverberates around the kitchen and I run for the stairs before anyone can come back inside. I hate that I'm thirsting for the simple freedom I experienced earlier today. It's an itch I'm not allowed to scratch because the more I give in to my dark desires, the bigger a hold they have over me.

I sit on my bed to breathe through the pain of fighting with my voice. It's like trying to swallow a ball of glass that's been dipped in vinegar. I concentrate on Aaron's scent, from his sneaking in to hold me at night. Being tangled with him keeps the nightmares at bay but he only does it when the others aren't here. It's as much a taboo in his culture as the one I grew up in and that startled me at first. I didn't expect a society where everybody is so highly weaponised, to have so many...rules.

I get the feeling he follows the rules more for me than for himself, though and I get it. If my human parents were alive, he wouldn't be allowed in my room with me. I wouldn't get to experience his electric kisses after waking from a nightmare, or the heat of his skin on mine. His embrace is everything when I wake panting in fear, skin slick with sweat. When I kiss him, he never pushes for more, despite us both wanting it. He doesn't push and I don't try to take it beyond what we have. How can I, when I'm hiding the growing ice in my middle?

I'm terrified of losing Aaron, since I think he's the only reason I'm fighting that side of my nature. But how can I willingly tie myself to someone, when I know I'm becoming a monster? I'm petrified of turning into my mother but I'm scared of losing Aaron more. It's selfish to keep him but I can't live without him either.

I slide a hand under my pillow and pull out the gift I got him. He's going to be upset when he realises I used my lyre to fetch it, since he made me promise I wouldn't use it without him. But I didn't want to be the only one not giving him a gift on his birthday. He claims the cake I made was my gift but I hated the fact everyone else was allowed to get him something special and I wasn't.

Aaron knocks on the doorframe. 'Can I come in?'

I jolt to my feet and spin to face him, hiding his gift behind my back. He's in the doorway, eyes bright from fighting. A crimson line is already healing along his left cheekbone, skin shining with sweat. It makes his scent more potent and my mouth waters, the memory of tasting him on the Flowery Isle that day suddenly stark in my mind.

Frigid, darkness rises through me but I shove it down and croak, 'Aaron.'

He steps into the room, smile fading. 'What's wrong?'

I aim for casual. 'I, er... Nothing.'

He smirks at my crappy lying. 'What are you hiding? Is it for me?'

I back against the wall when he stalks in my direction, suddenly realising what a bad idea it is to gift him what I've chosen. He grabs me before I can make a run for it, caging me against the wall. I lock my fingers around his gift as he slides his hands down my arms. Goosebumps prickle over my skin, desire flaring bright inside me.

'It won't work,' I breathe.

He chuckles, gripping my waist. 'I don't know what you mean.'

He presses his lips to mine, and warm, delicious electricity stings through me. My knees buckle at the sensation and he pulls me closer. His chest presses to mine and I whimper at the sensation of his heart pounding. His kiss turns hungry, like he's trying to devour me whole. I want to devour him too, force him to be a part of me forever.

I sink into his hold, let his taste infuse my senses. It's the closest I can get to that day on the Flowery Isle, when I tasted his blood and was drenched in everything Aaron. I groan at the memory and thread my fingers through his hair, tugging him closer. My skin grows hot, desire spiking through me. Something flexes outward from the perpetual inferno in my centre and I open my eyes in dazed confusion.

Aaron's eyes snap open when I gasp and he goes rigid, blue gaze beautiful against the golden light shining around us. I glow like the sun when I'm healing but this feels different. There isn't any pain, just aching and a delicious yearning for more of Aaron. His taste, his touch... The addictive shiver of his warm electricity.

He shoves away and stares at me with suspicion. He thinks I'm trying to heal him and hates the pain and weakness it causes me.

'I'm not doing this; not on purpose,' I say.

He touches his injured cheek then frowns at the smear of blood on his fingertips, knowing that if I were healing him, his wound would already be gone.

'Then what is it?' he demands, stepping up to run his hands over me. 'Are you injured...hurting?'

'I think you're the reason for this, Aaron.'

He snaps his hands back like I've stung him. 'What?'

'Not in a bad way! I think it happened because you... I mean...' I look at the floor, face flaming.

He puts a finger under my chin and tips my gaze back to his. 'Talk to me.'

I grimace. 'It really isn't that important—'

He looks crestfallen. 'Please?'

Gah, why is this so difficult? I don't want him to be upset that I can't talk to him like this. I'm hiding the monstrous side of myself but I *should* be able to talk to Aaron about stuff like this, right? I wish Helen were here right now. She'd know what to say to make me less of a coward.

I blow out a breath and say, 'It's because... I think it's because I... want you.'

'You...*want* me?'

He stares at me blankly and I huff, 'A lot, Aaron. I want you a lot and this light is because of that fact.'

My words sink through his thick skull and a triumphant smile lights his face. I groan and look away, face feeling hotter than the sun.

He cups my jaw. 'Don't be embarrassed, love. Gods, if I shined each time I felt that way about you, I'd look like a walking torchlight.'

I meet his gaze. 'Really?'

'Yes!'

I give a shy smile then look down at my skin. 'I should stay out of sight though until it wears off. I don't want to explain this to anyone else.'

He shuts the door. 'Fine by me.'

'You can't stay in here when everyone came to see you, Aaron.'

'I don't want to spend my birthday without you,' he scoffs and pulls me over to the bed. 'Everyone will understand.'

'It looks like it's fading anyway,' I say as I sit next to him.

He grins. 'Damn.'

I wonder how just one word from him can make my insides ignite. I bite my lip and the light shines a little brighter.

He tilts his head. 'Are you going to give me the gift you're hiding now, or will I have to wrestle it from you?'

I look at the parcel in my hand then sigh and hand it to him. He turns it in his hands then stops and rests it in his lap.

'I have something for you first,' he says.

'For me?'

He digs into his pocket. 'It's my gift from Logan.'

I frown. 'I don't understand.'

He hands me a small, leather box. 'Open it.'

I gasp at the gold pendant inside. It's in the shape of a butterfly, intricate wings spread wide and dainty. The body between is made from three green jewels.

'It's beautiful.'

'It was my mother's,' Aaron says. 'I begged Logan to gift it me because I want you to have it.'

'Aaron,' I breathe, overwhelmed.

'The gold wings remind me of yours and the emeralds are like your eyes. It's kind of perfect for you.'

Emeralds? 'I can't accept this.'

He takes it from me. 'It isn't like Logan or I can wear it and it's just been gathering dust since my mother passed.'

'But it's your birthday and you're gifting me priceless heirlooms,' I scoff.

He cups my jaw. 'Your acceptance of it will make me happy. What more could I want for my birthday, Inara?'

I sigh, 'Fine, you win.'

I turn and hold my hair up for him to fasten it around my neck. The butterfly rests above the dip of my collarbone, glistening green against the tan of my skin. All that sun on the Guardian Isle left me a nice shade of gold like my father and it hasn't faded. I release my hair and turn back to face Aaron.

He smiles. 'The emeralds match your eyes.'

'Thank you,' I say then point to the parcel in his lap. 'Your turn.'

I chew my lip as he tears through the paper then pulls the leather wristband free. He holds it for a long time, fingers running over the surface of the silver Saint Christopher embedded in a thick band of leather.

'It was Grandfather Thompson's,' I say quietly. 'He gave it to Daniel on his twenty-first birthday. Twenty-one is sort of a milestone for humans. This Saint Christopher has been in the family for generations and is supposed to carry the wearer of it to safety.'

His gaze meets mine. 'Where did you get this?'

I flinch at the prickle of his anger against my skin. 'I was only gone for ten minutes—'

'That's all it would take, Inara! Gods, how could you be so stupid?'

The light fades from my skin, my own anger flaring. 'If you wanted to keep me prisoner, you should've left me on Anthemusa, Aaron. I was gone such short a time you didn't even know I'd left.'

'You could've been attacked and I wouldn't have been there to protect you!'

'I just wanted to get you something special for your birthday.' I reach for the wristband. 'If you don't want it, give it back.'

He holds it from my reach. 'I didn't say I didn't want it.'

'Where are you going?' I demand when he gets up and nearly yanks the door from its hinges.

'You could've been attacked and I wouldn't have been there to protect you; wouldn't have even known where to look for you, Inara. I'd rather you hate me for keeping you safe than risk losing you again.'

'What the heck is that supposed to mean?'

He stalks away and shouts, 'I'm confiscating your lyre until I know you're safe.'

I shove from the bed to chase after him. 'You can't do that!' I sprint down to the kitchen but the lyre is gone from the worktop. 'Where's my key, Aaron?'

'You'll get it back when this is over,' he growls.

My voice rings with rage, freezing the others watching our argument but I'm too angry to care, 'When what's over? When my mother and sister find me? When they drag me back to where I belong? Maybe when the gods finally get what they want and end me!'

I want to hurt him, so he'll understand how much he's hurting me. He loves me and wants to keep me safe but locking me away isn't working. Aaron saved me from the Flowery Isle but trapped me in this house and he's the only thing keeping me sane. He doesn't understand that I can't afford to hate him.

He flinches and reaches for me, like he needs comfort from what I just said. 'I need to keep you safe, Inara.'

'Give me my lyre.'

His pupils dilate at the ringing of my voice but he holds firm. 'No.'

Icy rage floods my veins and clouds my vision with black mist. My throat throbs with the need to subdue him like the others and I teeter on an edge I've been battling to stay away from for months. I glance at the frozen faces of the others in the kitchen and self-loathing permeates the dark lust for control.

'This is your fault,' I hiss, tears streaking my face as I turn away.

I bolt back upstairs and slam my bedroom door, punching the wall instead of screaming the way I want to. Pain splinters through my hand, giving me an agony other than that of my Siren rage to focus on. Icy claws, rake my insides for release, as I fight through my emotions. I pant through it, each inhale laced with acid as hot tears spill down my face.

I retrieve the other item I stole from Aunt Gertrude's house from under my pillow. The photograph was taken three years ago on a family trip to the beach. Tears splash the happy image as my chest aches with homesickness. I miss my family and Aaron is the only thing that really takes that pain away. I hug the picture to my chest and curl up in a ball on my side, grief swallowing me whole.

I WAKE face-down on an unforgiving surface and push up to find myself sprawled on marble flooring. Fear prickles my spine as memories of Anthemusa bombard me. I remember closing my eyes on my bed and this is way too vivid to be just a dream, which means it's a visit. I stand up, trying not to panic and look around. I haven't visited Anthemusa this way since the night before I got trapped there but this place isn't anywhere I recognise.

I turn a slow circle, studying the stately room. It has the black-marble flooring of the Grecian buildings on Anthemusa but feels different. There's a sunken pool in the middle of the room, like the ones the Sirens liked to bathe in and I back away from the low-lit water.

My bare back meets a cold surface and I startle, spinning to face a set of glass doors, leading to a balcony. I frown at the realisation that my back is bare then glance down at the folds of blue-green silk hugging my body. The dress splays at the knee into a fishtail design and isn't what I wake in during my visits to the Flowery Isle.

I step through the ornate doors, floor-length dress whispering over the marble. I notice the lack of stars as I walk to the wall, skirting the balcony. I stare out at palatial gardens of pristine marble and glowing turquoise pools.

The gardens end at the curve of a translucent dome and my panic comes roaring back. This isn't Anthemusa but I have no idea where I am. I turn to the building I just exited and look up to the glowing façade of a towering structure: a palace, umbrellaed by a dome of darkness. It reminds me of the dome that lit up over Anthemusa, when Zeus sealed it with lightning the night I escaped.

I close my eyes and try for a while to wake up. When that fails, I head back to where I started in hopes it will help. I can get hurt during my visits, so need to lay low and maybe find somewhere to hide.

I freeze at the glass doors, when a light flicks on inside. A boy comes into view, tall with a crown of curly blond hair. He's carrying weapons and dressed in armour, and my body locks with fear.

'Your father will kill me, Dante,' he scoffs.

'I just want to go for a swim,' another male, presumably Dante, answers from view. 'Can't you send one of the guards to look for something so I can slip out?'

'Go swimming in one of the billion pools within the dome,' Blondie answers.

'It isn't the same, Milos.'

'Imagine one of the escaped Sirens killed you and it was discovered that *I* helped you get out? The answer is no, Dante.'

'How in hades are they going to get down here?' Dante asks.

'They escaped Anthemusa and have a god helping them. Need I say more?'

'Fine. Don't let the door hit you on the way out.'

Milos snorts. 'I take it I'm dismissed.' He rolls his eyes and saunters out, closing the doors behind him.

I'm edging towards the wall at the side of the glass doors when Dante steps into view. He has his broad back to me, dark hair and stature similar to Aaron's. I reach the edge of the door and step from view. I scrunch my eyes shut and focus all my energy on waking. It works and I feel myself lifting, the feel of bedcovers against my skin...

Dante steps through the doors to my left, jolting my awareness back to him. He walks to the edge of the balcony and I flatten myself against the marble beside the door. My heart races as he stares out at the gardens below and I frantically look for somewhere to hide. He sits on the wall and pulls something from inside his shirt. I watch his profile as he examines it in his palm. Long eyelashes, blade-straight nose, high cheekbones and an angular jaw.

Vivid, green eyes fix on me, every green I can think of, seemingly crammed into his irises. Glittering, neon flecks shimmer amid the pretty disks as we stare at each other and I take an unconscious step in his direction. He stands and I back up against the wall, wondering what the hell I'm doing.

'I won't hurt you,' he says.

My mouth drops open at the deep, rich resonation of his voice. That resonance presses against my flesh, seducing the Siren burn to galvanise in my throat. The resonance is a quality only Sirens can detect in this dormant form, a chime-like property that exists even when a Siren isn't singing. Aaron and the others don't seem to notice but since I transitioned, I've been able to hear it clear as day.

But what does Dante having it mean? Male Sirens don't exist, since they don't inherit the deadly traits, so the females devour them shortly after birth. But I'm hearing his voice with my own ears.

'I haven't seen you in the palace before,' he says. 'Are you new?' He frowns when I shake my head. 'Did my father send you to my chambers?'

Instead of asking who his father is, I shake my head again. I don't know what will happen if I talk but if I can hear the identifying chime in his voice, he'll be able to hear it in mine. Milos mentioned the escaped Sirens earlier and seemed afraid, so I'm not taking any risks. My spine creaks as my wings push for freedom. I don't know how or why Dante exists but I want out of here.

His smile fades. 'Then how did you get here?'

We stare at each other as I think of a way to answer. It becomes apparent that there is no other way, though. My only option out of this is to wake up and that's obviously not happening, so I need to speak.

I blow out a breathe. 'I'm not entirely sure.'

Dante's eyebrows reach for his hairline the moment I speak, confirming that he can detect the resonance in my voice. His expression darkens, turning hostile.

'You finally found me,' he snarls. 'But where's the other?'

'The other what?'

'Two of you escaped the Flowery Isle, so don't try lying to protect your sister.'

He thinks I'm my mother or sister. 'I'm not—'

'Tell me which god is helping you,' he snarls, prowling closer.

He stalks me as I back into the room, trying to keep some distance between us. The guy is huge and doesn't seem to want to hear me out.

'You've made a mistake. I'm not—' His fingers are suddenly around my throat and I didn't even see him move.

'You won't get chance to relay what you've seen here,' he says, lifting me from the floor by my throat until our gazes draw level.

Black stars dance across my vision as my higher brain function gives way to baser instinct. I kick him hard in the knee and his grip loosens as he loses his footing. We crash to the floor and I rip free, scramble away. I shove to my feet and dart towards the balcony.

Pain slices my shoulders as I draw on my wings, readying for freedom. If I make it to the wall I can fly away but Dante grabs my ankle and I face-plant the marble. He drags me towards him but I kick him in the face with my free foot. He curses and grabs for me again but I scramble from reach. I wipe the sweat from my brow as he dives for me. He's relentless, as strong as Aaron or Logan and I mostly lose to them in training.

I flip onto my back and curl my knees into my chest as he comes at me. I kick out at the last second, punching my soles into his gut. I grip his shoulders in the same motion and use the momentum to throw him over me. He slams into the marble, me straddling his waist but he snags my forearm. I draw my free arm back and punch him square in the nose. Dante reaches for his broken nose, thanks to my signature move and I huff a laugh that it keeps paying off.

He growls, hands whipping out to grip my throat again. Panic flares through me in response and I lose the tenuous hold on my wings. A scream wheezes from my constricted throat, as my wings tear from my back. Gold feathers rain around me, as familiar weight tugs at my shoulders.

Dante releases me, his pretty eyes growing wide as he stares at my wings. I jerk away, stumbling over my dress as I stagger for the balcony doors. He snags my wrist before I make it outside and I swing around to punch him again. He catches my fist and just...stares at me.

'It's you,' he breathes, green-on-green gaze drinking in the sight of my wings. 'You're...a girl.'

The room trembles and I breathe in relief when I realise what's happening. 'Oh, thank the gods.'

'Wait!' he shouts as I fade. I meet his desperate gaze before the room disappears.

3

A girl. Female. The other demigod Siren is female?

My father conveniently forgot to mention that little detail. I think of his speech about no female being able to understand me enough to accept what I am. Except, there's one just like me, even down to her having wings and being sired by a god.

I summon my wings, hands still tingling from the heat of her skin against mine. Ebony feathers join her gold ones littering the floor and I stare down at the black and gold blanket. I pluck a golden feather from the marble and shiver at the sensation of her energy. She's a perfect match for me, beautiful and soft and warm like the sun. I haven't seen the sun in a very long time and had forgotten how it feels.

I drop into my private pool and sit beneath the surface, waiting for my feathers to dissolve. I could wait for her to visit again but I just tried to kill her, so she probably won't come back. I should go to her and explain my mistake; find out what she came here to say. Father won't like my leaving his realm but I don't have a choice anymore. I *need* to find her.

4

I knock on Inara's door, my jaw so tight my teeth ache. I'm still mad about what she did but can't end my birthday without making sure she's okay. She barricaded herself inside her room after our fight and hasn't been down for lunch or dinner.

The door inches open and she peeks out, eyes luminous amid a golden curtain of tangled hair. Her lashes are spiked from crying, her expression wounded and my heart hurts at the sight.

'What do you want?' she asks.

'Can I come in?'

She debates my request then turns away, leaving the door open. I accept the invitation and follow her inside. Her sunny fragrance fills the room, warm and wild like midsummer. I discern her shape in the darkness and sit beside her on the bed. It's quiet and awkward for a long moment and her luminous gaze meets mine.

I know what she wants from me. 'I'm sorry.'

She sighs, 'I'm sorry for ruining your birthday, Aaron. It was stupid to use my key without telling you and it won't happen again.'

She doesn't yet comprehend how true her words are. Apology or not, I'm keeping her lyre until her sister and mother are neutralised. Even after everything that's happened, Inara doesn't take her safety seriously and I'll be damned if I let her risk herself again. The memory of her standing on the beach that day, after sacrificing herself for my freedom, still keeps me awake at night. I'd felt so powerless on that boat, sailing away from my reason for breathing.

I pull her into my lap, relieved when she comes willingly and curls against me. She's soft and mine and possessiveness thunders through me. I've never felt this kind of connection to another being and I will never get enough. I crave her in ways I can't explain; want to bind her to me in every way possible. She's my greatest weakness but also my salvation.

'You should sleep,' I say when she yawns.

'I know the others are here but...will you stay with me tonight?'

I lift her onto the bed in answer and we lay on our sides, her back to my front. She twines her legs with mine and her warmth infuses my body. I comb my fingers through her hair and she sighs, her breathing levelling out in minutes. When her breaths grow shallow, I whisper three words I never understood until I met Inara.

'I love you too,' she murmurs in our native language.

So far, she only speaks the language when sleeping. Part of her brain is rebooting dormant information, stored inside by the divine half of her heritage. I've seen this happen in demigods raised in the human realm before. Her conscious mind will catch up eventually and then I'll have to be careful about arguing with Logan around her. I won't expose her to his crudeness.

SOMETHING IS MISSING when I wake. I sit up and look around, pale sunlight highlighting the empty space beside me. I bolt from the room, terrified Inara's found her key and used it to leave. The connection we share flutters from deep in my chest though, settling that fear.

The house is silent, everyone sleeping in the earliest hours of the day. I hurry along the hallway as silently as possible then pause at a strange noise. I follow the sound to the bathroom, in time to hear a string of whispered curses from within.

I press a hand to the door. 'Inara?'

There's a beat of silence before she answers, 'Aaron?'

Her panicked tone fills me with dread and I test the handle, finding it locked. 'Let me in.'

'It's best if you just stay out there,' she says.

Fear that she's using her key strikes through me. 'Are you decent?'

'Yes, but—'

'I'm coming in,' I warn, ready to break down the door if she refuses.

She huffs and the lock clicks. 'Fine, it's open.'

I push inside to find her sitting on the edge of the bathtub, looking like she's been caught doing something she shouldn't. Her hands are behind her back and there's a scarf around her neck.

'Going somewhere?'

She glares at my question. 'And how would I do that from here?'

'Then what are you hiding?'

'Not my lyre, if that's what you're suggesting.'

She can't tell a direct lie to save her life but she's still hiding something. 'Why are you so upset?'

'Because you've barged in here like you have the right then accused me of trying to leave, even though you've stolen my means to do it,' she hisses.

'Forgive me if your history with bathroom-related excursions makes me paranoid.'

'I deserve my privacy, Aaron.'

'You do but you're hiding something from me,' I say.

'Because you aren't going to like it,' she huffs.

'I already don't like it,' I scoff.

She shoves to her feet and holds out her hands in frustration. It takes a second to register what I'm seeing and a growl tears out of me. I take her hands and stare at the purple marks staining her tanned skin beneath the bracelets around her wrists. She winces as I turn them to examine the underside, eyes widening as I recognise the shape they form. I lightly shackle her wrist with my hands, aligning my fingers with the bruising. Handprints—They're gods-damned handprints.

'I was hoping they'd heal before you woke up,' she says.

'But you didn't leave your room for most of the day... How did this happen?'

'I fell asleep after our argument yesterday and visited someone who thought I was an escaped Siren.' She shrugs like it's nothing. 'I've never had to fight during my visits to Anthemusa. I guess I should've known it would hurt my body if I did, since I've woken up with grazed knees from climbing the rocks there.'

I stare at her in horror. She hasn't visited Anthemusa since before she sacrificed her freedom to save me. I never considered the possibility of her visiting anywhere else, or the fact she'd get hurt doing it. Gods, how am I supposed to protect her?

I unlock my jaw enough to ask, 'Where did you go?'

'I don't know,' she says then tugs the scarf from her neck.

I snarl at the purple handprints staining her throat, rage welling inside when I think about anyone taking her from me. I'd been a staircase away while she'd been fighting for her life.

She gasps when my fist hits the mirror, glass exploding in a tinkling shower to the floor. I use the pain to stop the building bolt of lightning in my core form escaping.

'Aaron,' she breathes.

I stare at her bewildered expression and shake the anger away, realising I've frightened her. She stares at my still-clenched fists and I follow her gaze. Blood drips from my knuckles and is pooling on the tile at my feet.

'When I think of someone hurting you...' I shut my eyes and force the lightning back. 'Gods.'

A gentle hand cups my jaw and I force myself to meet her

gaze. She stares up at me, emerald gaze framed by all that pretty, golden hair. She slides her arms around my waist and hugs me. I breathe her sunny fragrance and let it tranquillise my lightning. She's the only one who has this effect on me and I rest into her hold.

The bathroom door crashes open, Alexander and Logan shoving inside. I look at them over the top of Inara's head as they glance between us and the broken mirror. Logan's gaze is fixed on Inara, scrutinising her as something furious passes like a shadow through his dark gaze.

'What in hades happened to her?' he growls, gaze glued to her bruised throat.

She untangles herself from my embrace and says, 'Calm down, Logan.'

He stares at her. 'I'll *calm down* when you tell me who did that to you and I've beaten them to death.'

'He isn't here, so punch a mirror like Aaron just did and calm the hell down. Your anger is giving me a headache.'

Logan growls but she huffs and shoves past him. He watches her go then turns with Alexander to look at me.

'She doesn't like to make things easy, remember? She'd rather die than let any of us fight to protect her.'

Logan snarls and sheaths his sword before stalking away. Alexander shrugs then follows him out, both going back to their rooms. I rinse the blood and glass from my hand then go to my room for fresh clothes.

Inara is sitting at the kitchen table eating a slice of cremated bread when I make it downstairs. She pushes a heaped plate of food in my direction and I smile. I sit, trying and failing not to look at the stark bruising on her throat.

'I don't want to talk about it,' she sighs when I growl for the third time.

'I can't just ignore it, Inara.'

'Then we'll discuss it when you can look at me without wanting to hurt someone.'

I drum my fingers against the table as I eat, knowing that even after the bruises are gone, I'll want to kill the being that hurt her.

'You'll tell me everything and I won't promise not to break more furniture,' I say.

'I'll make sure we're nowhere near my room then.'

'This is serious,' I growl.

'You think I don't know that?' she scoffs. '*I'm* the one with the bruises, Aaron. I survived yet you sit here acting like I can't defend myself and expect me not to be insulted.'

The following silence turns awkward until I sigh, 'I'm sorry. I just hate that you had to do it alone.'

Her eyes fill with fear and she opens her mouth as if to say something but sighs and looks away. It isn't the first time she's looked at me like that lately and I want to ask what's going on but, when she meets my gaze again, the fear is gone. Her whole demeanour has shifted and that feeling that she's hiding something surfaces again.

She reaches for my hand. 'I've been wondering...' she says but trails off, cheeks flushing.

I love that shade of pink. 'What?'

The colour darkens and this shade becomes my new favourite. 'Never mind.'

She tries to pull her hand back but I don't let her. 'Please talk to me, Inara.'

Her gaze darts around the kitchen, before her tortured gaze meets mine. She leans close, heat radiating from her skin and I wonder if sunlight will burst from it like yesterday when we were kissing. My worry eases and I smile in understanding.

'What is it, love?'

'I was thinking about your room.'

I blink in confusion. 'My...room?'

She nods. 'It's big enough to fit two beds and just seems silly to waste two rooms, when we can both fit into one.' She sighs, 'I don't want to sneak around anymore, Aaron. It makes me feel guilty, like I'm taking advantage of you or something. Everyone already knows we're together, so I don't see what the problem is.'

I resist the feral need to kiss her now-crimson face. 'You want to *share* a room?'

'Only if you want to. We did it on the Guardian Isle and it wasn't a problem but now...' She shrugs and stares at me with wide eyes, like she's terrified of my answer. Is this really the reason for the fear in her eyes just now?

'I suppose I *could* make an exception, for you?' I tease.

Surprise paints her face. 'Really?'

'On one condition.'

'What?'

'We push the beds together.'

Her smile fades. 'Oh.'

I feel like an idiot for taking it too far. 'You know I'd never—'

She puts a hand over my mouth. 'I just like squeezing onto my bed with you,' she admits.

I kiss her palm then drag her from her chair, into my lap. Her giggle resonates around the kitchen, like chimes in the breeze. Her love for me makes me immune but the sound is still intoxicating. I kiss her slowly, her lips warm and sweet against mine. Faint sunlight shimmers from her skin and I smile into our kiss.

Inara is my everything; the balm to my short temper and I don't know how I've lived so many years without her. Navigating a relationship is new and I don't always get it right, but she makes me want to try.

5

DANTE

The last time I ventured into Father's armoury, he went ballistic. He'd lectured me for weeks about there being no need for me to fight, since I'd never be leaving his domain. We both knew the real reason was because combat makes my darker side surface and the almighty Poseidon was getting worried at how easily I'd been beating my opponents. The look he'd given me had been fleeting but jarring because I'd realised, he'd begun to fear his own son.

The armoury hasn't changed much, still smelling of blood and rust despite the meticulous cleaning each weapon receives after use. I pick through the items, shoving what I need into a canvas bag over my shoulder. At the next wall of gleaming weapons, I close my eyes and pick one at random. I stifle a snort when I find a trident in my grasp. Like father, like son. I concentrate and it starts to glow. The blue light shines brighter and brighter, until it flares and disappears, becoming a silver cuff on my right wrist. It shimmers with iridescent light beside the key I've also stolen.

I slip back into the hallway and quicken my pace. The next rotation of guards leave for the Guardian Isle soon and I don't want to miss it. I keep to the shadows, only relaxing when I make it back to my room uninterrupted.

I empty the bag onto my bed and start applying layers of leather and metal to my body. It's the armour worn by the palace guards, to make me blend in. I rub charcoal paste under my eyes then glance at myself in the full-length mirror. My eyes are going to give me away because even an idiot will recognise the glittery, sea-green irises the same shade as my father's.

I glance around for an answer then spy the small dagger by my bed. I remember how the soldiers at the border reacted to Milos when he returned from the surface once with a tattoo. They're a waste of time for demigods, since our fast healing pushes the ink from our skin before it has chance to take. The stronger the linage of the demigod, the shorter the tattoo lasts. Milos's bloodline is diluted enough that his tattoo lasted nearly a week. Being Poseidon's son, mine should last an hour at best. Long enough to hopefully distract attention from my eyes.

I pull on a helmet then look in the mirror. Other than my eyes, I look like a palace guard. I stare down at the small blade in my hand and take a deep breath, hissing as it slices my skin. It stings like hades but I need to keep going if I want to see my Siren girl again.

I'm sweating by the time I drop the blade, spattering crimson over the marble. I take a shuddering breath before smearing charcoal paste into the crudely carved image on my forearm. I snarl at the burn of the paste, sweat dripping down my face. I wipe the excess away, leaving the blackened image of a trident in my weeping flesh and collect my stash of weapons with shaking hands. I just need to keep my eyes down and mouth shut and maybe I'll actually pull this off.

I reach the transfer station with barely a minute to spare, joining the group of off-duty guards waiting for transport to the surface. A few eye me curiously, before dropping their gazes to my homemade tattoo.

'The first thing I'm going to do this rotation,' the male in front says, 'is visit this cute little demigod in the human realm. Five-five, curly red hair and the most perfect pair of—'

'We don't need such vivid descriptions, Hector,' his superior cuts in.

Hector grins, laughing with the others. 'I was talking about her eyes.'

'Sure you were,' one of the others bellows.

'Think what you want,' Hector chuckles. 'She's a Daughter of Aphrodite and she's gorgeous.'

'How in hades did a minotaur-faced moron like you score with one of Aphrodite's daughters?'

Hector laughs. 'Gods know but she's smitten.'

'It's time,' the superior says. 'Line up or miss the boat.'

I file onto the transfer grid with the others, keeping my gaze on the ground. I'm thinking of how easy it's been when an alarm sounds from the palace grounds.

One of the guards groans. 'So much for your demigod, Hector.'

The superior nods as he listens to the communication being fed through his earpiece. He grimaces at the guards then says, 'Milos can't find Lord Dante and they've found a bloody dagger in his bed chamber.'

I keep my gaze on the floor as I mentally curse Milos from his toes to his idiotic smirk. Why can't the curly-haired moron stay the hades out of my room? Sweat beads my brow as the other guards growl their frustration around me.

'Come on, Stefan!' Hector whines. 'Everyone on the grid has been on duty all day under your watch. You know none of us are involved. Tell them you've already activated the transport and we'll report to you happy and refreshed in six weeks.'

'Please, Stephan,' someone else pleads.

More guards beg him to activate the grid, moaning about how

tired they are, until Stephan huffs, 'Fine, but if any of you speak a word of this I'll gut you myself.'

'We love you, Stephan,' a guard shouts, imitating a feminine voice.

A female guard elbows him, cutting him off and Stephan laughs, locking down the grid. 'Enjoy your break.'

The guards chat in relief around me as the grid fills with blinding light. It floods the space, pushing and pulling on every cell in my body. There's a flare of heat before the light fades and the doors of the grid reopen. I step out in the middle of the guard rotation, shielding my face from the light of a sunny day.

Sunlight warms my skin for the first time in over forty-five years and I grin up at the blazing ball in the sky. My shoulders itch to take flight and for the first time in forever, I feel free.

'I can't wait to sink a cold ale,' one of the guards says, brushing past me.

Others in the group grunt their approval and I follow them into the main square. I remember this place from when I was very young. Father had transported us here using one of his keys and it reminds me of the stolen key on my wrist. Now I'm out of his domain, I can use this key without him being able to track me. I just have to figure out where my Siren girl is and I can use it to get to her. It's simple, except that she's being hunted, so is actively trying to disappear.

I loiter in front of the statues in the middle of the square. The rest of the guards disappear, most into a tavern, no doubt to get inebriated like in the tales Milos loves to regale me with about his trips to the surface. I pull off my helmet and stare up at the statues depicting my father, Zeus and Hades. It's a good likeness and I remember meeting the Muse who designed it. She designed the statues in the gods' temples too, like the one in the centre of the Temple of Apollo I visited as a boy. My father went there to visit the Oracle of Delphi and I wonder if my Siren girl would go to visit her father there too.

I weave between the labyrinth of white buildings, frustration growing. The last time I was here, the red-haired girl had guided me to Apollo's temple while Father ran an errand. She'd walked a few paces ahead and I'd asked why she was crying. She'd glanced back with teary eyes then started sobbing. I'd caught up with her, horrified I'd made her cry, and taken her hand. She'd balked at her hand in mine, then smiled shyly. It was the first time a girl had ever smiled my way.

Without warning, we'd been standing in a different place. The girl was still holding my hand but was also in front of me, hugging a red-haired woman on the sand.

'That's my mother and me on the beach in Delphi,' the girl holding my hand had whispered. 'They made me leave her when they discovered I'd been touched by the Fates. I live in the temple now.'

'You're the new Oracle of Delphi,' I'd said remembering my teachings about the gifted seers. She'd nodded, fresh tears brimming in her eyes. 'Couldn't your mother come with you?'

She'd shaken her head and pulled her hand from mine. The scenery dissolved, leaving us back between the rows of white houses. The girl started walking again and I'd stared after her, feeling the pain of her loss. I hadn't known my mother, so couldn't really relate but it still hurt.

I'd caught up with the girl and taken her hand again. 'I lost my mother, too. I don't remember her but still miss her in here,' I'd admitted pressing a hand over my heart.

She'd looked up at me with profound understanding. 'This place is strange,' she'd whispered. 'It's full of warriors and smells funny.'

'It's just different but you'll adapt,' I'd told her. 'A place is what you make it. Where I live, I never see the sun or stars but it isn't so bad. I get to swim in the ocean, which is filled with other kinds of light.' I'd smiled down at her. 'You can be happy here, you just need to find the good in it.'

She'd smiled at me again. 'Thank you, Dante.'

I smile at the memory, as I turn the corner and the golden dome of Apollo's temple glitters ahead of me. I climb the stone steps but frown when I can't get inside. I push against an invisible barrier blocking my way then stand back and stare at the doorway, perplexed.

'The House of Apollo is sealed to males,' a soft feminine voice states from behind me.

I spin to the beautiful female behind me, golden thread woven through her thick braid of fiery hair. Her brown eyes are like chestnut shells against creamy skin. She's wearing a long dress, held in place by gold ornaments worn only by the Oracle of Delphi.

She scrutinises my armour. 'Have you come to find a new patron, Guard of Poseidon?'

I stare at her in shock, trying to marry my memories of the red-haired girl with the vision standing before me. 'Delia?'

Her eyebrows pinch in confusion before those doe eyes widen. 'Dante?'

I grin. 'Yep.'

She huffs a laugh then hurries up the last few steps to me. I catch her when she throws her slender arms around my neck and hugs me tight.

'I'd know those eyes anywhere,' she breathes against my neck.

'I can't believe it's you, after all this time!' I say, grinning down at her as we part.

She grins back, an attractive shade of pink staining her pale cheeks. 'What are you doing here? I'm surprised Poseidon allowed you to the surface at such a dangerous time.'

'He didn't.'

'You snuck out?' I grin but she doesn't share my enthusiasm. 'Dante, do you know there are Sirens loose? You've chosen a perilous time to discover your rebellious side.'

'You sound like my father,' I scoff, then look at the temple door-way. 'Why can't I enter?'

'Apollo gifted his House on the Guardian Isle to Artemis, as a sanctuary for the Daughters of Okeanos.'

'Why would Artemis send her daughters here?'

Nervousness flashes in Delia's gaze. 'Why did you sneak out?' she asks, avoiding my question.

'Is there a place we can talk in private?' I ask wondering what she's hiding. I'm guessing it has something to do with my Siren girl. As a virgin priestess of Apollo, Delia will do anything to protect the deity she serves, even hide his hunted offspring from the other gods.

'We can go for food in the main square,' she says.

'I arrived here with a rotation of palace guards,' I say. 'They're getting drunk in the square and if they recognise me, it will be a short visit.'

She purses her lips then smiles. 'There's a place on the cliff we can go. It belongs to a friend who is visiting family in the Human Realm.'

'They won't mind us being there?'

'No,' she says and turns to lead the way down the steps.

I stare after her, mesmerised by her graceful movements and elegant form. Delia has gotten, as Milos would say, *hot*. Too bad she's a temple priestess and off limits. Not that she'd want someone like me if she ever discovered what I am. The only female who'll accept me for the monster I am, is my Siren girl.

6

I collapse on the grass at the top of the hill and tip my face to the sky. It's so good to be out of the house; fluffy clouds lazing above and the space to think. I push onto my elbows and look down at the house in the valley below. I used Aaron's constant growling over my bruises as leverage to guilt him into letting me have this time. I almost caved and told him about my strengthening Siren traits this morning but chickened out and asked to share his room instead. It's all I could think of to shift the conversation onto something that would wipe the worry from his expression.

I sigh and breathe the fresh air, the anxiety easing from my chest. It's getting warmer, the grass no longer getting frosty at night. Wildflowers dot the hillside, making it pretty and lush. I close my eyes and listen to the birds. A distant plane drones overhead, the sun warming my face and I wonder if my dad's watching right now.

'Sunbeam,' he says, as if answering my unspoken question.

I pop my eyes open and smile. 'Hi, Dad.'

He chuckles, golden light around him shining brighter as he lays back with me on the grass. 'Dad is so informal.'

My smiles fades. 'I can call you Father or Apollo if you'd prefer—'

'I like Dad.'

I relax and look back at the clouds. 'Dad it is.'

He looks more like an older brother than my dad, until you peer behind the carefree visage of tousled hair and notice the ancient quality of his gaze. It's...unsettling.

'Are you going to tell me how you received those remarkable bruises?' he asks.

I match his casual tone, 'From a male Siren.'

His jaw ticks but he doesn't look surprised by my declaration. 'So, you've finally met.'

I sit up and scoff, 'When were you going to tell me there are male Sirens?'

'I didn't tell you because Poseidon asked that I keep his existence secret. And there aren't male Sirens, just Dante.'

'Poseidon's his father?' Apollo nods and I ask, 'Is he like me then?'

'He's the only other Siren like you.'

I mull over the new information. 'I suppose it makes me less of a freak.'

'You're not a *freak*, Inara.'

'As my father you're obliged to say that.'

Apollo frowns. 'I say it because it's true.'

I stare at him, wanting to tell him my worries over my Siren side. But what if he decides I'm a danger and takes me back to Anthemusa? It was his plan, way back when he and my mother were on speaking terms. He has no issue with locking away the female he had a child with because he deems her monstrous enough and I'm scared he'll feel the same way about me. I keep thinking about the original three Sirens and how their only crime was losing track of Persephone long enough for Hades to steal her away. They didn't start off as monsters either and look what happened to them.

I look away and sigh, 'Thank you.'

'Where's Aaron?' he asks after a moment of silence.

'He didn't like looking at the bruises Dante gave me, so stayed in the house.'

Apollo's tone is concerned, 'You told him about Dante?'

'Why wouldn't I?'

He frowns. 'What did you say?'

'That I visited a place I've never been and someone attacked me, thinking I was either Mila or Callista.'

He smirks. 'Dante thought you were a regular Siren?'

'He heard the resonance in my voice and didn't give me chance to explain.'

His smirk widens into a grin. 'You bested him in a fight?'

'Does it look like I won the fight?' I huff. 'You can at least act less pleased that I ended up in a smack-down with a large male who almost killed me. He only stopped attacking when he saw my wings. Then I woke up.'

'I'm not happy you were injured,' he says. 'I keep forgetting you aren't like other demigods, who'd boast about such things.'

I pull a face. 'They do all seem to love fighting.'

'You cannot tell anyone about Dante, Inara.'

'You want me to lie to Aaron?' Even if I could, I wouldn't.'

'It's for his safety. Think of the things that would join the hunt for you if it were discovered there are two god-sired Sirens; a matching pair.'

I don't like his terminology. Being part of a pair insinuates that we belong together; that to be separated would make us incomplete, when Aaron is the other half of my whole. *He* was the one who mended my shattered heart, saving me from the abyss. Not some Siren boy who tried to strangle me.

'I won't lie to Aaron.'

'Even though he's lying to you?'

I spear him with a *look*. 'What do you think you know?'

'Go back to the house and find out,' he says then disappears in a flare of blazing heat.

'You're wrong,' I yell into the sky but shove to my feet and start running. I hate how dramatic Apollo can be. He's older than dust but can act so childish.

Adonia is reading at the kitchen counter when I burst inside. Talia is sitting at the table, lovingly cleaning an array of weapons.

'You're back early,' Adonia blurts earning a glare from Talia.

'I didn't realise I was being timed,' I say.

'Do you want to help clean my blades,' Talia asks.

I stare at her in disbelief because I've never witnessed another living soul allowed to even breathe on her blades unless it's to cut them with one.

I narrow my gaze. 'Where's Aaron?'

'Training with Logan and Alex outside.'

My internal lie detector starts blaring and I have to force my tone to stay calm. I've never revealed that I can tell when someone is directly lying because I've never needed to.

'Oh? I didn't see them on my way back,' I say.

'They must've moved beyond the valley.'

My lie detector all but explodes at the answer and it takes everything I have to stop my voice from ringing. I turn and head for the stairs.

'Okay.'

'Where are you going?' Adonia asks.

'I'm tired,' I say since it isn't a lie. I'm tired of this house and the pain of hiding half of who I am.

They can't hide their relief at my words and it makes me feel sick. I make my way up to my room and shut the door, seething so much my throat throbs in time with the beat of my heart. I try to find the faint fluttering that's been in my chest since I brought Aaron back from the dead. It only disappears when he's far away and it's gone now. I open the door, ready to confront Talia and Adonia.

'They'll be back before she discovers they're gone,' Talia says from the kitchen.

'She'll be furious when she finds out,' Adonia says.

'How will she find out?'

'She isn't stupid, Lia. She could figure out he left.'

'Just show her the lyre. She doesn't know he has his own key, so won't suspect he's no longer in this realm.'

Aaron has his own key?

Hurt strikes through me, followed by disbelief then anger and betrayal. He confiscated my key and is doing the exact thing he got mad at me for doing. My anger boils into rage then syphons back into hurt when I realise, he's been lying to me from the start. He's had his own key all along and never told me.

I quietly close the door, tears burning my vision. Hurt and betrayal fight for supremacy that it isn't just Aaron. All of them know he has a key, which means they've all been in on his lie. I feel like such a fool. They think because I don't like to fight, I'm weak and treat me like a fragile piece of glass. If only they knew of the undiluted rage I carry; always there, scratching at the underside of my skin.

My throat burns, acid licking my insides at the disrespect and betrayal. It's so painful when I hold it back but what choice do I have? I need to calm down but Aaron waited for me to leave before sneaking away. I pant against the pain. It begs for release, a sweet voice curling through me, telling me to relent. I can't risk it with Talia and Adonia in the house but the voice tells me they deserve it for lying.

I take a leaf out of Aaron's book and punch the mirror. Sharp agony webs through my hand as my seething reflection splinters in front of me. I meet my gaze in the broken glass then blink at the dark-green shade of my irises. Instead of bright emerald, they're a deep, forest green. I step closer for a better look but startle at the sound of knocking.

Aaron's voice comes from the other side of the bedroom door, 'Inara, are you awake?'

Dark mist hazes my vision as I turn to the window. I climb onto the sill and loosen the latch to ease it open, craning my neck to look up into the eaves. I crawl outside and climb, back cramping as I reach the roof. I pause when I hear the window burst open below and Logan ask Aaron what's going on.

'She isn't here,' Aaron says, worry drenching his tone.

'She's probably in the attic again,' Logan says.

Aaron grunts an answer and the window bangs shut.

I crawl up to the chimney, slate tiles warm beneath my hands and sit with my back against the stack. The warm fluttering has returned to my chest and I hate how relieved I feel that he's back. He's made such a fool out of me and it hurts in a way I didn't know it could.

The dark mist clears from my vision as I sag against the brick, adrenaline replaced by frustration. I can't believe Aaron thought I wouldn't eventually realise he was gone. It can take a while to notice the absent connection if I'm not expecting it but the sensation of something being missing, grows more intense the longer we're apart. I gave myself ten minutes to retrieve the Saint Christopher for this exact reason.

I hug my knees, feeling stupid and betrayed and wonder how many times he's left like this. I've been feeling so guilty that he's trapped here with me, giving up his life, when really he's given up nothing. He's guilted me about asking for simple freedoms, while flaunting the rules *he* set.

I scrub at angry tears and rest my head on my knees, physically and mentally exhausted. I'm so damn tired of fighting what I am all the time and for what; to protect people who don't even respect me? I shut my eyes to close out the world, to pretend for a while that it doesn't exist. In my mind, I'm just a normal girl, visiting universities with my parents and worrying over which course to pick. The heat of the sun warms my back, soothing my anger until my throat stops burning and I can breathe again. I slip deeper into the fantasy I'm weaving, pushing reality to the periphery for a while.

I don't realise I've fallen asleep until I blink into a familiar sun-filled room. I push to my feet and look around. Warm sunset floods Aaron's bedroom on the Guardian Isle and I feel like I've come home. I press my palms to the heated glass of the window and watch the glittering ocean foam against a ribbon of black sand.

Aaron's scent is fresh in the air and I growl at the stark evidence of his lie. I shove the resulting anger deep, refusing to let it ruin my visit and head for the door to go see Delia while I'm here. I startle when I bump into a silver shield, propped against the wall by the window. It clatters to the wooden floor and I bend to collect it. I glance up at the sound of footsteps and find a familiar figure filling the doorway.

I back against the window as Dante stares at me, green eyes wide. He's dressed in armour, skin less pale in the sunlight as he steps into the room.

'You're here,' he breathes.

I take a defensive stance and snarl, 'Don't come any closer.'

'I won't hurt you.'

'You said the same before doing this to my neck,' I scoff.

'I didn't realise who you were back then,' he defends, gaze raking me from head to toe. 'My father neglected to tell me you were female, so I was expecting a male, like me.'

I let his explanation digest then admit, 'My father didn't tell me about you until this morning.'

'Seems they've kept us both in the dark,' he says.

'Apollo let me believe I was the only one,' I agree unsure what to do now. I've felt so out of place for months, alone with no one to talk to but Dante is like me. He'll understand the things I'm scared to tell the others about.

'I thought the same, until he sent my father this,' Dante says pulling one of my feathers from his tunic. 'I knew the moment I touched it, I had to find you.' He smirks. 'I didn't think you'd find me first.'

I stare at my feather between his fingertips, weighing up my options. If he really wanted to hurt me, he would've tried by now. He's been deceived as much as I have and probably just wants to know the truth like me.

I ease my defensive stance and say, 'Apollo said Poseidon is your father.'

'You asked him about me?'

'He visited this morning and asked how I got my bruises. He admitted who you were then.'

His smile fades. 'You haven't healed since this morning?'

I glance at the fading bruises on my wrists then the sunset filling the room and understand. 'It's still morning where I am.'

He frowns. 'Where you are?'

A wave of dizziness hits me, like the reminder that I'm not really here is drawing me back to my body. The ground shudders beneath my feet but Dante isn't affected.

'I'm not really here, like when we met,' I say. 'Sometimes I visit places like the gods do, while I'm sleeping. I can't control where I go like they can though.'

'Can you come here when you wake?'

It should be that easy but my key is being held hostage by my lying boyfriend. 'I don't have my key.'

I stumble when the ground tilts but Dante catches me. I gasp at the startling feel of his energy; cool and fluid to my blazing heat.

'You're leaving,' he says.

'Because I'm waking up.'

'Tell me where to find you.' His voice barely a whisper as he fades with the scenery around me.

'The Human Realm!' I shout back.

My eyes fly open at the sensation of falling. I slide from the roof and don't have time to unfurl my wings before I hit the ground with a sickening crunch. Pain explodes through my body as I try to breathe. I'm face-down on the grass, several bones broken. Each time I try to move it's excruciating and I bite back a sob because it hurts too much. All that time in the Gaming Zone last year and a fall from a roof is what will kill me.

Laughter bursts free at the sheer irony then I wheeze at the resulting pain. Aaron calls my name from somewhere close by and relief blasts through me. Then I remember he's the reason I'm even here and scowl into the grass. I grit my teeth, determined to wait out the healing alone.

7

I pace the kitchen, furious at myself for letting Logan talk me into leaving. I should've broken more furniture instead because the tension I worked off fighting Logan is back tenfold.

I slam Inara's key onto the table and growl, 'Taking this from her was supposed to stop this from happening!'

'I don't understand,' Adonia says glaring at me. 'We were in the kitchen, so we'd have seen if she came back downstairs.'

'We searched all the rooms upstairs,' Logan repeats.

'She could've climbed out the window,' Alexander suggests.

'She was up there maybe five minutes before you got back,' Talia argues. 'Unless she just floated away—'

I bolt outside, wondering why I hadn't thought about it sooner and search the sky.

'We already searched out here,' Logan says following me out.

I shield my gaze from the sun as I search. If Inara flew away, she could be anywhere by now. The others wouldn't have thought to search the skies because they don't know she has wings and I curse myself for letting her keep this secret.

A burst of laughter sounds close by and I spin in its direction. 'Inara?'

I follow the sound around the house, calling her name but she doesn't respond. Her scent grows potent and I start to jog. Logan joins me as I turn the corner to the rear of the house, then he slams into my back when I stop dead in my tracks. I stare at Inara lying face-down on the grass; body twisted and unnaturally still.

I drop to my knees at her side, hands shaking as I brush tangled hair from her face. The relief huffs out of me when her gaze meets mine and I mentally thank the gods that she's okay.

'What happened?' I ask, gently picking her up.

She whimpers at being moved then turns her face from mine, ignoring my question. I'm transported to the night I carried her through the woods during her transition. She'd lost her voice but I didn't need to be a mind-reader to know she was furious. She's wearing the same expression now but I don't know what I've done to deserve it.

Talia and Adonia crowd me as I carry Inara inside. I growl for them to back off then stalk up to my room. Inara's anger means her voice will be dangerous to anyone but me and I need to know what's going on. She hisses in pain when I lower her onto the bed then turns her face away. I arrange her limbs so her broken bones will set correctly then sit on the edge of the bed to wait out her healing.

Panting fills the silence as her bones knit back together and I watch in awe. I've witnessed grown men scream while healing from injuries less severe than this but she hasn't made a sound. Despite her fragile appearance, Inara's strong and it fills me with pride. She survived days in the Gaming Zone and forced a Son of Athena twice her size to yield. She was broken and exhausted by the time I'd found her but was still fighting to save Alexander's life. I remember her scream as her shoulder dislocated under his weight. I'd thought I'd lost her then but she'd been dangling from the cliff when I'd reached the edge.

Hours pass before her breathing slows and she visibly relaxes. She closed her eyes a while back and is now pretending to sleep.

'Are you going to avoid speaking with me for the rest of the night?' I sigh.

'I've got nothing to say to you,' she scoffs, voice ringing with rage.

The last time I heard it this devastatingly-beautiful was back on Anthemusa, when she'd been facing off with Callista. There's nothing that can truly describe the sound. It's so many things: a plucked harp, chimes in the breeze—the zephyr through tall grasses on a spring day. Inara's love for me makes me immune to the paralysing affects but it's still difficult to concentrate at the sound. The angrier she gets, the more beautiful it grows, meaning she's furious right now.

'At least tell me what I've done to upset you so much.'

Her glare is cutting when she finally looks my way. 'When were you going to tell me that you have your own key that you've been sneaking off with?'

'How did you—'

'You know, I've been lying here wondering how many times you've deceived me like this while we've been here. How many times have you left on the sly, while I've been trapped in this house with zero outlets to keep me sane?'

'Inara—'

'You went ballistic at me for going on a ten-minute trip without you, Aaron,' she snarls.

'That was different, you were alone—'

'You've been lying to me from the start!' she yells, angrier than I've ever seen. 'You took my key for doing something you've been doing all along and had the audacity to make me feel guilty about it.'

She gasps as she pushes from the bed, dodging my attempts to make her stay.

'You need to stay still until the healing is complete, Inara.'

She slaps my hands away. 'Don't touch me, and don't you dare come into my room without my permission.' She hobbles to the door as I stare in disbelief. 'And tell the other liars downstairs to keep the hell away from me too.'

She limps away and I stare after her, wondering what I'm going to do. I trace the leather cuff she gifted me, smoothing my fingers over the Saint Christopher before sliding it from my wrist. With a thought, the silver cuff hidden beneath, flashes into the shape of a thunderbolt in my palm. Inara can do this with her key but I never showed her, not wanting her to ask about the cuff on my wrist in response.

I toss it onto the bed and pinch the bridge of my nose, the scathing look she just gave me forever scored into my memory. Everything I've done is to protect her, even though I know she can protect herself. The problem is, given the choice, she won't.

I palm my face, remembering the sheer emptiness of waiting by the Acheron for Charon to collect me. I hadn't understood the bone-deep hollowness at the time. All I'd known was that I'd forgotten something so important it made me ache.

Then warmth had come, wrapping around me like a blanket and seeping into my vacant insides. It infused my being, growing hotter and hotter, until the searing heat blinded my senses with pain. And from the pain came Inara. She'd spoken my name and I'd opened my eyes to find her sitting on top of me like an angel. The love in her gaze as she'd stared down at me, made it impossible to look away. She'd brought me back from death and we've been connected by a deep fluttering in our chests ever since. We're connected in a way beyond the physical and relief rushes me at the memory. She will forgive me because she loves me, all I have to do is remind her of the reasons why.

I FROWN at the empty space beside me when I wake. I'm confident Inara will forgive me but know it will take time. Her distance is already difficult to deal with but I've lost her trust and need to prove myself again. I rub at the place on my chest where the gentle flutter of our connection resides and determination pulses through me to fix this.

I follow the sound of voices to the kitchen and relief floods me when I see Inara sitting with the others. She glares my way then quickly averts her gaze and I fight a sigh.

'We'll be back before you know it,' Adonia says squeezing Inara's hand.

She's forgiven Adonia then. Frustration winds through me that she can forgive their lies but not mine. Of course, they were only lying because I'd asked it of them.

'Which lucky person got nominated to babysit me this time?' Inara asks.

Alexander grins. 'Me, and maybe Helen if she arrives in time.'

Inara's face lights up. 'Helen's coming?'

'She's going to text when she gets home,' he says. 'I'll collect her then.'

'Tell her to hurry the hell up,' she says.

He pulls a phone from his pocket and hands it to her. 'Text her yourself. Helen only takes orders from you and I don't want to be shot if she disappoints you.'

She takes the phone, fingers flying over the screen with practiced ease. She's pleaded more than once over the months to get her a phone but I've denied her each time. If someone finds Helen, they could use it to find Inara but she doesn't seem to care. She never cares about her own safety and I'd had to use the risk to Helen's safety to get her to understand.

'We need to go,' Logan says.

He slides Talia a curious glance as he gets up. Talia moves to his left while Adonia steps up to his right and he reaches for the lyre.

'I'll take you,' I say needing to get out of here. Maybe if I show Inara that I trust her to be alone, she'll be less angry with me.

I summon my key and meet her fascinated gaze across the kitchen. She chews her lip as everyone except Alexander gathers around me. Her emerald gaze locks with mine, as electricity heats my flesh. We stare at each other before she looks at her key then her wrist and sadness fills her gaze. She looks away as she figures out another one of my lies and I sigh. I let the building electricity surge through me then direct the lightning into my key. It teleports me to the Guardian Isle, along with anyone I've chosen to bring along.

'Thunderbolt—fastest way to travel,' Talia says then, 'Sorry to run but I'm late.'

Logan practically chases her from the room, muttering something about being late too. I look at Adonia when I realise, she's watching me with narrowed eyes.

'It's because she loves you that she's so angry,' she says.

'I know.'

'Yet, you still don't trust her.'

I frown. 'I trust her.'

'Since she tricked you into leaving her on Anthemusa, you haven't trusted Inara to decide her own fate,' she argues.

'You're wrong.'

'Am I? Think about it, Aaron. You've essentially locked her away in that isolated place under the guise of keeping her safe but she's suffering. We all try to visit so much because we see what you cannot.'

'Which is?' I scoff.

'What's the point in living, if you have no life?' she huffs like it's obvious. 'Are you so arrogant that you won't admit your failings, even to save your relationship with her? Your efforts to *protect* Inara are going to be the thing that pushes her away, Aaron. You know she doesn't need the so-call protection you're inflicting on her. You're just punishing her for choosing to save your life over her own and it's a matter of time before she figures it out. And then what? What will you do when she realises the person she loves most is hurting her on purpose?'

She stalks out before I can respond and I stare after her. Is she right? Am I...punishing Inara for sacrificing her life for mine? I turn to the warmth of the midday sun as I relive the memory of that day. She'd been standing on the white sand, watching as we rowed away. The image of her in that blue dress, hair tangled and sprayed with onyx blood, is a sight I'll never forget. Even across the growing distance, I could see she'd given up and I was furious.

I scrub at my face and groan, realising Adonia is right. I haven't forgiven Inara for sacrificing herself that day; for tricking me into leaving then trying to end her life before I had the chance to rescue her back. If I'd made it to Anthemusa a moment later, she'd have been out of my reach forever.

I don't know why I've been treating her so poorly or why it took Adonia to wake me up to the fact. Inara only did what I'd have done if our roles had been reversed. I'd do anything in my power to give her a long and happy life, even if it meant my own demise. It's all she wanted for me that day, yet I've been punishing her for it since. I've locked her away in that house for saving my life and now I have to fix it.

I go to where her belongings are piled in the corner. There are the clothes she was wearing the first night I brought her to the Guardian Isle and the armour I purchased to replace the set she left on Anthemusa. I'll purchase furniture to store her things in now that she knows I've been leaving and my trips don't have to be so short. I'll bring her here for visits to escape the house in the valley but first, I'll give her some of the things she's been asking for.

I frown around the now-scattered leather and metal, wondering where it could be. The phone Helen gave Inara last year is no longer with the rest of her things. I scan the room in confusion and see the black rectangle on the floor beneath the window. I stalk over to pick it up and my spine stiffens, hackles rising at an unfamiliar scent. I tuck the phone into my pocket and draw my sword.

I follow a faint thread of the foreign scent into the hallway. It's only detectible if I inhale deeply and smells a few hours old. I pause at Logan's bedroom door when I hear movement inside. I tighten my grip on my sword then crash through the door.

'What the hades!' Logan snarls, throwing a book from his nightstand at me. It sails through the broken door when I step left.

I lower my sword and avert my gaze. 'I thought you'd gone out.'

Talia smirks as she stands from the bed and pulls on one of Logan's tunics.

'Did I say I was going out?' he barks.

'I didn't mean to… Since you're here, I need your help. Someone's been in my room and I need to know if you recognise the scent.'

I retreat to my room without waiting for a response. Logan and Talia follow minutes later, dressed and less ruffled. No wonder they've been acting strange around each other lately. I regard Talia with a fresh perspective. She's the only female Logan has ever brought into this house and I'm intrigued.

She locks her silver gaze with mine and asks, 'Where?'

I point to where I found the phone. 'It's strongest by the window.'

They move to the window and frown in unison.

'You're right but I don't recognise it,' Logan says.

'Nor do I but it's demigod and a powerful one,' Talia adds.

'They had Inara's phone,' I say. 'I left it with her things after the Games last year, switched off and I just found it by the window, switched on.'

Talia takes it from me and starts tapping the screen. 'The call log says it phoned Helen yesterday at ten, Human Realm time.'

'We were here then,' I say.

'We were out in the square, talking with Delia,' Logan corrects.

I take the phone and dial Helen's number. 'There's one way to solve this.'

I activate the speaker and the dial tone sounds twice, before Helen snarls, 'Listen, you sick prick! I don't know how you got a hold of this phone but I'm not interested. Call me again and I'll find you and gut you.'

'It's Aaron,' I say.

There's an ellipse of silence then, 'What the hell is going on? Is Inara okay?'

'I need to know who contacted you from this phone yesterday.'

'Update me first,' she scoffs.

'This is important, Helen—'

'My friend is important!'

I pinch the bridge of my nose and resist the urge to snarl my response, 'Inara is safe at the house in the valley but I've come to get her phone and realised, someone called you from it yesterday.'

'So...you don't know who that was?'

'What happened?' Logan asks.

'Is that Logan?'

'And Talia. You're on speakerphone.'

'I guess you do get network service there,' she mutters then, 'Someone phoned but when I asked who they were, they didn't answer. I could hear them breathing, so I yelled at them and hung up.'

'Where are you?' I ask.

'My parents and I got home late last night. I've been texting to arrange for Alex to pick me up.'

'I'll send Alexander to collect you now,' I say.

'Are you sure Inara's okay?'

'She's safe,' I say dodging the question.

'I guess I'll see you in a few minutes then.'

8

DANTE

I stare at the place my Siren girl was standing, palms tingling from the sweet burn of her energy. She was so beautiful in the sunlight that I never thought to ask her name. I savour her delicious scent as I look around. She'd seemed relaxed like she'd been in this room before but the masculine space doesn't really suit her.

Sunlight glints off a small pile of gold in the corner. I'm drawn to its shine because it's the only thing in here that reminds me of her. I shudder when I touch the armour, her latent energy shivering through my fingertips in a delicious caress.

I pick through the items: strange clothes, armour and a shiny, black rectangle. I pick the rectangle up. It's smooth like glass, except it isn't like any kind of glass I've encountered. I take it to the light of the window and turn it between my fingers, wondering what it is. I press a thin button on the side and it lights up, displaying a series of foreign symbols on the flat surface.

I frown at the strange squiggles before recognising them as

numbers from a Human Realm language. I tap a finger against one and the rectangle chirps in response. I experiment with pressing more numbers, each making a sound, as I try to recall the names of each character. It's been years since I studied any of the human languages and the answers don't come readily. Speaking is one thing but written language is another.

I grip the rectangle in frustration, inadvertently causing a string of symbols to appear. A new sound comes with the sequence of numbers displayed and I lift the rectangle to my ear in fascination. A female voice cuts off the shrill ringing and I drop the device in surprise.

'Hello?' she says in the same human language my Siren girl speaks. During our encounters, she's alternated between my language and this one, making me wonder if she was raised in the Human Realm.

I collect the rectangle from the floor and press it back to my ear. The female sounds confused, like she's expecting a response and I realise the rectangle is a communication device. This device was with my Siren girl's things, so this female must know her.

'For heaven's sake, Helen what on Earth's the matter?' a male asks through the device.

'It's just some pervert messing around, Dad,' the female—Helen huffs and ends the communication.

I stare at the device wishing my key could take me to specific people, instead of places then startle at Delia's call from downstairs. I drop the device and hurry from the room, making it to the top of the stairs at the same time Delia does.

'Did you find your friends?' I ask.

She frowns. 'What are you doing up here?'

I gesture to the restroom in answer. It isn't a lie, since I'd come up here for that purpose when I'd heard noise from one of the other rooms. I'd been curious since Delia claimed the house was empty.

'I was using the facilities.'

Her frown eases. 'I'm ready now.'

I sit at the kitchen table while she makes us warm milk and

honey. I watch her slender hands as she works, skin smooth and pale like she's a marble carving come to life.

'You were telling me why you sneaked out,' she says, smiling as she joins me at the table.

Instead of asking outright if she knows the location of Apollo's daughter, I reach across the table and take her hand. Delia's hiding something and I want to prove she can trust me enough to share what she knows. She gasps as my fingers curl around hers, those whiskey-coloured eyes going wide.

'Dante,' she breathes.

It's forbidden to initiate contact with the virgin priestesses of the temples but Delia is my friend. I would never betray her by acting on *those* kinds of impulses.

Energy blasts from her and the kitchen seemingly, melts away. I stand up as a new destination rises around us. The room has lilac walls and soft, indigo flooring. Unusual furniture fills the space and there's a bed to one side. The door is ajar, voices leaking in from beyond; the air laced with the scent of human female and male demigod.

'Helen's room?' Delia murmurs then seems to remember I'm here.

She pulls her hand from mine and the room dissolves away, until we're standing back in the kitchen. She stares at me wide-eyed but my brain is still fixated on her words. Helen is the name of the female who spoke on the device and that was her room. Now I have seen the destination, I can use my key to go there. I want to grin because it's too fortuitous, as if the Fates designed this to happen.

'I don't understand,' Delia says.

'Understand what?'

'That vision was of the Human Realm.'

'Do you not have visions of the Human Realm?'

'Your touch triggered it Dante, meaning it's linked to you. I know that place and... Why are you going to the Human Realm?'

She knows that place, meaning she knows Helen and my Siren girl.
'I've never been, nor am I planning to go to the Human Realm,' I lie.

She stares up at me, brown eyes scrutinising my face. 'Promise you won't go there.'

I choose my words with care. 'You told me once that your visions are never certain, that we shape our fate by the choices we make,' I say. 'Just because you had a vision that I might go there, doesn't mean I will, Delia.'

She smiles at my answer, despite my not making the promise she wanted. I feel a surge of guilt for lying but smile when I think that her vision has confirmed I'll reach Helen's room. I'm one step closer to finding my Siren girl and wonder what it will be like to really touch her. She was so warm, even when she wasn't physically there and I swallow at the memory.

'It's good to see you again, Dante,' Delia says drawing my focus from the sudden burn in my throat.

I smile at my oldest friend. 'I've missed you,' I say meaning it. Pink infuses her cheeks and it's a lovely colour.

THE SUN IS ALMOST RISING AGAIN by the time we step outside and breathe the salty air. I stare up at the stars, like fragments of sunshine in ink. Delia offers to walk me back to the square but I tell her I need to go to the water. She doesn't question my response, knowing my aqueous nature.

I wait for her to disappear into the maze of white buildings, her elegant figure like poetry in motion. It's been more than good to see her again, like a deep inhale of surface air. She's grown so beautiful and, once again, I regret that she's a temple priestess. If there were a female out there that might possibly accept me, despite knowing I'm half Siren, it's Delia. The fear of her shunning me is palpable though, so I've kept the secret to myself. She's my oldest friend and I don't want to lose her now we've finally reconnected.

I follow a grassy path from the top of the cliff, down to the black sand. The calm lapping of the surf tells me all I need to know about whether my father has been notified of my disappearance. Milos is probably dehydrated from the sweating he's doing at the concept of relaying the news.

I smirk at the thought and summon my key. A pearly shell forms in my right hand and when I blow into it, luminous water rises around my ankles. I picture the human girl's room from Delia's vision, as the ground disappears beneath my feet, dropping me through a watery doorway. I float in liquid light before pushing back to the surface and climbing out at my new location.

I stand and stare down at the strange purple fabric covering the floor. The room is exactly as it had been in Delia's vision, down to the shade of sunlight shining in through the window. I turn a slow circle then go to a cluster of pictures on the windowsill. I grin at the image of my Siren girl. She's with a human in all the pictures, the girl's hair colour differing except for in the ones where they're both really young. It's evidence to the theory that my Siren girl grew up in the Human Realm, when it should've been impossible. How did she cope with transitioning amid beings that don't know of our existence?

I pick up a picture to get a closer look but my spine prickles, drawing my focus to the doorway. Voices leak in through the gap between the door and frame and I search for a place to hide. I duck into the closet and pull the door almost shut, as someone bursts into the room beyond.

'You shouldn't throw away your chance of going to university, for the sake of some hot boy, Helen,' one of the two females harps at the other.

I peer through the sliver I've left between the door and frame, to see the younger of the two stop midway through stuffing items into a bag on the bed.

'I'm not throwing anything away, Amy! Alex and I love each other and he understands there are things I want to do.' She yanks the fastening of her bag closed. 'Stop meddling in my life.'

The girls share similar features, making it obvious they're related; perhaps sisters. It's the younger one that draws my focus though, as she's the one in the pictures with my Siren girl. Helen was the name of the girl who answered the communication back on the Guardian

Isle too, adding evidence to the theory that Helen knows where my Siren girl is.

'So, you're not ditching uni then,' Amy says.

'When *I* decide what *I* want to do, I'll let you know,' Helen snarls.

She shoves Amy from the room and slams the door in her face. She punches a pillow on the bed then pulls something from her tight-fitting leg-wear. I stare intently as she taps the surface of her communication device then holds it to her ear.

'I'm ready, Alex. I'm fine, just come get me.'

She stuffs the rectangle back into her pocket then stares into the middle of the room. A moment later the air wrinkles, sending sound-less waves crashing against my skin. Helen doesn't notice the atmosphere crumpling around her, only reacting when a distinct doorway appears to her left.

A large male with curly hair and amber eyes steps through and Helen shoves from the bed. He catches her when she tackles him, lifting her from the ground to crush his lips to hers. His eyes snap open a second into the kiss and he lowers Helen gently to the ground.

'Alex...?

He presses a finger to her lips as his nostrils flare. He moves around her, stepping deeper into the room and I know he's detected my scent. He drops a gold object onto the bed and lifts his right hand. A hammer fashioned by Hephaestus, flashes into his grip and Helen's eyes widen in alarm.

The other demigod's muscles tense and my chest starts throb-bing, my Siren half salivating at the prospect of a fight. I grit my teeth against the icy burn and force it back. I don't know how my Siren voice will affect a full human and I'm not monstrous enough to risk harming Helen. There are other ways of fighting Alex that will leave her out of the bloodshed and still feed the icy parts of me.

'What the hell is happening?' Helen whispers.

'He's been in your room,' Alex says.

Helen pales. 'The boy from the phone call yesterday? Alex; Amy and my parents are downstairs.'

He looks down at her, expression softening. 'I'll check the house before we leave.'

She nods and he takes her hand, his hammer flashing back into a bronze cuff on his wrist as he leads her from the room. I creep from the closet and examine the lyre he left on the bed, excitement thrumming through me when I realise, it's an Apollyon key. My Siren girl told me during her visit that she didn't have her key and this must be why. I touch the fizzing metal and bite back a groan, when a massive jolt of her energy zaps through me. This is it, this is how I'll find her.

I tuck the small picture still in my grip, into my tunic then summon my key. I pick up the lyre and press my key to it, a bolt of power drawing them together with a magnetic snap. It takes force to yank them apart again, the tether they've formed so powerful I panic for a beat that I'm not strong enough to part them.

I put the lyre back on the bed and return to my hiding place in Helen's closet. I've witnessed a key tethering only once but remember the link formed is good for one trip. It will tie my key into the next destination of the lyre and I pray Alex is going wherever my Siren girl is hiding.

'She isn't alone,' Alex is saying when he leads Helen back into the room. 'Logan, Aaron and Talia are with her.'

'She told me what Aaron did,' Helen huffs.

Alex retrieves the lyre and says, 'He only did it to keep her safe.'

'We both know that's absolute crap, Alexander. He took her key under the pretence of keeping her safe but was gallivanting to God knows where using his own, secret, key.' She narrows her gaze. 'Do you have a key I don't know about?'

He snorts. 'Not all gods are as generous as Apollo and Zeus, little love. If Hephaestus chose to gift a key to all his offspring, he'd never have time for anything else.'

Helen smirks. 'You've got a lot of siblings?'

'Many,' he agrees before pain flashes in his amber gaze.

She cups his jaw. 'I'm sorry, I didn't mean to make you sad about your sister.'

He holds her hand to his face and smiles. 'I miss her is all.'

They share a tender moment before Helen says, 'I thought Zeus was attracted to anything with a pulse. How hasn't he got a billion kids?'

'Even if the human myths you've been reading weren't exaggerated tales, Zeus and Apollo don't sow their oats as much anymore. They don't sire as many heirs, so have more heirlooms to bestow upon favoured children.'

Helen smirks. 'Their oats?'

He grins and tucks her into his side. He slings her bag onto his other shoulder then strums the lyre. Silent waves kiss my skin, as a doorway opens. I wait for Alex to guide Helen through then blow into my key. The magnetic pull of the lyre decides my destination this time, as luminous water rises around my ankles and delivers me somewhere new.

9

Aaron, Logan and Talia talk amid themselves as if I'm not sitting with them at the kitchen table. They haven't realised I can understand a lot of what they're saying and I've decided not to tell them. My grasp of their language has grown over the months and I practice speaking it in private. They've spent the last hour pretending they're not freaking out, so I've sat pretending I'm oblivious to what they're saying. From the outside, they look calm and collected and I realise they're all practised liars.

I turn the next page in my book to keep up the pretence of reading and maintain a neutral expression, while they basically describe me as being defenceless. It's rude to talk about someone the way they're speaking about me, even if they think I can't understand. I hold back from reminding them I'm a god-sired Siren: the whole reason we're hiding.

I sigh and stand to get a glass of water. Aaron's gaze snaps to me the moment I get up. I fight a growl at his reaction, wondering how I can love someone enough to die for him but have the urge to smash his face against the table. I thought he'd apologise when he got back but all he's done is ignore me. They're all surprised at detecting an unknown demigod's scent is his room, when I'm actively being hunted. Logic dictates that they'd track me to his house and maybe if he weren't being such a dick, I'd tell him the scent is Dante's.

I look to the middle of the room when the air creases with familiar vibration. The others look over in response to my reaction, as a doorway opens and Alex pulls Helen through. I told myself I wouldn't cry but the relief at seeing her is too potent. I go straight to her and she shoves around Alex to hug me back.

'It's okay,' she says knowing exactly what I need to hear.

I meet her gaze. 'God, I've missed you.'

Her gaze darkens and she snatches the lyre from Alexander's hand. She pushes it at me, as Aaron shoves to his feet. Helen rounds on him before he has chance to speak, meeting his glare with her own.

'You hypocritical prick,' she hisses. 'How dare you use her love for you as a weapon to get what you want!' She pushes me to the stairs and snarls at Aaron, 'Don't you dare come near us while I'm here.'

I grin as we climb the stairs, wishing I had her ability to articulate what I'm feeling when I'm angry. We sit on my bed together and she picks up the picture I cried myself to sleep over the night before.

'I remember those shorts,' she laughs. 'I hope you burned them.'

I gasp and throw a pillow at her head, smiling properly for the first time in days.

We hide in my room for the next few hours, skirting around anything too serious, which rules out anything to do with my life. So, we talk about hers and the more she talks, the more my mood sours. I start dwelling on everything I'm missing out on. I want to ask her to stop but I'm scared of upsetting her and making her leave.

Her stomach rumbles and I realise how selfish I'm being. 'You should go eat with Alex,' I say.

She stretches as she stands. 'Great, I'm starved!' She pauses on her way to the door. 'Aren't you coming?'

'I'm not hungry.'

She looks like she wants to argue but reigns it in. 'I'll bring you something.'

'Tell Alexander I'm sorry for hogging your time.'

She snorts, 'You make it sound like a chore.'

I pull my knees to my chest once she's gone and let the tears I've been holding back fall. She'll be gone again soon and I'll be stuck in my room because I can't bear to be around Aaron. I pick up my lyre and think about leaving. I could use it to escape and nobody could stop me. Then I think about the panic it would cause and sigh. I want to stick it to Aaron but can't do that to Helen.

I wonder if he'll demand my key back once she's gone. If I deny him, will he take it by force again? I think about where to hide it and remember how his key had been a silver cuff on his wrist until he'd wanted to use it. I stare at my lyre wondering if it can do the same thing... It bursts into a flare of golden light at the thought then forms into a band of gold beside the bracelet on my right wrist.

Son of a...

I startle at the sound of tapping on my bedroom window. Fear freezes me in place at the armour-clad figure staring in at me, until his features register. I shove from the bed and stare back at Dante in disbelief; palms pressed to the glass like he wants inside. I glance at my bed, wondering if I'm dreaming but he's still there when I look back.

I stumble over and press my palms over his, gasping when his cool energy shivers up my arm. If it feels this powerful through a layer of glass, what will it feel like to actually touch him? His gaze drops to follow my hand, as it curls around the latch. Spring air rushes in when I push the window open, bringing Dante's delicious scent with it. He smells like the ocean: salty, cool and free. He leans in until our faces are inches apart, then grips my waist and pulls me outside.

His scent curls around me as my brain flat-lines against the cool press of his energy. He wraps me in his arms like I'm precious and I let him. I know it's wrong but it feels so right. Everything about him feels *right*, like a balance is being gained by our coming together.

He steps back from the window ledge and I gasp, burying my face in his shoulder for the fall. I look up when he chuckles and stare at him. He stares back amused, as huge, ebony wings beat rhythmically behind him.

'You have wings like me,' I say, my voice a resonating purr beneath the onslaught of sensation.

Touching Dante is like finding peace while breathing fire. His cool energy has activated my Siren side, forcing it to surface from where I keep it locked in my middle. It feels delicious, like sliding into a hot bath on a cold night; muscles unknotting at the sensation. It's a stark reminder of how much I have to hide from everyone else, including Aaron. An insidious thought snakes into my mind, asking whether Aaron even loves me or if he only loves the parts I let him see.

Dante's brow creases, before a rush of his energy infuses my insides. It spreads a wave of calm through me and my mouth pops open when I realise, I can feel his emotions. Does it mean he can feel mine?

We shift in the air, my hair tangling around my face as he guides us back to Earth. The grass is sun-warmed as we alight at the top of the valley, the house visible below. He loosens his embrace and I take a measured step back, disconnecting from his delicious energy. I bite my lip hard, worried at the visceral sensations he's causing.

He flexes his wings then tucks them against his back and I can't help but stare. He tilts his right shoulder towards me in invitation, freaking me out with how he seems to know what I'm thinking. Even so, I can't resist. I slide my fingers along the sleek black feathers, fascinated by the blue-black colour as his energy tingles against my fingertips.

He shivers and I withdraw my hand, face burning at what I now realise, is an intimate action. I've never explored my wings in this way but I do know they're sensitive. I shouldn't have touched Dante that way but he's so...magnetic. Even now, I want to reach out and touch him again.

'You feel it too,' he says, voice husky and resonating.

I nod, guilt riding me at the admission. I'm not supposed to react this way to anyone that isn't Aaron; but then this is different—isn't it? I don't love Dante. It's more like discovering I'm not the only one of my species and I'm curious.

'May I see yours again?' he asks.

I blink at his request because I don't willingly show my wings to others. They're another item on the long list of things that make me different. But I'm not different where Dante's concerned and he's looking at me expectantly, with those green-on-green eyes, like his request is the most natural thing in the world. It probably is for a guy sporting his own set of wings.

I relax my shoulders and bite back a wince, as my wings unfurl. Gold feathers sprinkle the ground as I flex them out behind me, repressing a groan at how good it feels to free them. It's been so long since I let them out like this and I tug the back of my vest top down, until it sits comfortably beneath my wing-base.

Dante steps in close before I can protest and touches my left wing. A bolt of pleasure shoots through me at his cool, delicious energy and I gasp. He mirrors my reaction when gold light explodes from my skin and I jerk back. The light snaps off and I look around, half expecting Aaron to be behind me.

'What was that?' Dante breathes, voice so beautiful with Siren song it sets my body on fire. He reaches for me again. 'It felt like sunshine.'

I lurch from his reach. 'Don't!'

He looks devastated. 'I'm sorry, I didn't mean—'

'It's just too much too fast,' I say. 'Touching you feels... I've never... It's very overwhelming.'

'I've never touched another Siren,' he agrees.

'It isn't like this,' I say gesturing between us.

He looks intrigued. 'You've been around other Sirens?'

'I've been to the Flowery Isle.'

'How did you... I'm sorry, I only know the little information my father gave me and what I've garnered from our interactions. I don't even know your name.'

'You don't know my name?'

Inky hair falls across his right eye when he shakes his head. 'No.'

I resist the urge to sweep his hair back and say, 'It's Inara.'

He smiles and his whole expression lights up. 'It's good to finally meet you in the flesh, Inara.'

I smile back because I can finally be around someone without having to worry about hurting or surprising them in some weird, Siren way. I have a million questions I've been too afraid to ask but Dante is different. I'm hoping he has answers about my strengthening Siren side. He might know how to control it or maybe even stop it.

'Inara,' he hums, his resonating voice turning my name into a musical sound.

I lower onto the grass in answer, wings arcing at my shoulders and folding around my body. Dante sits at my side, his wings mirroring mine as we gaze down at the house in the valley. He tells me the story of escaping Poseidon's domain then using his key to track me down. He's been kept prisoner by someone he loves like me and I resonate with the pain in his voice as he speaks. When he describes the fear in his father's eyes at how powerful his Siren abilities were getting, I bite my lip. I frown down at the house, wondering if that's what's in store for me on revealing my increasing abilities to Aaron. Dante thinks his father keeps him locked away as much for his own safety as for everyone else's and that's one of my biggest fears. Aaron has already isolated me so much for my own safety. What will happen if he ever decides the others need protecting from me? Will he stop them from visiting?

My gaze snaps from the house when Dante's fingers curl around mine. I glare his way then realise, he isn't paying any attention to me. His gaze is still fixed ahead as he talks and I don't think he knows he's reached for me. I stare down at our hands, debating whether to pull free. Maybe he feels the magnetic pull too and it would explain this. It's a powerful draw to get close to him; an insistent itch beneath my skin.

Instead of pulling away, I ask why he didn't just use his key to leave Poseidon's domain. He says Poseidon can sense if it's used there and I nod like I understand. I look at our hands again and tell myself I'm not pulling away because I'm enjoying his cool energy and not his touch.

My insides are pulsing with Siren fire but for the first time in a long time, it doesn't hurt. I'm not fighting against it, terrified of hurting the person next to me and this simple freedom is everything. I know I should take him back to the house to meet the others but I haven't felt this free since before I transitioned. That life feels like it happened hundreds of years ago but it was the last time I felt this sensation of peace.

10

I step in Helen's way before she can reach the stairs and hold out a hand for the plate of food.

She glares up at me. 'She doesn't want to see you, Aaron.'

'Give me the plate, Helen.'

Alexander shoves away from the table when she squares her shoulders and comes up behind her. He plucks the plate from her hands and thrusts it at me.

'Hey!' Helen yells.

'Inara will starve before either of you backs down,' he huffs.

I smirk at her outraged expression then turn and climb the stairs. I admire Helen's bravery but she's a thorn in my side.

'Leave them to sort their own issues,' I hear Alexander say as I knock on Inara's door.

I knock again when she doesn't answer and press an ear to the door. Maybe she's sleeping and I should leave the food outside. I consider taking it back downstairs then I think of Helen's smug reaction.

'Inara, I'm coming in,' I warn, waiting a few more seconds before letting myself in.

Her room is empty.

I drop the plate on the bed and stalk to the window, frustration streaking through me. I climb onto the windowsill and look up into the eaves. My annoyance fades when I realise, at least on the roof we'll have privacy to talk. Then I wonder why I'm annoyed at all. I promised myself I'd give her more freedom and I should celebrate the fact she even left her room at all.

I climb onto the roof but find it empty too and panic threads through me. Inara has her key and is upset enough to use it. She promised she wouldn't but that was before she knew I'd been using mine. She could be in danger and it's all my fault. I should've apologised and given back her key as soon as I returned from the Guardian Isle.

I drop from the roof onto the grass, taking the quickest route back to recruit the others. A familiar fragrance hits me as I land and I reach for my weapon. My spine arcs before I get chance, a blade slamming into my back and bursting out between my right ribs. I stare down at the bloody tip as my knees buckle.

Cold fingers grip my hair and yank my head back as the blade jerks free. Mila's upside-down face fills my vision, her resemblance to Inara still jarring. She lacks the softness of Inara's beauty though, mouth sharp and jaw more angular. She has those cold, dark eyes and a mane of midnight hair like their mother.

'Hello again, Warrior,' she purrs.

I smirk at her ringing voice. 'You know that doesn't work on me, Noisemaker.'

She snarls in frustration and thrusts the blade into my back again. 'At least if you're immune to my song, I know my baby sister is still alive,' she says. 'Tell me where she is and I'll make it quick for you.'

She twists the blade when I take too long to answer and I cough a mouthful of blood. She leans close when I try to speak, bringing her ear close to my lips.

'I'll die a slow death before I give her to you.'

She grins down at me. 'I was hoping you'd say that.'

She leaves the blade wedged in my back and wipes a trickle of blood from my lips. She sucks it from her fingertip and shivers at the taste.

'Do you remember how much fun we had the last time I got to play with you like this?' she asks. 'The mere thought of doing all those things again, makes my mouth water.'

'Can't wait,' I wheeze then grab her wrist and yank her over my shoulder.

She slams onto her back and I pin her to the ground. She reaches over my shoulder and yanks the dagger from my flesh. Blood pours out in its wake, suctioning my shirt to my skin and filling my right lung. It gets hard to breathe, as we both freeze in our struggle at the sound of Inara's voice.

I look up, heart in my throat, terrified that she's here right now. I growl in pain and glare down at Mila to see her gripping the hilt of the dagger she's buried in my only working lung. Air hisses out around the blade as she shoves me away. I land on my back, fingers sliding awkwardly over the dagger's bloody hilt. Mila stands and smirks down at me before slinking away.

'No,' I rasp, lungs filling with blood.

Black stars burst through my vision as unconsciousness presses down on me. I try to get up but can't. All I can do is watch Inara fly towards me, wings beating like gold fire behind her.

Mila laughs as she watches me struggle. 'That blade was meant for my sister and has been dipped in Milk of Morpheus. It's a shame you'll be dead before you wake from the effects, as I was so looking forward to playing with you again, Son of Zeus.'

Her words register through the haze in my head and I look back to Inara. I mentally beg her to turn around, suddenly understanding why she tricked me that day. If I could trick her to leave right now, I would. Not because I want to deceive her but because I'd do anything to save her from this fate. She's my everything; my heart and soul and all that's between.

Lightning prickles my skin as I try to move but it's futile, so I turn my full focus to Inara. I memorise her beautiful face, vowing that when I stand waiting for Charon to collect my soul, I'll remember her. I'll wait on the banks of the Acheron River, even if I have to wait an eternity for her.

Our gazes meet across the distance, her golden hair sticking to tear-drenched skin. Even now, seeing Siren tears fills me with wonder. A dark shadow stretches out behind her and for a moment, I think Charon has come to claim what's mine. Then tanned arms circle her waist and send her crashing to the ground.

'Impossible,' Mila breathes.

A tangle of black and gold hit the ground before Inara struggles from the male's hold and scrambles to her feet. She runs at me but the male chases. Fear coats my tongue but there's nothing I can do.

He grabs her around the waist and yanks her back, growling, 'She's one of the escaped Sirens!'

'I know!' Inara growls back, fighting to get free.

The exchange fills me with relief because, even though I don't know who he is, he's obviously trying to protect her.

'Aaron,' Inara screams and I blink awake, unsure when I'd even closed my eyes.

'Goddess,' I whisper.

She's frantic, fighting the male's attempts at restraint and reaching for me. 'Fight it,' she tells me. 'Don't you dare leave me again!'

Mila chuckles. 'When you're dead and your bones picked clean, I'll gift her your skull as a reminder of this moment.'

I snarl and summon the remaining strength in my core. The lightning barely forms a bolt but I use it to fill the remaining space in my lung.

I shift my gaze to the winged male and rasp, 'Get her out of here.'

I collapse against the grass and Inara screams, 'Aaron, no!'

The agony in her voice hurts more than the dagger in my chest. I watch from my prone position on the ground as Mila hisses and starts running towards my love. There's a flash of light and the winged male lifts something to his lips. Another flash and he drops with Inara through a portal in the ground.

Mila's beautiful face eclipses my vision when she crawls over me and snarls, 'Where did they go?'

I smirk in answer, knowing she's lost and she hisses at the same realisation. Darkness creeps around my vision as she starts to feast, wet warmth slipping over my skin. She groans her pleasure at the taste of my flesh and I sink into the heaviness of death. I wait for the cold to find my bones and my feet to press into the mud of the riverbed.

A familiar voice tugs me from the growing silence and I claw past the numbness to find Logan standing above me. One hand is clasped over Mila's mouth, while he holds a blade to her throat with the other. She claws at his arms leaving bloody grooves but he doesn't even flinch. I stare up at him as he stares back, eyes burning with black fire.

A cruel smile curves his lips and he purrs, 'You're a long way from home, pretty Siren.'

Mila jerks against his hold and Logan laughs. He turns her face so he can meet her furious gaze with his own, as he slides a blade leisurely along her shoulder.

'I heard you like death to come slowly and I wouldn't want to disappoint.'

Her eyes widen when he jams the blade into her shoulder, her cries muffled by his hand. Black blood oozes around the hilt and he uses his now-free hand to grip her nape, forcing her gaze to me.

'That was for my brother,' he snarls against her ear then rips the blade free. 'And this is for the female you attacked in the house.'

Mila stills, eyes rounding, before she explodes into a mist of black blood. Logan drops to his knees beside me, body smeared in a mix of black and red. He looks me over then eases the blade from my chest. Bubbles froth from the wound and he presses his hand over it to form a seal.

'Where's Inara, Aaron?'

My lips work but no sound comes out. The heavy veil of drugs is numbing the pain but it's hard to breathe and my consciousness is fading again.

I see fear in Logan's gaze as he looks at me. 'Rest,' he says in the same tone he used with me in the days after my mother died. 'You're no good to her dead.'

He pulls something from his pocket and presses it to my nose. The heavy fragrance of the purple petals pull me under.

11

We drop beneath the surface of the gateway, into the liquid light between destinations and Inara goes rigid. Her fingernails press into my flesh as our wings dissolve in the ethereal liquid, her fear bleeding through me. I stare down at her in surprise because I just watched her trying to rescue the male in the valley from a Siren but she's afraid of this?

I swim us to the exit portal and look around in confusion because we're not where we're supposed to be. Inara shoves away while I'm distracted, her rage and sorrow overwhelming my senses. I wipe an unexpected tear from my face and wonder what's going on. This isn't the destination I requested my key take us to.

A flash of gold light draws my focus and I glance back at Inara in time to see one of her bracelets turn into a lyre. I lunge at her, gripping her wrist before she has chance to strum the strings.

She twists in my grip and snarls, 'Let go!'

'You can't go back there,' I growl and yank the lyre from her grip.

Her anger blasts through me, hot and fierce. 'You don't decide where I go! Aaron needs me!'

'I didn't make the decision for you to leave, he did!' I say assuming Aaron is the male from the valley. 'I did as he asked to keep you safe.'

Her emerald gaze widens and her rage dissolves into grief. A pained sound rips from her, her sorrow raking through me and I gasp for breath. It's all-consuming and I suddenly wonder what her relationship was with this Aaron. I pull her into a hug, wondering if I did the right thing as she sobs against my breastplate.

I've spent every waking moment since discovering Inara's existence, dreaming of finding her. She's like me—seemingly made for me and not once, did it occur to me that she'd be involved with another. I thought it would be as simple as finding her and for me, it had been. When we'd first touched, it was as if the world aligned. It felt like I'd been off-kilter my entire life, until we came together—As if we were *meant* to find each other.

I stare down at the top of her head, wondering if what happened to Aaron was fated too. Maybe I was there to save Inara from the Siren that killed him because the Fates designed it to happen. My easy escape from Father's domain, meeting Delia, the phone call with Helen and Alexander leaving Inara's lyre for me to tether—Each event catered to our meeting in time for me to be there in the right moment.

Inara fits against me like she was designed that way, adding proof to my theory that she's supposed to be mine. I comb fingers through the soft gold of her hair and breathe her sunny fragrance. She will be my sunshine in the darkness of my father's domain, once she's had time to let go of the male in the valley and sees what I already see.

I look around as I soothe her, wondering again why my key didn't take us to the location I'd been thinking of. I meet her watery gaze when her sobbing ebbs. She looks from me to the room and recognition flows through her. Shock spears me when I realise, Inara is the reason we're here.

'You know this place?' I ask.

She studies the pale green walls and says, 'How did you know I used to live here?'

'I didn't,' I say. 'I've never been here.'

She looks around again, eyebrows pinched. 'You're saying I brought us here?' When I nod she says, 'I didn't know your key could bring us to a place *I* was thinking about.'

'Nor did I.'

I think of Inara's warm energy tingling my skin and wonder if it's how it happened? Are we so connected that our thoughts can be confused by my key? I like the idea of her thoughts and essence being mingled with mine.

I look around with fresh appreciation at the knowledge that Inara once lived in this space. I pull the framed picture I took from Helen's room from within my armour. The walls are a different colour but it's the same window Helen and Inara are posing under in the picture.

'Where did you get that?' Inara asks taking it from me. A tiny smile creeps onto her tear-stained face as she studies it.

'From Helen's room when I was trying to find you.'

Shadow passes over her features and she sighs, 'We should get out of here.' She pulls me to the doorway then glances at me over her shoulder. 'And we need to find something less conspicuous for you to wear.'

I look down at my armour. 'What's wrong with what I'm wearing?'

'People don't dress like that in the Human Realm and we should at least try to blend in.'

My grip tightens on her key. 'You no longer want to go back to the valley?'

Sadness pours from her as she says, 'The Siren in the valley is my sister and the other roaming free from Anthemusa is my mother.'

I blink at this new information realising, there are more things my father neglected to tell me. These are things I should have asked Inara about while we were talking earlier, instead of spending the time talking about myself.

'They were released by one of the gods to hunt me,' Inara says. 'Somebody wants to use me for what I am, Dante and once my sister reports your existence, they won't just be hunting me anymore. They'll want us both—the matching set.'

Delight rakes through me at her description of us being paired like that. We're a set; her words, not mine. After years of being locked away in my father's domain I'm finally going to be exposed. Everyone will know I exist and what I am.

'Why are you smiling?' she scoffs.

'I don't care that they'll know about me, Inara.'

Her eyebrows reach for her hairline. 'Don't you get it? You're in danger because of me, Dante. Everyone is *always* in danger because of me. I'm a magnet for this stuff and Mila was in the valley—in the house because of me. I'm the reason Aaron is...' she scrubs fresh tears from her face and growls.

I cup her jaw and bend to bring our gazes level. 'I'm in danger because of *me*, Inara. Because of what *I* am, what we *both* are. You aren't alone anymore. I'm here now and we're the same.'

'I'm a monster,' she argues.

'No more of a monster than me.'

She stares at me in shock before a wave of her gratitude washes through me, warm and shocking as it fills me up. Even my father, whom I know loves me considers me a monster. His view is plain as day when he speaks of my mother and other Sirens. It seems Inara has been victim to the same stereotyping but I vow to rid her of the negative feelings they've caused her.

'We really should get out of here,' she says.

'Other than a short time in Helen's room, this is my first time in the Human Realm,' I admit.

'Really?'

'I travelled from the Guardian Isle to Helen's bedroom, then followed her to you,' I say then blanch. 'You don't think Mila followed me to you, do you?'

'Mila was as surprised to see you as Aaron was,' she counters then frowns. 'I never got the chance to tell him about you. We were fighting and I—'

Her gaze snaps towards the sound of voices. She grips my hand

and tugs me through the doorway. We creep along a short hallway then through another doorway at the end. Inara eases the door shut and scans the room. Her sadness blankets me as she pulls me to the window and climbs onto the sill. She pushes the window open and drops onto the enclosed garden below. I follow her out, landing silently beside her then grunt when she tugs me sharply to my knees.

'What—' She clamps a hand over my mouth and points up.

I follow the direction of her finger to glimpse a human wandering past the downstairs window we've landed in front of. Inara's burning heat licks my skin, palm still pressed over my lips as we wait for the human to pass. She releases me the second the coast is clear and runs to a small wooden structure at the opposite end of the garden. I hurry after her, ducking into the mouldy-smelling dwelling. It's some kind of storage unit, housing strange contraptions, littered in mud and dry grass.

'Give me my key,' she says holding out her hand.

I give her a wary look. 'Where are we going?'

'We stand a better chance if we go somewhere we're both familiar with, don't you think?'

'The Guardian Isle?'

She nods. 'We need a place where we'll have time to think and we can't stay here because you have no idea how to blend in.'

She's right. This place is strange and intriguing but we need somewhere I can focus on protecting her. I didn't wait my whole life to find Inara, to have her taken from me. I reluctantly pass her the lyre then grab her free hand to make sure she takes me wherever she has in mind. She gives me an annoyed look as I strum the strings for her and let her pull me through the shivering doorway it creates.

12

I stand in Aaron's bedroom, feeling like my heart will shatter if I breathe his lingering scent too deep. I want to breakdown but Dante is watching. It's bad enough knowing he can feel my emotions the way I can his. I *feel* that he wants to comfort me but I need time to process.

I tug my hand from his and head for the door. 'I'm going to the bathroom.' I drop the lyre on the bed on my way out, so he won't have reason to follow.

I shut myself in the bathroom and slide down to the tile. When I close my eyes, I see Mila torturing Aaron in the valley. My head and heart pound at knowing there's probably nothing left of his body. Even if I went back, there'll be nothing to resurrect like last time. He's gone and there isn't anything I can do to change it.

I think of Talia, Logan, Alexander and Helen and scramble across the floor to retch into the toilet. I left them all there for Mila, when I could've done something to help.

'Inara,' Dante calls through the bathroom door, voice pained.

I glare at the door because he dragged me away when I could've saved them. The anger fades as fast as it flares though and a sob rips free. This isn't his fault, it's mine. I knew this day was coming but had grown complacent. I let meeting Dante distract me; had been the one to suggest we stay on the hilltop a while longer.

I curl up on my side and let familiar numbness fill my chest. Flashbacks of the accident that killed my family play like a horror movie in my head. It's happening all over again, like a nightmare I can't wake from. I never should have let Aaron or the others past the walls I'd built. Not only are they gone but I'm the reason for it.

The bathroom door creaks open as the sunlight begins to fade, Dante's scent trickling inside. He sighs then comes to scoop me from the floor, cradling me against his chest as he carries me from the room. Guilt claws at me at how right it feels when he holds me and I close my eyes.

The softness of a bed surrounds me and Aaron's spicy scent fills my nose. Fresh pain threatens to choke me but the tears won't come. I scrunch my eyes shut and concentrate on breathing in and out. In and out, until I'm drifting in a sea of cerulean blue.

I WAKE in the house in the valley and look down at the Siren-style dress I'm wearing. The dream is so vivid it feels real and I slide my hand under the pillow to pull out the photograph hidden there. It feels real and solid and exactly how I remember it.

I shove from the bed when it occurs to me that I'm visiting, hurrying across the hallway to Aaron's bedroom. I falter in his doorway, tears welling when I find him sleeping on the bed. I creep closer and stare down at his perfect face. He seems real too and, though this is only a dream, relief floods me that I have the ability to remember him so well.

I climb onto the bed and curl around him. He's warm and electric like in real life and it's beautifully painful. I want to stay in this dream forever, pressed to his warmth and surrounded by his scent. But I'm not here and reality pushes down on me at the reminder, trying to wake me from this gift. I dig my fingers into his chest and close my eyes, desperate to stay.

'Please,' I rasp.

His arms wrap around me and he sleepily murmurs, 'Love you.'

I cup his jaw and say, 'Let me see your eyes before I wake.'

His eyebrows pinch together. 'Why are you so far away?'

'Just one look,' I plead as the room shudders. I tighten my grip on him in desperation. 'Please, not yet!'

His eyes snap open, cerulean fire burning into me as he smiles and breathes, 'My heart.'

I smile back as my tears splash his face. 'I love you, Aaron.'

His smile fades as the dream continues to crumble. 'You aren't really here.'

I sob, 'Why would you tell Dante to take me away? How am I supposed to live without you?'

His frown deepens, voice now barely a whisper as I wake, 'Come back to me, Goddess.'

My skin prickles as I wake for real, shudders of awareness rippling down my spine. I scramble from the bed, blinking in the darkness of the room. The air is alive with foreign energy and Dante is nowhere to be seen. I hesitate, wondering if I should just go present myself to whomever is here. Maybe they'll kill me and I'll go join Aaron on the river bank. Maybe I'll explode into a sticky, black mist like the other Sirens. Either way I don't care, if it will end this pain.

Siren burn scolds my throat as I step into the hallway. I inch towards the stairs, bracelets illuminating the way as my bow activates in response to impending danger. I realise my lyre is missing from my wrist and glance back to the bedroom, remembering I left it on the bed. I consider going back, until voices draw my focus to the stairs. I press my spine to the wall and silently descend the first two steps.

A hand clamps over my mouth as an arm bands my waist, lifting me back onto the top step. 'It's me,' Dante whispers by my ear before peeling his hand from my mouth.

He releases his hold and I turn his way, nearly falling backwards down the stairs when I see what he's wearing. The black shirt and dark jeans belong to Aaron. He's been dead less than a day and this is not okay.

Dante grabs my hand and pulls me back to the bedroom. I realise why when the prickling sensation increases on my skin, footsteps sounding on the stairs. A flash of blue light illuminates the room as Dante lifts a curly shell to his lips. I panic at the sight but before I can bolt, luminous water rises around my ankles and sucks me under.

Like last time, we're suspended in blinding liquid until Dante pulls me towards the exit. I thank God as we break the surface, lungs burning to take a breath—except we're still in the water, only now it's crushing and devoid of light. All I see is Dante's sparkly eyes, like green fire in night.

I feel his confusion at my panic before his voice sounds in my mind. 'It's okay, we're safe here.'

I shake my head and grip my throat, mind growing numb with fear as my body shuts down. He doesn't seem to understand that I'm drowning, so I push away from him and try to swim for the surface. But there is no surface and we're so far down, there isn't even sunlight to tell me which way is up.

My arms and legs get heavy and the fire to keep fighting goes out. All these months, it's Aaron and my friends I've been fighting for anyway. Without them, I'm back to being an empty shell.

I close my eyes and think of Aaron in my last moments. He taught me to swim so I'd no longer fear the ocean but the ocean isn't done with me yet. The sound of my heart slowing is strangely hypnotic. I feel the throb of it in my throat and chest, as I imagine Aaron's arms curling around me. He tugs me close and cups my face, his lip pressing with mine. They're warm and salty and he breathes cool breath into my aching lungs. My insides light up at the sensation and I curl my fingers through his soft hair, as I deepen the kiss.

The fog slowly clears from my brain, reason returning and I open my eyes in confusion. There's a haze of gold light around me and through it, I meet Dante's startled gaze. I jerk away when it registers, he was the one kissing me. I open my mouth to berate him but falter when I realise, I'm breathing water. I stare at Dante dumbfounded, my shining skin illuminating his worried expression.

'*I'm sorry,*' he says and I flinch at the sound of his voice inside my head. '*I assumed we were the same in all things but I suppose I inherited water-breathing from my father. You seem to be managing well though, considering.*'

Because it isn't my first time breathing water but I don't see the point of going into it. '*Can you hear me, too?*' I think back as the light fades from my skin, drenching us back in darkness.

He takes my hand when I panic and pulls me close. The heat of his skin is intense compared to mine and I suddenly realise how cold I am. Even so, I try to pull away.

'*Why are you fighting me?*' he asks.

'*Because you kissed me.*'

'*That was not a kiss until you made it one,*' he defends.

'*Pressing your lips to another's isn't considered kissing where you're from?*' I scoff.

'*It's the only way of imparting the Breath of the Ocean,*' he says. '*And I did it to stop you from drowning.*'

I stop struggling. '*You mean it's the reason I can breathe water now?*'

He nods then mentally sighs before admitting, '*I've never been kissed like that by anyone until now.*'

I stare at him in surprise then horror, as I realise I've stolen his first kiss. '*Dante, I'm so sorry! You never gave me permission and I—*'

'*You didn't know it was me,*' he says dismissively.

'*How...did you know that?*'

'*Your emotions were...intense.*'

'*Oh,*' I answer, shivering as I look away.

'*You're cold down here,*' he says, his worry weaving through me. He bites his lip in the same way I do then pulls me into a hug, sighing, '*I didn't think this through.*'

I give in and plaster myself against his warmth. '*Why are you still so warm?*'

'*Poseidon is my father and water is my element. My body regulates automatically to whatever temperature the water is.*'

'*Can we go somewhere that won't involve me freezing to death?*'

He thinks for a moment then says, '*I know a place.*'

He tucks me tight against him, enough that I feel his muscles coil before we shoot through the water. We fly so fast it stings my eyes and I have to bury my face against his shoulder. I look up when we slow to see a wall of rock, rise from the ocean floor like a shadow in the already dark water. We glide parallel to the sheer face before Dante pulls me in through an almost invisible fissure. We barely fit through the gap, rough walls closing in, skimming our bodies as we move along the narrow passage.

Dante squeezes me even closer, his muscular frame undulating as he guides us forward. He's confident in the dark water and I notice how visible he is despite the lack of light. I study him the best I can in the tight space. He's peppered in speckles of neon blue and green; freckles of starlight decorating his skin. I brush a curious finger over one on his cheek and his luminous gaze snaps to mine. His eyes are like jewels down here, burning neon like the freckles of light on his skin.

I look away as the passageway spits us out into an enormous cavern, the walls alive with twinkling lights. I look around in awe as Dante swims us deeper into the space. I realise the lights are tiny sea creatures, lining the ledges and crevices that form a honeycomb structure up to a smooth, domed ceiling.

Dante swims to one of the ledges and sits me on the edge. I push a cloud of hair from my face to study him as he sits beside me. He's covered in those glowing freckles, glittering in the darkness like the shimmering creatures on the walls.

'*There's an active volcano below this cavern, warming the water inside,*' he says not meeting my gaze.

I remember how easily he located the hidden entrance and ask, '*Do you come here often?*'

'*It's part of my father's domain but some areas, like this one, are not on his radar.'* His shyness blooms through me before he says. *'This place is the closest thing I had to escaping.'*

'Before you actually escaped to find me,' I say.

He smiles and meets my gaze. *'You understand.'*

Because I understand feeling so devastated about your life that you need to escape it. If I'd had a secret place, I would've gone there too.

I rest a hand over his. *'Thank you for bringing me here, Dante.'*

His fresh energy spreads through me in response, smoking into the emptiness in my middle. It's a temporary salve, like sticking tape over a fault line and expecting it to stop the Earth from shaking.

13

I wheeze as I sit up and look down at the bruising from Mila's blade. The wounds will take several more hours to heal but I can breathe again. One of Inara's tears, drips from my chin and I remember how upset she'd been. She thinks I died from the attack and is alone somewhere, without my protection.

I ease from the bed and stagger to the door, remembering what she'd tried to do the last time she thought I'd died. I have to find her before it's too late. I use the wall for support as I shuffle to the top of the stairs then falter at the sound of Delia's voice amid the ruckus below. I make my way gingerly down the steps, unsure why the Oracle of Delphi is here but glad since she'll be paramount in locating Inara.

The kitchen is packed with soldiers, Logan in the centre, weapons drawn and face like thunder. Delia's standing between him and a male with curly blond hair. The shadows gather around Logan and his eyes are glinting, meaning more than one warrior will be bleeding soon.

'I already told you, he isn't here,' Logan snarls at the blond. 'Now give me that before I'm forced to take it from you.'

I follow Logan's glare to the lyre in Blondie's hand and see the other warriors shift with unease. Logan's bad mood is summoning dark, unearthly smoke to roll across the floor but Blondie seems oblivious. Lightning prickles my skin as I stalk up to Logan's side and stare at the lyre in Blondies grip.

An arsenal of weapons swing my way as I growl, 'Where did you get that?'

'And who might you be?' Blondie sneers, directing his weapon from Logan to me too.

'Aaron, Son of Zeus,' I say allowing a sliver of lightning to snap over my skin. 'The question is, who are *you* and why do have that key?'

Blondie's eyes widen as he looks from me to Logan then back again and figures out who we are. Every weapon in the room except Logan's is sheathed and Blondie takes a nervous breath. I breathe deep too, tasting the air. The only demigods in the room are Logan and I, though Blondie has a faint odour of the divine weaving his scent. He's far less than god but more than human—perhaps a child or grandchild of a demigod. Whatever he is, Logan and I can easily take them all if we have to.

'I'm Milos and I'm following direct orders from Poseidon,' Blondie says.

'What orders?' I ask looking pointedly at Inara's key.

'He's been charged with finding Dante, Son of Poseidon,' Delia says when Milos hesitates. 'Milos and The Guard followed Dante's trail to your house on the Guardian Isle and discovered Inara's key on your bed, Aaron. I only brought them here because I'm worried about her.'

I glance at Logan and know from the look on his face that he's thinking the same as me. The unfamiliar scent we detected in my room yesterday suddenly has an owner.

'I didn't know Poseidon had a living son,' Logan says, failing to hide his excitement.

For years now, the only real challenge Logan and I face is fighting each other. But Dante is Poseidon's. He'll be as strong as Logan and I, and Logan is practically drooling at the thought.

'Not many people do,' Milos says.

'What the hades was Dante doing in my home on the Guardian Isle?' I demand.

Milos huffs, 'All I know is he got out two nights ago with a rotation of guards and we've been despatched to retrieve him.'

Logan raises an eyebrow. 'He...got out?'

Milos looks terrified that he's divulged too much then admits, 'Poseidon doesn't allow Dante to go...unaccompanied outside of his domain.'

'Why not?'

Milos frowns like he didn't expect the question. 'That's Poseidon's business.'

'So you don't know,' Logan decides and looks at me. 'It must be serious, for Poseidon to hide Dante's existence from the other gods.'

I stare at Milos then down at Inara's key, mind whirring. Apollo kept Inara a secret because he'd known what would happen if the other gods discovered her existence. The dark-haired male that saved Inara had enormous ebony wings, like a midnight copy of hers... Has Poseidon been hiding a Siren offspring too? It fits, except for Dante being male and Siren women only birth females.

I glance at the many eyes watching us then back to Milos. I need to speak to him alone about Dante, without implicating Inara in the process. She isn't on my father's Most Wanted list anymore but doesn't have his protection either. The less warriors that know my connection to her, the better.

'I'll help you locate Dante but you won't like what I have to say,' I tell Milos.

He catches my meaning and barks, 'Dismissed.'

The soldiers file outside and we wait for them to reach a distance where overhearing us would be unlikely.

'I'm not helping him,' Logan snarls the second they're out of range.

'Who do you think has Inara?' I scoff.

His jaw flexes and a growl vibrates my aching chest. Whatever happened between Logan and Inara during the Games has given him a soft spot for her that I've never witnessed. I don't know if it's something I should be worried about or if he's just drawn to her like everyone is. Even other Sirens seem captivated by Inara's allure and it's something she hates. She dreams of blending into the crowd but knows it will never happen. Her allure was something I despised back when we first met too. It infuriated me that I could be attracted to such a monstrous thing and fuelled my rage. It was her kindness that ensnared me though, not her hypnotic beauty.

'You let the Son of Poseidon take her?' Logan snarls.

'I didn't *let* him take her,' I snarl back. 'She was trying to save me from her sister, so I had no choice.'

'Mila was here?' Delia gasps. 'My gods, is everyone okay?'

'Alex and I were upstairs when she tried to get to Helen but Talia got in her way,' Logan says. 'I killed her for what she did.'

'Helen and Talia?' Delia rasps.

'Alexander used my key to take Helen home and Talia is...healing upstairs,' Logan says, voice tight with rage.

I thought his relationship with Talia was just physical but it seems I was wrong. I remember what he'd said to Mila before he slit her throat; that her death would be painful because of what she'd done to Talia. It's Logan's love language and I pray his feelings are reciprocated. Not many females dare to entangle themselves with the Son of Hades for more than a claim to have liaised with Death. I always thought he enjoyed the fear he caused them but maybe I was wrong about that too.

'Who's Mila?' Milos asks.

'How do we know we can trust him?' Logan says glaring at Milos.

'He knows Dante better than any of us, which is why he's managed to track him this far,' Delia says. 'If we want to find Inara quickly, we need his help.'

'She might come back of her own accord,' Logan says.

'The last thing she and Dante saw was Mila torturing me to death,' I argue. 'He wouldn't allow her to return even if she wanted to because they think it isn't safe.'

'Callista could make her way here too,' Logan murmurs then, 'I need to move Talia to the Guardian Isle.'

'I'm Dante's oldest friend and your best chance of finding him,' Milos cuts in seeming annoyed that he isn't a part of the conversation. 'If you want my help then you're going to have to reveal what you know.'

I sigh because time isn't our ally right now. 'If you tell anyone what I'm about to reveal, I'll kill you,' I promise.

Milos nods. 'That's fair.'

'Mila was one of the escaped Sirens,' I say.

'But this is the Human Realm,' he argues. 'Why would she come here?'

'To hunt Inara.'

'Your girlfriend...' Understanding slackens his jaw before he says, 'Inara is the god-sired Siren.'

'She is.'

He sneers, 'But why would you...with that... She's a filthy flesh-eating—'

'Hold your tongue,' I snarl; lightning snapping around me.

He holds his hands up in surrender. 'I'm not judging, it's your life.' He glances nervously at Logan, whose rage has filled the room with shadow and dropped the temperature several degrees. 'I just want to get Dante away from her before he gets hurt.'

'For such a close friend, Dante didn't confide in you much, did he?'

Milos narrows his gaze on me. 'What's that supposed to mean?'

'This is the part you won't like,' I warn.

'What could be worse than knowing Dante is with that thing?' he scoffs then starts choking when Logan grips his throat.

'I think you'll enjoy his reaction to what I have to say, Logan.'

Logan gives me a lazy glare then drops Milos. He lands on the floor, wheezing and clutching his bruised throat and we stare down at his dramatics.

'Fine, I'll keep the insults to a minimum,' he rasps as he shoves to his feet. 'Just tell me so I can continue tracking Dante.'

'Dante escaped his father's domain to find Inara,' I say.

'Poseidon ordered to keep her existence from him, so why would he come looking for a being he knew nothing about?'

'Have you never wondered why Poseidon kept Dante a secret?' I ask. 'Apollo tried to do the same with Inara because look how well it turned out for her when her existence was revealed.'

He stares at me with an incredulous expression. 'Are you honestly trying to tell me Dante is some kind of monster?'

'I'm *trying* to tell you that Inara and Dante are the same.'

He starts laughing. 'Okay, this is getting ridiculous. Didn't anyone ever explain that Sirens only birth female offspring? Sorry to disappoint but Dante isn't curvy enough to pass as female.'

'That...isn't entirely true,' Delia says. Logan, Milos and I turn to stare at her. She fidgets under our gaze. 'I suppose Inara didn't tell you then.'

'Tell us what?' Logan demands.

'Sirens *do* produce male offspring, they—they just don't make it past infancy.'

'Why?' I ask, already dreading the answer.

She winces. 'They...eat their male offspring shortly after birth.'

Milos gags. 'Why would they do that?'

'They don't inherit the deadly traits of the females, so are deemed useless. They even consider them a delicacy.'

Bile burns my throat at this new information. Inara doesn't like to talk about her time alone on the Flowery Isle but I know it was traumatic. She talks in her sleep and sometimes, she repeatedly apologises to me during nightmares. She blames herself for my death on that island and won't fully accept when I tell her it wasn't her fault. Something happened during her time with the Sirens and apparently finding out they eat their young was part of it. No wonder she refuses to speak about it and my heart aches with the need to hold her.

'Have you heard yourselves?' Milos scoffs. 'Male Sirens don't exist! I've spent most of my life babysitting Dante, so don't you think I'd have noticed if he was one?'

'How can you be sure, have you ever met his mother?'

Milos blanches then shakes his head. 'No... It's too crazy.'

'What do you know?' Logan says.

'I don't—'

'Please, gift me the pleasure of beating it from you,' Logan purrs.

Milos hesitates, swallows then looks around to check we're still alone. 'I have met Dante's mother,' he admits. 'I just never understood what she did to deserve her fate.'

'Her fate?'

'Poseidon had the gorgon Euryale turn her to stone and now her body stands in a shrine-like room in the main palace. She—she was very beautiful,' he whispers then shakes his head. 'But Dante, he's so normal—'

'So is Inara,' I say.

14

Inara is sleeping in one of the many hollows lining the cavern walls. It's been at least a week since we took refuge here and she's spent most of that time staring into space, lost in her grief. It's been a special kind of torture and I don't know what to do. She's growing weak but doesn't touch the food I bring her. I can feel that she's giving up and I need to think of a way to make her want to live again.

I go to the opening that leads out into the ocean, hoping a swim will help me think of something. Maybe if I find different food for her, it will coax her into eating.

Her fear prickles through me as I reach the exit and her voice breathes into my mind, *'Where are you going?'*

I glance at the slender fingers gripping my forearm then meet her gaze. *'You need food, Inara.'*

'I'm fine.'

'You aren't.'

She hesitates because she knows I'm right. She's barely been awake the last two days and it's only a matter of time before she doesn't wake up at all.

'*I'll come with you then,*' she says.

'*The ocean is crawling with guards. If they discover me, I'll be fine but I don't know what will happen to you.*'

'*And what will happen if you don't come back?*' she argues.

I hand her my key. '*If I don't return within a few hours, use this to leave.*' She stares at my key like I've offered her salvation and I snatch it back. '*You can't go back there!*'

She doesn't deny that she was contemplating returning to where we watched Aaron die. '*I have nowhere else to go, Dante. You have the option of living a happy life with your father and should take it.*'

'Happy?' I scoff. '*Would you really throw your life away, knowing I didn't understand happiness until I met you?*'

She stares at me in shock. '*How can you say that when you don't even know me?*'

'*I've spent a week feeling your emotions.*'

'*That doesn't mean you know me, Dante.*'

'*But I understand you.*'

'*You think?*' she sneers, angry now but I'll take her anger over the grief and apathy.

'*We are kindred spirits; connected by what we are and the similar hardships we've experienced because of it. We've both felt the loneliness being what we are causes and if you leave, you'll force me to go back to that existence.*'

Her anger switches to despair. '*I'm broken, Dante. Trust me when I say, your life will be brighter without me in it.*'

I brush a swirl of golden hair from her face and say, '*Won't you at least give me the chance to decide that for myself?*'

Her despair thickens, coiling through my insides and gripping tight. '*I don't know if I'm strong enough.*'

I pull her into a hug. '*I think you're stronger than you give yourself credit for, Inara. You won't know until you try. I thought I'd spend my life alone in the depths of the ocean and now look at me.*'

'*You're still in the depths of the ocean,*' she scoffs.

I smirk. '*My gods, was that a joke?*'

A glimmer of amusement shines from her but she shakes her head and backs away. The wall she's learned to create over the past week, rises between us and she uses it to shutter her emotions from me. I already felt the sliver of hope she's trying to hide though and it proves she's capable of crossing the threshold of her sorrow. There's light growing in the darkness of her grief and all I have to do is guide her from it.

'*I'm not letting you go out there without me,*' she says after an awkward moment.

'*And I won't risk you getting caught,*' I say.

She glares at me, hair a pretty halo of gold around her perfect face. Her fury is magnetic, filling me with the need to feel her lips on mine again. She apologised for stealing my first kiss but I found it startlingly glorious. Her lips were so plush and warm and her taste...

'*Then what do you propose we do?*' she huffs, pulling me back to the moment.

'*We cannot return to where your sister is, nor to the Guardian Isle,*' I say, '*and my father's domain is still swarming with guards.*'

'*That leaves us with the Human Realm but we'll have to go somewhere nobody knows to look for me.*'

'*A place no one knows you've been,*' I agree.

'*There's a place I've been that only Aaron knew about.*'

Her sadness presses down on me, so I take her hand. '*I'll open the doorway and you can navigate.*'

I LIFT Inara from the pool of light, drenched clothes clinging to our skin. She looks around the rectangles of stone jutting from the earth, as fading sunlight streams through the leafy trees above. Birds chatter from the branches but there's a sombre feel in the air.

'What is this place?'

'A graveyard,' she says distractedly, as she picks her way around the epitaphs.

I stay close to her, while studying the place humans bury their dead. The stones transform from rectangles into monuments, each growing more elaborate before she stops. I follow her gaze to a stone woman perched atop a marble plinth, wings arced around her, head bent in prayer.

'A Siren?' I rasp, thinking of my mother's frozen form.

'It's a depiction of an Angel,' Inara corrects. 'Humans believe they watch over them.'

I stare at the angel's beautiful face, wondering what it would be like if Sirens protected people the same way. What would my life look like now if I were revered instead of feared?

Inara drops to her knees and retrieves a bouquet of rotting flowers from the grave. She hugs them to her chest and closes her eyes. Sunshine engulfs her frame and I shield my eyes from the glare. When it fades, I blink at the fresh flowers in her arms.

'How?' I breathe in awe.

She places the flowers back on the grave and sighs, 'It's a gift I inherited from Apollo. I can heal things, make them live again.'

'Are you serious?'

'Yes,' she rasps and a tear slides down her face. Another wells in its wake, then another and another. She's thinking of Aaron again.

I read the inscription on the gravestone. 'Who was she?'

'Aaron's mother.'

She unclasps the pendant from around her neck and fastens the chain around the bouquet, so the tiny butterfly is nestled amid the blooms. She hangs her head and lets her tears feed the earth. I think she's saying goodbye to Aaron, so I retreat to a wooden bench on a path winding through the graveyard. I can still see her from my seat but it's the only privacy I can offer right now. I study a bronze plaque embedded in the wooden bench, dedicating it to someone's lost love.

Inara comes to find me as the sun slips beneath the horizon. Her eyes are puffy and her skin is pale. I stand and pull her into a hug, letting her sob against my shoulder. The barrier is down, her emotions battering me like a raging storm.

'Everyone except Delia and Adonia are gone and I can't go to them because they're on the Guardian Isle,' she says.

'I'll protect you,' I vow.

She shoves away. 'No!'

'Inara—'

'This stupid curse!' she hisses, 'Luring people in and making them feel the need to protect or kill me. I'll get you killed too, Dante and then you'll be gone like the others.'

She tries to pull that damned wall up between us but I grab her wrist and snarl, 'Don't.'

She struggles to get free. 'I thought you were immune but we aren't the same, Dante. You'll fall victim to my curse like everyone else.'

'I won't.'

'It's already lured you in,' she argues. 'It's only a matter of time before it takes you too.'

'Then I promise I'll never leave!' I growl, voice resonating with my frustration. When she stills I know I need to cement my idea in her mind. 'I'll never leave you, Inara. We're the same, you and I; kindred spirits walking the same path. We were destined to find each other and will face what's coming *together*.'

'You don't know what you're promising,' she breathes.

'I do.'

'I loved him so much,' she rasps. 'I thought the Fates gave me a second chance but they took him away and I don't know how to live without him.'

'He'd want you to be happy; would want you to live.'

Tear-drenched eyes stare up at me. 'My dreams of him are so real, Dante. He doesn't feel gone, just...far away.'

'I used to dream about my mother in the same way. She would hold me and sing me to sleep but I never even knew her,' I say. 'Sometimes dreaming of the ones we want is just a part of letting them go.'

She looks back to where she left the pendant. 'Letting go?'

'I promise it gets easier after a while.'

She rests her head on my shoulder and I hug her tight, waiting for her to process her emotions. The barrier dissolves between us and I hide my relief at her show of trust.

'We should go,' she says after a while.

She's shivering as we leave the graveyard, so I pull her into my side and wrap my arm around her shoulders. Our clothes are still damp and the temperature is dropping, tall lights blinking on along the pavement as we walk. The roadway is a continual strip of hard grey stone, with a broken white line marking the centre. I stare when a shiny chariot-like vehicle glides by. There aren't any horses pulling it and it makes a rumbling sound as though it contains a great beast.

'It's called a car,' Inara says taking my hand to tug me along faster. 'Stop staring or you'll draw too much attention.'

'Where are we going?' I ask unable to hide the fascination from my tone.

'There's a university up ahead where we should blend in more; plus, students are notoriously lax with their security.'

'I don't understand anything you just said.'

A wan smile tugs at the corners of her perfect mouth, the first I've seen in days. 'We need clothes and somewhere to sleep for the night. We can decide where to go in the morning.'

'Of course,' I agree, though I still don't fully understand.

15

The evening is coming alive, people bustling in and out of cafés and restaurants. Dante is gazing around with a look of wonderment, despite his efforts to hide it. My stomach growls at the alluring smell of food in the air and I can't remember ever feeling this hungry.

'Look!' Dante says, snagging my arm.

I follow the direction of his gaze, to a group of artists busking around an antique fountain in the cobbled market square.

'We don't have time for this,' I huff when he pulls me towards them.

I'm so hungry, all I can think about is food. Dante, of course, ignores me and drags me over to the crowd that has formed.

'What are they doing?' he asks, watching patrons drop money into an empty guitar case.

'It's called busking. They're making money using their talents.'

He takes a moment to study the musician, then tugs me to the next busker: an artist drawing caricatures for tourists. He smiles at the girl when she offers to draw our portraits.

'Dante,' I whine, trying to pull him from the crowd. 'We need to find food.'

'I have an idea,' he says guiding me to a vacant spot in front of the fountain.

'What are you doing?' I hiss when he pulls his shirt off.

'We need something for them to put money on,' he answers arranging the shirt on the ground in front of his feet.

I drag my eyes from his ripped torso and ask, 'Why?'

'I'm going to use one of my talents to make money for food.'

I grip his arm. 'Humans don't know about us,' I whisper, glancing at the crowd already forming in front of us. 'You can't just do things that they think can't happen.'

'I know,' he scoffs and gestures to a busker opposite, a tall man attempting to pull something out of a hat. 'But they believe in magic, do they not?'

I stare at the magician. 'Sure, but—'

Dante cups my jaw to regain my focus. 'Trust me, Inara.'

His cool energy stings my skin and I nod dumbly. Something about his touch is instantly soothing and I have to stop letting him use it on me.

He climbs onto the edge of the fountain and more people gather around. He addresses the crowd, voice strange with just the non-lethal resonance only Sirens can detect. I still find it enticing and wonder how he's holding his voice back when we're so close. I haven't been holding mine back around him and now it hurts when I try. His proximity draws it from me and the more I'm around him, the harder it is to fight that part of myself. His immunity to my song has made me complacent and I need to stop it. I like that I can be myself around him but don't want it to isolate me from everyone else.

'I need a volunteer from the crowd,' he shouts.

A young girl raises her hand eagerly, waving it alongside the many volunteers willing to do whatever Dante wants. Even without using his voice, he's captivating to watch but it's all part of his Siren charm. He gestures the young girl forward and jumps down from the fountain to take her hand. Her face flushes and the crowd leans in. I feel a surge of Dante's energy from where I'm standing and the girl looks startled when he pulls his hands away. A tiny bird made of ice, sits in her palm. She spins to her parents, brandishing the delicate carving and gasps fill the air. Money rains onto the shirt Dante laid out on the cobbles and he grins my way.

I feel chastised and impressed as I watch him work. The crowd thickens around him, people requesting their own sculptures made from ice. I move away as they circle him and smile at his expression, as he tries to decipher the human words from a group of chattering girls. He's very alluring and I perch on the low wall of a café, watching his shirt overflow with coins. A group of excited girls wander by, each holding an ice ornament.

'When he held my hand I felt a connection,' one says.

'He's the hottest guy I've ever seen,' another responds.

'I'm sure your boyfriend will love to hear you say that,' the first scoffs.

'Just because I'm taken doesn't mean I'm not allowed to go window shopping.'

The first girl giggles, then they're gone. I stare after them, wondering why hearing them talk like that about Dante bothers me. I gaze at him, holding the hand of a tall girl with raven hair. An uncomfortable sensation curls through my stomach and Dante's eyes find mine across the cobbled square. A bright smile lights his face and I smile back. The girl says something and he looks away and that feeling comes back.

A loud crash snaps me from my thoughts and I spin to find Joshua staring at me; a tray of drinks smashed on the floor at his feet. He steps over the wrecked coffee mugs and out into the square.

'You're here; you're okay,' he says before throwing his arms around me and squeezing me tight.

'Joshua—'

'Josh, you idiot!'

Joshua glances at the male standing by the pile of broken mugs. It looks like his older brother Michael but before I can really look, he grips my hand and pulls me away from the café.

'I've got to go. Cover my shift!' Joshua shouts.

We round the corner, leaving Michael's objections behind. Joshua pulls me into a narrow road leading to the back entrance of the café. He spins me to face him and backs me against the wall. A light flickers overhead, reminding me of a distant lightning storm and I swallow.

'What happened?' he demands.

'I...'

'Don't you dare lie to me, Inara. I want answers. That day in the graveyard, I watched you disappear. I went to ask Helen about it and could tell she was hiding something.'

I stare at him, wanting to tell him everything but knowing it will be a mistake. After Helen he's the closest thing I have to family and Helen's gone. I won't tangle his future with mine and get him killed too.

I slide from between him and the wall. 'I can't tell you, Josh.'

He blocks my escape. 'If you're in some kind of trouble I can help.'

'I can't; I can't let you get involved in this.' I push him out of the way and try to leave again.

He catches my wrist. 'I promised Danny I'd look out for you, Nara and that's what I'm going to do.'

'What is it with guys thinking they can manhandle me in the name of protection,' I snarl making him flinch, a little too much of my Siren side seeping out.

It's all venom, no charm and I see his shock at glimpsing my monster. It's taking everything to hold my voice at bay though and it's all Aaron's fault. If he hadn't carried me off last year, Joshua wouldn't be acting this way.

Joshua lets me go. 'I didn't mean—'

'Noisemaker!' a familiar voice snarls.

A figure appears at the entrance of the dim, narrow road. My muscles lock at the derogatory term used for Sirens, scalp prickling at the danger.

I shove Joshua towards the back door of the café. 'Run!'

He moves in front of me instead and shouts, 'What do you want?'

'Stay out of my way, boy,' the female answers.

Where do I know that voice from? The figure steps beneath the flickering light and my eyebrows shoot to my hairline. 'Cali?'

She's wrapped in silver armour, chestnut hair like satin around her shoulders as her hazel eyes narrow. She always looks like she's on her way to a modelling shoot, even when she's glaring my way. Joshua glances between us and I know he's thinking Cali's armour-clad figure is like what I'd been wearing when he saw me last winter.

'Noisemaker, or would you prefer Cytheria?' she sneers.

'What are you doing here, Cali?'

She draws the sword from its sheath on her hip. 'I'll give you three guesses.'

I shove around Joshua. 'Are you serious?' I snarl, fighting the resonance from my voice at her audacity. 'I saved you in the Games last year.'

'You stood there and watched me get shot,' she scoffs.

'Pushing you from the path of a flaming spear counts for nothing then,' I grit out.

'What is she talking about?' Joshua asks.

'I never knew boys from the Human Realm could be so good looking,' Cali says. 'Maybe after I kill you, I'll stay and play with this one.'

A protective rage hazes my vision and I growl, 'Go back to the café, Josh.'

'That boy is my insurance policy that you won't start singing,' she argues. 'He's staying here until I'm done with you.'

My bracelets ignite, searing my wrists. 'Don't force me to hurt you, Cali.'

Her laughter echoes between the narrow walls before she leaps at me, sword high. My left arm snaps up, golden bow flashing out. A shimmering arrow appears between my fingers as I aim. Then Joshua crashes into my side, slamming us into the concrete and jarring my shoulder as his weight lands on me. I lose my grip on the bow and it dissipates.

I shove him away and roll to the side as Cali's blade impacts the concrete. She doesn't seem to care that she could've hurt Joshua, her sword singing as she swings for the rebound. I kick her legs from under her then scramble for her blade as it skids across the ground. She snares my ankle, dragging me backwards then climbs on top of me. She fists my hair and starts smashing my face into the concrete. I feel my cheekbone give way, the pain consuming yet...oddly satisfying. Ice, unfurls deliciously through my insides and I coil to strike.

Cali's weight disappears from my back and I wipe blood from my eyes at the sound of clashing metal. I stagger to my feet and think I'm seeing double, before Adonia's distinctive voice cuts through the chaos and confusion.

'I always knew you were an idiot,' Adonia snarls, swinging her blade to counter Cali's.

'I'm not the one defending a blood-thirsty Siren!' Cali snarls back.

'I told you, she isn't like the others! Put your weapon down and I'll explain.'

'You explained enough on the Guardian Isle.'

'I didn't think you'd freak out and start hunting her,' Adonia growls.

'I'm doing what I'm supposed to do, what *you're* supposed to do,' Cali hisses, blades locking in stalemate.

'Look around, Cali,' Adonia grunts. 'Not only have you exposed yourself to and attacked a human, Inara isn't even fighting back.'

'He's collateral damage and she's biding her time,' Cali hisses. 'Why can't you see that?'

Their words filter through the painful haze in my head and I look around. Collateral damage? I gasp when I see Joshua on the ground, body twisted at an awkward angle. Adonia and Cali's standoff separates me from him and I try to edge around them.

Cali's eyes narrow on me. 'Move and he dies.'

The wintry feeling flares bright inside me at her threat, a white rage infusing the perpetual heat in my core. I look from her to Joshua and images of Aaron lying on the stone table on Anthemusa bombard me. Somebody is always trying to steal the ones I love and I'm done with letting it happen.

I slam into Cali, throwing her to the ground. The ice in my middle purrs, as I grip her throat and lift her until she's looking down at me, toes grazing the concrete. Her weapon clatters at my feet, as her pulse throbs deliciously beneath my palm. The burning in my lungs grows unbearable with the need to taste her. And yet, a small voice amid the delectable rage tells me that I shouldn't.

I ponder my reasons for holding back, as her luscious, earthy fragrance teases my senses. The demigod twang perfumes her aroma, making me salivate and I swallow against the fire in my throat. It's starkly overwhelming, engulfing me like when I tasted Aaron on Anthemusa.

Aaron.

I drop Cali and stumble backwards. She crashes to the ground coughing and clambers for her weapon. I back away, wondering what the hell just happened and meet Adonia's shocked gaze. She just witnessed the part of me I've been hiding and I'm terrified her shock will turn to disgust.

Joshua's hysterical voice registers through the drumming in my ears and Adonia throws herself at Cali. I watch them grapple on the ground until Joshua grabs my hand. He pulls me to the end of the road, voice seeming far away. It feels like we're running through water and I can't seem to take a deep enough breath.

The fire in my lungs churns through the ice in my middle, both fighting for supremacy and making me nauseous. The ice I keep locked away has slipped its leash and tasted freedom. It doesn't want to go back into hiding and why should it? It hurts when I fight it and I keep wondering why I should have to.

We burst into the street beyond the alley, into the reassuring glow of the streetlights. I remember the blood on my face and wipe at it with the back of my free hand. Joshua looks at me with concern, then grunts when someone smacks into him so fast they blur.

I stare at Dante, pinning Joshua to the wall by his throat before my brain kicks in. 'Dante, stop! He's my friend, stop!'

I pull against his iron grip until his gaze turns to me. His pupils are blown wide, his anger raking at my insides. It take a few more seconds for him to actually *see* me and he finally lets go. Joshua doesn't move and I register his serene expression. I was so caught up in the moment I forgot to keep my voice in check.

'Joshua?' I rasp.

He gazes at me dreamily and it's the reminder I need for fighting this part of myself. I slap him across the face in desperation when he doesn't wake from my song and he blinks, rubbing his cheek.

'Did...you just hit me?'

Relief blasts through me and I hug him tight. 'You scared the hell out of me!'

He hugs me back, voice hoarse, 'What just happened, Nara? What the hell was that back there? Please, I just want the truth.'

Where do I even start?

'Those women were dressed in armour, like you were last year when you—'

'Adonia!' I squeak at the reminder and start running back to help.

I slam into an armour-clad body as I turn the corner and the impact throws us to the ground. Dante picks me up and hands me to Joshua, before pinning the other body to the tarmac.

'Tell this moron to get off me,' Adonia growls.

'She isn't the one who attacked us, Dante. She's my friend too.'

He helps her up and she glares at him before her nostrils flare and she looks at me. 'What are you doing here and where is Aaron?'

Grief slams into me and I rasp, 'Mila... She found us.'

'What?'

'Mila found Inara's hiding place,' Dante says when I can't bring myself to speak. 'I managed to get her out but the others—'

'No,' she rasps face ashen, then her eyes widen. 'Helen?'

'I tried to save them,' I sob. 'I'm sorry, I'm so—'

'Talia?'

'And Alexander and Logan and...*everybody*.'

She leans against the wall for support and I reach to comfort her but Joshua gets in the way. His right eye is swollen shut and his bottom lip is bleeding.

'What happened to Helen? Who is Mila? Why the hell was that girl trying to kill you and why is *she* dressed like that?' he demands pointing at Adonia.

'Walk away from this while you can, Josh,' I rasp.

'You know I can't do that, Nara.'

'I don't think he has a choice,' Adonia says. 'Cali knows he's connected to you now and might use him as bait.'

'She escaped?'

Adonia nods. 'She has a talent for getting away when the odds are against her.'

I look from her to Josh, wondering how I'm going to tell him he's probably going to die. How it will be all my fault. Dante's cool energy stings my flesh, his fingers curling around my hand. His emotions rush in: concern and encouragement. I take a deep breath and pray Joshua won't hate me.

16

I blink in the lamplight and register the warm body nestled against mine. Recognition breezes through my weariness and I wonder if I'm still dreaming. I dare to look down and a tangle of golden hair quivers against my exhale. She's here; she's alive and I feel winded with relief. All week I've stayed in my home on the Guardian Isle in case Inara came back and it just paid off.

Her tears splash my chest as I relish the sensation of having her close. I've missed the warmth of her soft skin on mine, the burn that only her presence ignites. But I can't bear her weeping, so I comb my fingers through her tangled hair.

Her head jerks up, emerald eyes startled. Confusion knits her brow, then her eyes focus and we stare at each other. She scrambles up my body, meshing her lips with mine. Our kiss is hot and hungry and I groan at her taste. That sweet, indescribable fire tingles my flesh; burning raindrops quenching arid earth. Her fingers find my hair, my face...my chest. She draws away, sweet breath cascading my skin as she traces my face. Her eyes are glassy, tears like jewels on long lashes. She looks as if she expects me to vanish.

I kiss her again, hands roaming her body. She certainly feels real enough. Her lips are salty from her tears but she's hungry for me. I turn us, until I'm gazing down at her, trapping her between my body and the bed. Something settles in me now she can't escape, can't leave me again.

Her hair fans around her like a glorious halo but I bite out a curse when I realise, she's injured. She winces when I examine the gash on her forehead and across her cheek. Her top is torn and crusted with blood. A growl builds in my throat but she presses her fingers to my lips. Fresh tears brim in her eyes, streaking her temples then soaking the pillow.

'Please,' she whispers.

That voice, enticing...pleading. How can I resist? Her fingers curl into my hair and pull me in.

$$\sim$$

I DON'T WANT to open my eyes.

It's the only thing between indescribable joy and the harsh truth of reality. My conscious mind is telling me Inara is gone, yet my dream was so vivid. Her fire still infuses my skin and I groan. I never imagined burning alive could be so wonderful. Even dreaming about it was spectacular and I pray I get to act out my dream for real one day.

I sit up and swing my legs off the bed. My heart feels empty without her and I rub at my chest where our connection feels stretched thin. I frown when I notice golden feathers scattered across the room. They're jumbled with the clothing strewn across the floor, confusing me more. I collect a feather and smooth it between my thumb and forefinger and it dawns on me that Inara was actually here. Last night, easily the best night of my existence, was real.

'What are you so happy about?' Logan demands from the doorway. He frowns at the feathers. 'What did you do, kill one of your father's sacred birds?'

'Inara's alive!' I tell him.

His brow knots. 'And you know this how?'

'She visited me again last night. I swear she's getting better at it, Logan. When I saw her on Anthemusa I knew for sure she wasn't there because she looked out of focus, but last night she was so real.'

He regards me for a moment, then grins. 'I see you had fun *reuniting*. What was it like?'

The smile bleeds from my lips and I stalk past him. 'I'm not discussing this with you.'

He follows on my heels. 'I know for a *fact* she's your first, Aaron. It's healthy to talk about these things with your brother.'

'No,' I growl reaching the bottom of the stairs.

'I don't want details, just...a word. Sum it up in a single word and I'll leave you alone.'

I spin to face him, knowing Logan isn't going to leave this alone and huff, 'There aren't words to describe it.'

'Then prepare for more hounding,' he says.

I scowl. 'Swear you'll leave me alone if I do this.'

'I'll be so quiet, you'll have to keep checking I'm there.'

Sure I will. 'It was like burning in her essence, which is like nothing I can describe.'

Logan sighs, a smile tugging at the corners of his mouth. 'There's nothing quite like Inara burn.'

'And you'd know, how?' I growl.

'She kissed *me* remember. It's not my fault you left her with me last year.'

I brush his comment away because Inara admitted at the time to kissing Logan by mistake and I doubt Logan protested.

'Maybe we can concentrate on finding her now?' I huff, electricity snapping through the air as I rein my temper.

'Calm down, you're going to wreck the house again.'

I open my mouth to retort but the front door swings open. At first I think the girl Milos has with him is Amaryllis but then I realise my mistake. She could certainly pass for my friend but she's missing the decorative birthmarks covering the hands and wrists of all Demeter's children. Milos has his arm around her shoulders as he guides her inside. She has fading bruises around her throat and the pink line of a healing wound above her right knee. And she's drunk.

'This isn't a brothel,' Logan growls.

The girl's eyes widen as she looks at Logan, then her eyes track to me. 'You never told me your friends were the sons of Zeus and Hades,' she says, backing up.

'Relax,' Milos croons, ushering her deeper into the house. 'Logan and Aaron enjoy a good story as much as the rest of us.'

'What's this about?' I ask saving my judgement until I find out why Milos brought her here. I have to fight the urge to punch the carefree smile from his face as he tightens his arm around the girl. He really does rub me the wrong way, even when he isn't trying to.

'You'll never guess what story the gorgeous Cali here was telling in the tavern.'

'Oh?' Logan asks, flashing a mischievous smile. 'I love a good story.'

I grit my teeth, knowing I can't fake interest like Logan can. The second I realised Milos brought Cali here for a reason other than to hook up, my muscles tensed. If I speak now my voice will betray the situation and I can't risk it. Inara is alive but for how long? Why didn't I ask her about the injury on her head, or her bloody clothing?

'I was in the Games,' Cali says, unsure.

Logan puts his arm around her shoulders, glaring at Milos until he drops his and steps away. 'So was I,' he says smoothly. 'In fact, I think I remember you. I'm glad we never had to fight, Cali. I wouldn't have wanted to harm such a beautiful creature.'

'You think I'm beautiful?' she asks more confidently. She's beautiful and knows it.

'You must be a daughter of Aphrodite,' he says, guiding her into the kitchen.

I slip in behind them, watching as Cali gazes up at Logan. There's lust in her hazel eyes, glistening behind thick lashes. I have to hand it to Logan, he's charming when he wants to be.

'So, what happened?' he asks.

'I was teamed with the demigod Siren,' she boasts. 'That thing was actually posing as a daughter of Aphrodite.'

'The god-sired Siren?' Logan gasps.

'I was forced to yield because of her,' Cali huffs.

'That's not the best bit,' Milos adds from across the kitchen.

'There's more?' Logan asks.

Cali's smirks. 'I tracked her to the Human Realm last night.'

Logan's jaw ticks and the temperature drops. 'What happened?'

'I tried to kill her.'

'Where was she? How'd you find her?' I ask unable to stop myself.

She glares my way. 'If I tell you, you'll go steal my glory. I want to be the one to kill her. Killing that *thing* will be better than winning the Games.'

The temperature plummets, light withdrawing from the room as Logan loses his temper. He shoves her at me and my fingers lock around her throat. I slam her against the tabletop and she whimpers up at me.

'Tell me where she is,' I snarl.

She stares at me wide-eyed, when threads of lightning snap around us. 'I – I don't know what the place is called. It was my first time in the Human Realm.'

'*Think*,' I growl. 'What was she doing when you found her?'

'She was in a place where humans bury their dead.'

'Her family?' Logan suggests.

'What else?' I snarl.

'She was with a boy,' Cali rasps. 'I followed them to a courtyard. T-there were humans performing and selling their wares.'

'I've been to where Inara's human family are buried and there's nothing like the place Cali is describing.' I pull a dagger from the sheath on my hip and snarl, 'You're lying.'

'No!' she squeals. 'There was another boy, a human! She was trying to protect him, like she knew him.'

'A name.'

'I don't know!'

I raise the dagger. 'I'm sorry to hear that.'

'Joshua! She called him Joshua!'

It's the name of the male we saw when I took Inara to meet my mother. The relief is sweet at discovering where she is but I glare down at Cali, remembering Inara's injuries. I stab the dagger into the tabletop beside her head and reach into my tunic. Cali flails in vain when she sees the vial of Morpheus Milk. I force it into her mouth, emptying the contents past her teeth and rub her throat until she swallows. She slumps, eyes rolling back in her head.

'What was that?' Logan scoffs looking pointedly at my dagger.

I look at Cali, unconscious on the table. 'I won't kill her unless she forces me.'

'She tried to kill Inara, what more reason do you need?'

He's right, this time last year I would've killed Cali without a second thought for what she's done. But things have changed, *I've* changed and it's because of Inara. I try to remember when I'd hated her with every fibre of my being. She's the best part of my life and I'd almost killed her in the first few seconds of meeting her. I'd almost lost her before we ever had a chance and I'll never risk something like that again.

'She was only doing what we've all been taught to do since we were children,' I say. 'She's just a product of her teachings and if you and I can un-learn them, so can she. Besides, she told us where Inara is.'

'You know the place she described?' Logan asks.

'You should too, our mother is buried there.'

17

The pillow smells like *him*. His spicy scent is in my hair and on my skin and I close my eyes, tears seeping between my lashes, unwilling to let go of the dream. I press my teeth into my lip as I remember his electricity, his scent; the feel of his skin on mine. There's a sweet ache low in my belly and his voltage lingers in my flesh.

The delicious ache he's left, wars with the grief inside. I'll never forget the pure joy I felt but it was just a dream, a desire my subconscious brought to life. I didn't think I had the ability for such vivid dreaming but I pray it never leaves me.

I try to roll onto my back and register the weight against my shoulders. I open my eyes in confusion and hiss at the bright sunlight filling the room. I groan when I realise it's coming from me, probably triggered by the raunchy dream I was having.

I clamber from the bed and frown at my nakedness as I gather my clothing from the carpet. My top and bra are in tatters from wings unfurling and my jeans and underwear are missing. I search in vain before ripping the sheet from the bed in frustration. I wrap it around me and stalk to the door.

My sunlight floods into the dark hallway, as I tuck my wings to my back and squeeze through the doorframe. Expensive carpet muffles my footfall as I creep to the bathroom. Joshua's family are wealthy and the bathtub on this floor is huge. It's lucky his parents are on holiday somewhere tropical and Michael agreed to stop in the flat above the café tonight. I don't know how Joshua convinced him but right now I'm grateful.

I spin in the bathroom doorway, clutching the bedsheet to me. Joshua stares from the doorway opposite, mouth hanging open.

He blinks and asks, 'What next – a tail, or maybe some whiskers?'

His attitude has shifted since I explained what I am. I hate that I can sense his fear of me, since he's got a decent poker face otherwise. He's letting us stay here out of guilt for his promise to Daniel and I'm going along with it to make sure Cali doesn't come back to use him as bait.

'Sorry if I woke you,' I say.

'I was already awake,' he answers still staring at my wings. 'I came out to see what the light was.'

Said light fades, as if in response to his mentioning it. We stare at each other across the dark hallway, awkward silence stretching between us.

'I warned you not to get involved,' I huff. 'You're the one who kept insisting on it.'

I shove into the bathroom and Joshua follows me inside before I can shut the door on him. I don't really blame him for his reaction to finding out I'm a monster but it still hurts. He's the closest thing I have to a brother and his reaction feels like betrayal.

He shuts the door and flicks on the light. 'You look less freaky in the light.'

'I don't know how I'm supposed to respond to that,' I say.

'I didn't mean—'

'What exactly *did* you mean, Josh?'

'It's just a shock, okay! You aren't even human, Nara and with the wings and the light...' He shrugs.

'I already hate myself, so don't need it from you too. Look, I'm here until I know you're safe then I'll be gone.'

I bite back a growl and turn away as the first traitorous tear streaks my cheek. I'm so sick of crying. It feels like it's all I've done since I went into hiding and I feel pathetic.

Joshua turns me back to face him. 'I just need time to process, Nara. You're the closest thing I have to a sister and I love you. I won't let you go through this without me.'

'You're scared of me,' I accuse.

He sighs and hugs me. 'I'm scared *for* you; of the situation and what it means for you.'

'That makes two of us then.'

'Fear isn't always a bad thing, Nara. It keeps you vigilant.'

I pull away and go to the bath. 'You sound like Helen.'

'She knew about all this, didn't she?' When I nod, he huffs, 'Sneaky little witch.'

'She would've slapped you if she'd heard you still called her that,' I say, throat thick with grief.

He gives a sad smile then frowns when I plug the bath and turn on the water. 'Don't tell me you got up in the middle of the night to take a bath?'

'I need the water to get rid of my wings.'

He stares at me then shakes his head. 'I'm not going to pretend I understand but is there anything you need?'

'Something to wear?'

'What happened to your clothes?'

'Do you really want to know?'

'Actually, no,' he says retreating to the door. 'The fresh towels are in the cupboard and I'll leave you something to wear on your bed.'

I smile. 'Thanks, Josh.'

The water turns to liquid gold as my wings dissolve. I rest my head against the side of the tub, bubbles fizzing around my face as I remember the dream. Blue eyes and bronze skin; hot breath on my face as delicious electricity, rippled through me. I never thought anything could beat the sensation of tasting his blood last year but I was wrong.

18

I chew slowly as I watch Inara discuss our options with Adonia. She looks more radiant this morning but she smells strange in the clothes her human friend gifted her. My gaze moves to where he sits on Inara's other side and I wonder why his concern for her bothers me so much. She's concerned for him too – cares for this human. She meets his gaze and smiles, yet I feel the deep sadness she's hiding behind that happy façade.

My throat burns as I consider what happened between them to cause Inara's new glow. A dark haze mists my vision at the thought of her alone with him last night, my chest blistering in realisation. Inara flinches, her gaze finding mine as she presses a hand to her throat in question. She looks between Adonia and Joshua then stands and hurries from the room. Joshua stands up to follow but I get in his way, pressing a hand to my throat and shaking my head.

'Your voices are lethal?' Adonia guesses.

I nod then turn and chase after Inara, finding her in the room with a large, black rectangle bolted to the wall. She's curled up on one of the soft seats, face buried in her hands like she wants to hide.

'Are you okay?' she asks, voice beautiful. I get a thrill that I'm the only one able to hear her Siren song without succumbing to its allure.

'I came to ask you the same thing,' I say.

'Are you angry with me, Dante?'

I frown. 'Why would you ask that?'

'Your anger made my throat burn.'

I sigh and sit beside her, resting my hand over hers. 'I wasn't angry with you, Inara.'

She stares down at my hand but doesn't pull hers free. 'Then, what is it?'

'It doesn't matter.'

She lifts her gaze to search mine then sighs and rests her head on my shoulder. It's a sad sound and I wrap my arm around her, wishing I could take her grief away. Her pain weaves through me as we sit in comfortable silence. I stroke her silky hair and she lets me. She isn't pulling away anymore and it fills me with hope.

'I'm glad we found each other, Dante.'

The way she says it is the same as in the graveyard yesterday, when she was bidding farewell to Aaron. I frown, wanting to give her the hope she's given me.

'In more than fifty years, I've only seen the sun twice,' I say. 'Once when it was setting, and again when it was rising. I never thought anything would surpass that experience... until I met you.'

She looks up at me, that distracting mouth curved at the corners. Our faces are close enough to feel her breath on my skin and all I'd have to do is lean in...

'Thank you,' she breathes and kisses my cheek.

She gets up and walks away while I stare after her, cheek burning with the lingering press of her kiss. It makes me wonder what it would feel like to really kiss her. Not the simple press of lips when I was helping her to breathe underwater, but a real kiss. Meeting in the middle, hungry for each other.

She stops in the doorway. 'Are you coming?'

I join her in the doorway and stare down at her with longing. She stares back and a wave of her sadness rains through me, stealing my breath.

'Joshua is the closest thing to family I have left,' she tells me. 'He's like a brother, just like Helen was like a sister and I can't let him die, Dante. Not because of me.'

Relief spears through me that their love is plutonic and I brush a tear from her cheek. 'I'll protect him with my life.'

She smiles. 'Thank you.'

'IF CALI MANAGED to track you, others will do the same,' Adonia says. 'The reason Aaron chose the house in the valley was for the remote location and the surrounding hills. It was supposed to be impossible for anything to get close enough without being spotted.'

I take Inara's hand when sharp pain hits her at the mention of Aaron. Adonia glares at my hand on Inara's before she looks away. It isn't the first disgusted look she's sent my way when I've touched Inara in her presence.

'It was more effective hiding in plain sight on the Guardian Isle,' Inara says. 'The only reason you figured out my true identity was because you saw my lyre.'

'Too dangerous: Cali will be there, licking her wounds,' Adonia says.

'And no doubt she's told everyone I'm in the Human Realm,' Inara huffs, shoving to her feet to pace.

Her hips sway as she walks, each movement she makes a lesson in seduction. She doesn't even seem to know how beautiful she is and it's almost enough to distract me from the fact she's planning something.

'Then maybe we should go back there,' I say.

'Maybe, and I mean *maybe* Inara will blend in again but we can't take Joshua there,' Adonia scoffs.

'Why not?'

'Because it would take about five seconds for them to smell his humanity.'

'You can smell my humanity?' Joshua asks.

'We can dress him in my armour; my demigod scent will mask his human one.'

'And what do you propose we do about the swarms of your father's guards looking for you there?'

'They've already searched Aaron's house. Besides, once Cali starts spreading the word about Inara being in the Human Realm, they'll come here. My father knows I left to look for her and he'll send his search party after me.'

Adonia glares at me, the curl of her lip and lack of response making it obvious she knows it's a good plan.

'You want to stop in Aaron's house?' Inara rasps.

'We won't do anything you don't want to,' I say.

She looks to Adonia. 'It's a good plan and I can go to the Temple of Apollo to see Delia and my father.'

Joshua stands. 'I'm in.'

'But what about when we get there?' Adonia argues. 'You're still being hunted and your mother is still free.'

Inara flinches at her words and I decide to step in. The guilt Inara feels from putting those around her in the firing line, already claws at her and Adonia doesn't seem to care.

'At least we'll be in the opposite place to where everybody is searching,' I say.

'What would you know,' Adonia hisses.

'I know Inara has been running since Mila found her in the valley,' I growl, 'since she watched her sister kill the people she loves. She would be dead too if I hadn't done what Aaron asked of me and forced Inara to leave.'

Adonia stares at Inara. 'Is this true?'

Inara nods.

'Of course, it's true,' I say frustrated. 'I forced her, kicking and screaming, to leave the male she loves because he wanted her to live.

All Inara does is care for everybody else and is somehow berated for it.'

Adonia sighs, looking contrite and asks, 'How do you suggest we get Joshua to the Guardian Isle? It's at least three days travel from here for a demigod and we won't be able to cross the gateway with a human in tow.'

'What kind of gateway?' Joshua asks.

A flash of blue light illuminates the room and Adonia's eyes widen. 'You have a key?'

'I have my uses,' I answer.

19

'She was here,' I say kneeling beneath the stone angel.

I pick up the bouquet of flowers I left months ago and feel the soft burn of Inara's energy radiating from them. I close my eyes, the yearn to find her growing. She's given the flowers new life but left the butterfly pendant in their embrace. I tug it free, sunlight glittering from the faceted edges of the emeralds as it dangles from my clenched fist.

Memories of last night flash through my mind: words she'd spoken, soft and gentle, yet filled with pain. I'd been so full of joy I'd forgotten the things she'd said as we lay wrapped around each other on my bed.

'I left it by your mother's grave,' she'd whispered. 'It's all I had to leave as a tribute to your life.'

'Why would she leave that here?' Logan asks.

I get to my feet. 'She still thinks I'm dead.'

'How, after you two...?'

'I dream about her most nights, Logan. When I woke this morning, I thought last night was just that until I saw the feathers and some of her clothes. She must be thinking the same thing.'

'About the feathers—'

'No.'

'But—'

'We don't have time for this, Logan. I have to find her, before it's too late.'

I stuff the necklace into my pocket and stalk back to the path. I have to find Inara before she carries out the plan she told me about last night; the plan that means facing her mother and sister and not getting out alive. She thinks I'm dead and that she has nothing to lose. She thinks eliminating herself and her kin, will make everything right.

20

I stifle laughter at Joshua's attempt to put on armour. I'd been rusty putting it on again after so long but this boy doesn't have a clue.

'You've never worn armour before, have you?' I say taking a leather strap from his hands and fixing it in place.

He shrugs. 'It's not exactly required back home.'

'Don't you need it, when training to fight?'

'Most humans don't learn to fight and those that do, don't really wear this kind of armour or use the weapons you guys do.'

'Then what do you do when you're growing up?'

'Go to school, learn about maths and science and languages.'

'We learn these things too, but I meant beyond that,' I say, fastening the last piece of silver against his body.

'You mean in our free time?'

I nod. 'What do you do when you're not learning?'

'Go to the cinema, play sports, read—It depends on what interests you. I played league football with Inara's brother, Daniel on Saturday mornings and Tuesday nights.'

'You knew Inara when she was growing up?'

He grins. 'Since Grace and Adam Thompson brought her home from the hospital. I was really young, so don't really remember much but that day is one of my earliest memories. I think I was drafted in to keep Daniel occupied in the early days.'

The fondness in his voice speaks of his affection and I decide I like this boy. 'What was she like?'

He laughs, 'Awkward, shy but very sweet. She was Danny's little sister and I guess I always treated her like she was mine, too. She could make the room light up, even in the saddest moments. I don't know if that's a daughter-of-Apollo thing, or just a Nara thing.'

'It's an Inara thing. She's like sunshine.'

His gaze meets mine. 'You care for her.'

'I'd die for her.'

He frowns then asks, 'Are you really the son of Poseidon?'

I blow out a breath and stare out the window. Huge waves crash against the cliffs below and I can feel tremors rippling through the Earth from my father's anger.

'See the storminess of the ocean?' I ask.

His eyes are wide. 'Is your father really doing that?'

I nod. 'He's angry with me, for leaving.'

'Why?'

'He wants my existence to stay secret but I left to find Inara.'

'You'll be hunted like her, if they find out you exist?' When I nod, he says, 'So you're risking exposure to help someone you'd never met?'

'You don't know what it's like to be the only one of your kind. My father kept my Siren heritage secret because we are feared, even by the gods. It's the reason Apollo hid Inara in your realm.'

'Why would gods fear you when they're immortal, though?'

'Because immortality has its limits. Just because you have the potential to live forever, doesn't mean it will happen,' I say.

'I don't understand.'

'Inara and I have immortal parents but we can still be killed. It's more difficult to achieve than killing a mortal creature, but find the right weapon and you can kill anything.'

'Such as?'

'My mother was murdered by the gorgon Euryale: turned to stone to keep the secret of my existence. Our divine heritage means Inara and I have the potential of living forever, that we're durable against attacks and illness; but, like my mother, we can still be killed – albeit difficult.'

'But surely the gods know that if you wanted to hurt them, you would have by now,' Joshua says.

'Why kill something when you can use it?' I say.

Joshua frowns. 'Use her for what?'

'Power, greed, amusement... When you've been alive as long as the gods, you get bored. Our lives are cheap and they get caught up in their games, oblivious to how the rest of us will be affected. Inara has become a sought-after pawn. If she is found by a troublemaker god and refuses to help them, they'll kill her. If she sides with them, Zeus will kill her for it.'

'That isn't fair.'

'The gods only care about fairness when it directly relates to them,' I scoff.

He sits on the edge of the bed looking winded. 'I didn't realise how bad this all was. I mean, I knew it was bad but what chance does she have?'

'I don't have an answer to that but whatever happens I'll be there with her when it does,' I promise.

Adonia bursts into the room. 'Where's Inara?'

I frown at her frantic expression. 'Aaron's room.'

She shakes her head. 'I've searched the house, she's gone.'

I shove past her and go to Aaron's room. I look straight at the corner where Inara's armour had been piled. It's gone and so is her blade.

'Wherever she's gone, she's dressed to fight,' I say.

'We should try the temple of Apollo; maybe she went there,' Adonia says.

'I don't understand your language,' Joshua says. 'What's happening?'

'Stay here in case she returns,' Adonia tells him. 'Dante and I will go to Apollo's temple to look for her. Don't answer the door to anyone and don't go outside.'

WE CLIMB the stone steps of the temple and Adonia rushes inside. I'm pacing the entrance when Delia appears in the doorway. Her flame-red hair is loose around her shoulders, making her porcelain skin gleam. Adonia appears behind her as Delia steps outside.

'She isn't here,' Adonia pants still breathless from running.

Delia slaps me hard across the face. 'You promised!'

I rub my stinging cheek. 'I'm sorry.'

'You could have been killed, Dante! There are things after Inara and they'd be after you too if they discovered what you are.'

'You...know what I am?'

'It was you who rescued Inara from Mila, was it not?'

My eyes grow wide. 'How do you know that?'

She scowls. 'Because I've been trying to help Aaron and the others find her.'

Adonia grabs Delia's arm. 'Aaron's alive? Talia, Helen...the others?'

'They are all fine,' Delia answers. 'Logan killed Mila before she had chance to kill Aaron.'

'But Inara saw Aaron die.'

'We both did,' I say as my chest tightens. The boy Inara loves is still alive. She's finally lowered her wall to me and Aaron is going to take it all away.

'He *almost* did,' Delia says.

Adonia is sobbing, wiping tears with the heel of her hand. She cringes when Delia hugs her, then both girls look at each other and start laughing.

'Sorry,' Adonia says. 'Old habits can be difficult to kill. Where is Aaron now? We've been in his house for the last three hours and he isn't there.'

'He's in the Human Realm, looking for Inara,' Delia says shooting me an accusing glare. 'Apparently, Inara's been visiting him while sleeping but thinks it's all a dream. Last night she told him what she was planning.'

I forget my jealously and think about the breath-stealing sadness I felt from Inara earlier. 'What is she planning?' I rasp.

Delia's anger softens at my tone. 'She trying to find Callista and Mila. She thinks if she kills her mother and sister, it will make everything right again and the people she loves will be safe.'

'Logan killed Mila, so it will be a fair fight,' I say unsure if I'm trying to convince the others or myself.

'We've seen Callista in action,' Adonia argues. 'She doesn't play fair and won't go down without a fight, even if Inara *is* her daughter.'

'She isn't planning on surviving,' Delia breathes.

The blood drains from my face because I should have seen this coming. Her deep sadness and the way she'd hugged me before going to Aaron's room. She'd been telling me goodbye, like with Aaron in the graveyard. I'd known it at the time, I'd just refused to see it.

21

I stand in one of the fields Aaron trained me in for the Games, studying the shell of Dante's key. The likelihood I'll drown in the liquid between destinations is high but my lyre wasn't on Aaron's bed where I left it and this is my only option. I'll kill Callista and Mila before they have chance to tell anyone about Dante. He'll live without the fear of being hunted and everyone else will be safe.

I take a deep breath and blow into the shell. Soundless waves wrinkle the atmosphere like with my lyre and warm, luminous liquid rises around my ankles. My heartbeat counts the seconds – one, two – before I slip into the bright nowhere.

I look around the gleaming abyss in blind panic before remembering to think of a destination. My lungs burn for breath as a doorway opens above. I flounder to meet it and suck in oxygen when I break the surface. I claw my way from the opening then collapse on the kitchen floor, panting. The doorway closes and I stay on the floor until I've caught my breath, adding this experience to my growing list of trauma.

I pull the Artemis blade from its sheath as I silently search the empty house in the valley. My throat and lungs burn with Siren fire that will be useless against my mother and sister. Wintry excitement bleeds through me as I search though, my inner Siren purring at the possibility of violence. Deep down, I'm no better than the creatures on that island. I might hide it better, but I crave the same depraved things they do and deserve to be ended alongside them.

I think alot about what will happen when I die. I was raised Christian by my human family and always believed, without a doubt, that when I died I'd go to Heaven. I believed I was human and God gave humans eternal life. But I'm not human and everything I've learned... is it even true? Does the human God exist and is the Heaven He offers only for human souls?

Aaron's mother was human and I wonder if it's enough for him to get into human Heaven. Maybe he's with my family on the Isle of the Blessed, or the two places could be the same. Wherever he is, I hope he's happy. I want to believe I'll see him again but I still don't know if I'll turn to mist like the rest of my kind when I die.

I step around a trail of dried blood as I creep back downstairs. There's blood everywhere: Logan's room, Aaron's room and in the kitchen. There isn't anything definitive enough to tell me where to start looking for Mila and Callista though. I step outside, gaze tracking to where Mila took Aaron's life. Spring rain has washed away the evidence but the event will be forever burned into my memory.

A warning shiver prickles down my spine and I dive to the ground, as a huge spear strikes the glass door behind where I'd been standing. Glass rains over me as I stare back at the spear impaling the kitchen floor. It's as thick as my arm and twice my length.

I scramble to my feet and whirl to the enormous male pounding across the grass towards me. His blond hair is tied back and he's dressed in full armour. His footsteps shake the decreasing earth between us, as he throws his shield aside and slings a bow from his shoulder. He mounts an arrow from a sheath on his back without breaking his stride and fires.

His arrow slams into my shoulder before I can process what's happening, pinning me to the brick at my back. A scream tears from me, followed by a string of curses that would make a sailor blush. I try snapping the shaft, fingers sliding over the blood-slicked wood. It's too thick to break and I reach for the Artemis blade in desperation. Another arrow thumps into my right arm, nearly severing it at the elbow. I scream but it tapers into a sob, as a huge, sweaty hand grips my throat. The enormous male is on his knees but still has to crouch to meet my gaze.

He sniffs my hair then grins. 'Noisemaker.'

I struggle in vain as he pastes something pungent over my mouth, my airway cut off by the tight grip around my throat. The paste stings my skin as it solidifies over the bottom half of my face.

The males stands, peels the excess from his hands and snaps the arrows like they're twigs. My flesh slides over the wooden shafts in protest, as he yanks me from the wall. I groan in agony and he laughs at my pain.

'Don't worry pretty Noisemaker, you're too valuable to kill.'

The hairs on my nape stand tall at his words. He's obviously a bounty hunter but which god is he collecting for? He binds my wrists together then slings me over his shoulder, uncaring of the pain it causes. The ground is a long way down and I hurt so bad, I wish he'd just finish me off. My blood paints his back and I hope I bleed out before we reach our destination. It's moments like this, I hate that I'm so difficult to kill.

Halfway across the field, he stops and growls, 'Who are you?'

I think he's talking to me, until another male says, 'Hector, descendent of Ajax, you are a long way from home.'

'So you know who I am,' the enormous male says, gripping me tighter. 'What do you want?'

'I'm here for the Siren.'

Hector laughs, 'My prize is coming with me.'

'Who hired you to locate her?'

'The god I serve is known only to those worthy of the knowledge,' Hector scoffs.

'I'm disappointed,' the male sighs. 'When the war came, I expected you to choose the right side, Hector.'

I look up when shadow passes overhead, my eyes widening at the thick purple clouds blocking the sun. The air grows charged and my scalp prickles in warning. White fire slices the sky and strikes the ground, inches away. Hector's grip tightens when I try to recoil. More lightning meets the Earth, scorching the ground around us. It's raw power and panic bands my chest.

'Tell me who hired you and I'll consider sparing your life, Hector.'

Hector laughs. 'I didn't recognise you in that disguise, old man. She's Apollo's daughter, not yours. Fry me and she fries too.'

I'm about to get fried? Nausea rolls through me and I shut my eyes. It isn't the way I'd choose to go but at least I'll be dead soon.

'That would be true, if it weren't for the spark inside her,' the unknown male says.

'Meaning what?' Hector scoffs.

'Simple: you fry, she doesn't.'

White fire washes everything from view as lightning cracks directly down on me. Hector's screams are drowned out by the thundering roar. I'd scream with him if I could, as immense pain blasts through me. My divine heat swells to meet the lightning, joining the bolt that should be disintegrating my flesh. It's like Aaron's energy but so much stronger: painful and raw, ripping through every cell of my body.

Hector starts to melt beneath me and I gag at the stench of his burning flesh. Seared chunks, peel from his bones and thud to the ground. I squirm to get free but his body gives way, half burying me in his charred, steaming remains.

Someone plucks me from the mess and I struggle to get free, still blind from the whitewash. The arms are like steel bands though, as I'm carried away from the stench and placed on the grass. I blink neon spots from my vision in confusion and cerulean blue swirls into focus.

My heart stutters as I stare into his electric eyes. I grow dizzy until I realise, it isn't Aaron. This boy has his eyes, his features and his dark hair. He looks more like Aaron's brother than Logan, and I've mistaken Logan for Aaron twice already. I wince as he unbinds my wrists then kneels to examine my wounds.

'If I remove the gag, do you promise not to sing?'

I nod and he smooths his hand over the bottom half of my face. The gag turns back to thick, pungent paste and he wipes it away.

'T-thank you,' I rasp.

He sits on the grass, facing me. We stare at each other for a long moment and I wonder what the hell he wants.

'I've been watching you,' he finally says.

I wipe the remaining gunk away and ask, 'Which one are you?'

He smiles and it almost stops my heart again. He's so handsome, so much like... Zeus! He's Zeus! But why the heck is Zeus helping me?

He grins as if he knows my thoughts. 'You've figured it out. And, no, I shouldn't be helping you.'

'Then why?'

'The Moirai and Eileiythia gave me reason to save you. You're the holder of something precious to me now.'

'Which is?'

'You have the spark inside you.'

'The...spark?'

Instead of elaborating like a normal person, he curls his fingers around my injured arm. I scream when white fire shoots into my arm and across to my injured shoulder. I try to jerk free but he grips me tight. Electricity explodes through me but he doesn't let go until I'm about to pass out. I fight the urge to throw up when he finally lets go and look down at my healed wounds.

'While you carry the spark, my energy won't kill you. I'd also prefer to keep you alive from now on,' he says.

Just when I really want to end it all, Zeus decides to become my body-guard. 'W-why won't your energy kill me anymore?' I ask.

'Because my son gave you the spark.'

'Aaron did this to me?' I rasp.

He nods. 'He gave you a part of himself.'

My heart breaks with fresh grief. I don't really understand what Zeus is saying, other than Aaron has given me part of himself. It's inside me right now and it just saved my life.

Zeus helps me stand then says, 'Cherish the spark, Inara. Protect it with your life and stop wandering off alone. I saved you today because Olympus is focused elsewhere but I cannot interfere when the other gods are watching.'

'I'll go back to the Guardian Isle.'

'Go to where Mariah is buried,' he orders. 'Retrieve the necklace you left there.'

I backup when a bolt of lightning strikes him. It flashes bright and super-hot then is gone, taking him with it. I look towards the sky, skin stinging.

22

I sit on the bench under the trees, wings of the stone angel crowning my mother's grave, peeking above the mist. The sun is setting, bathing the leafy cemetery in warm light. Logan left to meet Talia over an hour ago but I can't bring myself to leave yet. This is the only place Inara's scent hasn't been diluted by the human populous and I want to savour it while I can.

I fish the butterfly pendant from my pocket and smooth my thumb over the emeralds, as if for inspiration. It took weeks to track her when I first discovered she existed and she wasn't trying to hide back then. My logic is skewered by my love for her this time round too, so I'm questioning every single decision.

I stand and kick the bin beside the bench, wondering what kind of warrior can't track the thing that means the most to them. I can't wait weeks this time. My need to find her isn't based on the need for revenge anymore. I feel...lost without her and I'm terrified something will happen to her while we're apart.

I sigh, knowing I need to leave and regroup. The longer I sit here, the more time she has to slip away. I allow the lightning to build in my core, ready to activate my key. I take a final glance towards my mother's resting place then frown.

Threads of dissipating lightning, snap around me as I release the bolt; key returning to its dormant form around my wrist. Blue light illuminates the mist clinging to the wings of the stone angel above my mother's grave. I creep towards it and pause when coughing punctuates the silence, followed by the sound of someone gasping for breath.

I weave around the ancient monuments, the last rays of sunlight glinting from my silently-drawn sword. I crouch behind my mother's epitaph before I strike and... Nobody is there and the silence is profound.

Inara's scent hits me a moment later, thick and delicious in the air. I breathe it in, greedy for each inhale then spin to the sound of fleeing footsteps.

Overgrown plants scratch at my skin as I dodge through the tall graves. Armour flashes between the stones as I close the distance between us, electricity burning hot inside as I anticipate the fight. I come level with my target, matching their speed as they blink between the graves to my right. I time my steps, then dive sideways and smash into them. We crash to the ground and I swear when they shove me away, slamming me into the corner of the nearest gravestone. I growl something my mother would've reprimanded me for, then roll to my feet.

And freeze.

'Goddess?'

Inara's eyes are uncertain and afraid as she stares back. Her mouth opens, closes and opens again, as if she wants to speak but can't find the words. There's something different about her but I can't put my finger on it. She's dishevelled, face etched with pain and her armour is smeared with blood; but she's...radiant.

She rubs her eyes with the heels of her hands then rasps, 'Aaron?'

I grip her nape and kiss her with all the longing I've felt since we've been apart. That delicious fire, stings my lips and bathes my soul. I taste her tears as she melts against me and sunlight burst from her skin. I break the kiss and rest my forehead against hers, our breathes mingling. It isn't enough; it will never be enough but we can't draw attention to ourselves here.

'I was terrified I'd never find you, but you found me,' I breathe.

She cups my face between her palms. 'Please tell me this isn't another dream.'

I hold her shaking hands against my face. 'I promise, this is real.'

'It feels like it,' she whispers.

She pulls her hands from mine and combs her fingers through my hair. She traces my face, lips and pushes onto her tiptoes and kisses me fiercely.

'Let's go home,' I pant as her sunlight fills the darkening cemetery.

She nods and I pull her close to summon my key.

'Please, don't let me wake up this time,' she breathes.

23

'We should check she hasn't gone back to the house,' Adonia says.

I nod but I'm still reeling over not realising what Inara was planning. I feel a like fool for ignoring the signs and Siren burn sears my lungs with each breath. I promised I'd never leave her side and she's forcing me to break that promise.

'I was wondering,' Adonia says.

I arch an eyebrow at her pleasant tone because I've never had it directed my way until now. 'Hm?'

Her smile makes me doubly suspicious as she says, 'Can I borrow your key once we've found Inara? I just spent two days thinking Helen was dead and I'd like to see her.'

I stop walking when I remember that I left my key at the house. I look at my bare wrist in horror then start running. Adonia chases after me but I'm too fast for her. My heart pounds as I crash through the door of the house. If Inara has my key she could be anywhere; she could be... No, I can't think like that.

Adonia nearly runs into my back as she burst inside on my heels. I head for the stairs but something crashes against the floor above. I look back at Adonia, as another loud thud shudders through the ceiling.

'Joshua!' she shouts.

I bolt upstairs, hackles rising as I reach the landing. The air is thick with the scent of demigod: musky like one of the scents belonging to a bedroom in this house. Adonia pushes around me when Joshua cries out and barrels into one of the bedrooms.

'Logan, no!' she screams.

The temperature plummets, shadow drawing in as if an invisible force is drinking the light. I should help but Logan is the name of Aaron's brother, the son of Hades and excitement rips down my spine. Another demigod from one of the top three means an actual challenge.

Adonia drags Joshua's prone form out into the hallway and a tall male with dark features and midnight eyes follows her out. His scent floods the hallway: thick and reeking of strength. He looks like the effigy of Hades my father showed me as a child.

'Stay back, Logan,' she snarls.

'I expected more from the son of Poseidon,' he scoffs. 'He can't even wield a sword.'

'This isn't the son of Poseidon! Gods, I think you've killed him,' she rasps.

'He's wearing Poseidon-crested armour and I can smell him from here,' Logan argues.

'We dressed him in Dante's armour to disguise his human scent. This is Inara's human friend Joshua. We brought him here for protection, you maniac!'

'I didn't know, he didn't say—'

'He doesn't speak our language,' I growl stalking over.

I scoop Joshua from the floor and take him to the room I first met Inara. I put him on one of the beds and press an ear to his chest.

'His heart's still beating but I think you've broken too many bones,' I say. 'Humans don't heal like we do and I'm not sure he'll make it.'

'I'm not stupid,' Logan growls. 'You think I don't know—'

His gaze snaps to the centre of the room and I look to the empty spot in confusion. I shield my eyes a moment later, when bright, crackling fire, flashes through the space. It leaves neon spots in my vision and delivers Inara in the arms of a dark haired male. He's holding her protectively and she's curled against him, like she doesn't want to be anywhere else.

She starts to smile when she sees me but her gaze tracks to Joshua and the colour drains from her face. 'What happened,' she asks hurrying over. She drops to her knees beside me and presses her ear to his chest. 'How did he get hurt?'

'We left him to go look for you at Apollo's temple,' Adonia says. 'We didn't know it was a possibility for Logan to return and our disguise worked too well. He picked a fight with Joshua, thinking he was Dante.'

'You did this?' Inara hisses at Logan.

He holds his hands up in defence. 'I thought he was demigod and he was in my home.'

Her jaw flexes and I feel the rage she's fighting. Siren burn, pours like acid through my veins in response and I grit my teeth.

'Everyone out,' she says barely holding it together enough to speak without putting them under her thrall. I honestly don't know how she's doing it, considering the icy rage radiating from her.

I curl my fingers around hers in silent support and her expression softens. Everyone files out, except for the dark haired male who rode in on a bolt of lightning. Even if I hadn't witnessed it, the scent of his electricity and strength confirms he's Aaron.

'I'm sorry,' she says as soon as the others are far enough away. 'I couldn't control my anger and... Does it hurt much?'

'No more than usual,' I say then look at Aaron in confusion. 'He's immune?'

'A side-effect of Inara being in love with me,' he says looking pointedly at my hand on hers.

I cup her jaw in response and ask, 'What can I do?'

She turns from my hold and climbs onto the bed with Joshua. She fumbles with the strapping on his armour, so I take over, removing the layers I helped put on this morning. Inara gasps when I remove the last layer, revealing his bruised and broken body. She holds her hands above his torso, unsure where to place them.

Aaron climbs onto the bed behind her and cradles her back to his chest. He leans in until his lips brush her ear and whispers something too low for me to hear. Warm emotion, floods from Inara in response and fresh Siren burn sears through me. Aaron's possessive gaze slides to mine and I look away, hating him with every fibre of my being.

She's supposed to be with *me*; exists to be with *me*. I care for her more than I care for myself – *love* her. I thought for sure she loved me back; felt it when we were alone together, before she discovered Aaron still lived.

I turn back to watch her lean over Joshua, her face filled with concern and my heart swells with affection. The strongest emotion I've ever felt floods my chest and I know I'm right. She and I were meant to be together, she's just blinded by Aaron right now. Once she spends time with us that isn't clouded by grief, she'll see the truth as I do. Our being together makes more sense than her relationship with Aaron ever will.

She presses her palms to Joshua's torso and bites her lip, fierce concentration lining her face. A wave of heat washes over my skin and I look down at myself in confusion. It's a tangible sensation, as if I've been dipped in warm water. It grows hotter and hotter, then an inferno ignites inside me. I growl in pain and hit the floor, as sunlight explodes from Inara's skin.

Aaron asks if I'm okay but I can't speak around the phantom fire, blistering my insides. It's impossibly hot and I don't understand what's happening, until Inara releases an agonised scream. This fire belongs to her, which means I'm only experiencing an echo of what she's feeling. I wonder how she held that scream in for so long and why Aaron is allowing her to heal, when this is what it does to her.

'She's burning,' I snarl at him. 'Stop her!'

The idiot hesitates, glancing between us before yanking her from the bed. The pain snaps off, like someone flicked a switch and I collapse against the hardwood. Aaron cradles Inara's limp form in his arms and stares down at me.

'Is she okay?' I croak, trying to stand but my legs give way and I hit the floor again.

'She'll be fine,' he says still watching me.

'What...was that?' I pant.

'You felt what she felt,' he accuses.

'Only a fraction but it was enough.'

'How?' he demands, possessive jealousy drenching his tone.

I use the bed for support and force myself onto my feet. Aaron is tall but I'm taller and I stare down at the male, holding the girl I love.

'She and I are the same,' I say.

A storm flashes in his neon eyes before he says, 'Thank you for saving her that day and keeping her safe.'

I expected his anger, can feel it ionising the atmosphere, so don't know how to deal with his thanks. He's standing between me and the girl I love and I can't hurt him without hurting her.

'I'd lay down my life for her,' I say.

His jaw ticks and he growls, 'You're not leaving, are you?'

I smirk. 'I promised Inara I wouldn't.'

24

S ilk, slides from my body and pools around my waist as I sit up, feeling dazed.

'Welcome, Daughter of Apollo,' a white-robed woman greets from the arched doorway across the room. She smiles when I hold my hands up to cover my nakedness and uses a burning torch to light the lamp on the wall beside me. Her ebony ringlets bounce, her milky-blue gaze kind as she hands me a square of white fabric. It unfolds into a dress, which I tug on while she just stands there, like a creeper. Only gods look at me like I'm some kind of pet or science experiment and I wonder which one she is.

'Thank you,' I murmur.

She offers her hand and says, 'You have nothing to fear, child. You're here because you need my help.'

I stare at her offered hand. 'Who are you?'

'The goddess Eileiythia and this is my home.'

I look around the white-marble room. 'Why am I here?'

'Because you carry the essence of Zeus inside you,' she says reaching down to take my hand when I still don't accept hers.

I sigh and don't fight when she helps me stand because what can I really do against a god? I study her profile as she leads me from the room. Like all the gods I've met, there's something ancient about her. She looks in her mid-twenties but there's deep knowledge in her gaze. It makes the hairs on my nape prickle when she catches me looking.

She gestures for me to sit in a plush chair and I obey. It feels like it's made from clouds; cradling my body as it moulds to my frame. Maybe I can suggest Aaron get one of these bad boys. I wriggle into a comfortable nook and hum in pleasure.

'Drink this,' Eileiythia orders materialising a tall steaming glass from thin air. When I just stare at the golden liquid she says, 'Ambrosia tea will nourish the spark.'

I sip the sweet, delicious liquid and fight a groan. It's the best thing I've ever tasted and gold light flares over my skin in response. It burns through my body like an injection of energy and I think I could easily get addicted.

'Drink it all,' she orders. 'Healing that human boy has drained your life-force, endangering the spark.'

'Is he okay?'

'The human boy?'

I nod, wondering who else she thinks I'm talking about and a pensive expression crosses her face, as if she's trying to hear a distant conversation.

'His life thread is long because of you, Daughter of Apollo but what you did was foolish. You must not use your life-force to heal while you carry the spark.'

While I carry the spark? It isn't a permanent thing then. I'd rather have Aaron than his spark though, and for a while I'll have both. It sucks that Zeus only wants me alive while I carry his precious essence but I'll take what I can get.

'I don't understand any of this,' I admit. 'Why can't I use my healing ability anymore?'

Eileiythia taps the empty cup and it dissipates, like it was made from mist. She takes my hands in hers and sits back, another cloud-chair materialising behind her.

'What you carry inside is precious, Inara. One day it will be a powerful thing but right now it's fragile. It needs your nurture and nourishment to make it strong. When you heal, you give away your life-force and it puts the spark in danger. Do you understand now?'

'Sort of but I still don't understand how I got it in the first place. How did Aaron pass on part himself to me?'

She smiles. 'When you made love, child.'

'But we've never; we haven't...'

'Are you forgetting your visits to him?' she asks.

I stare at her in shock. 'But they weren't real! I, I wasn't even really there!'

'Who told you that?' she scoffs. 'It's your divine half that visits other places, child. The more you do it, the more proficient you get. You may think your visits random but you took yourself to Aaron that night and took part of him back with you.'

'I can take things from the places I visit?'

'And leave things,' she says.

I think about the first time I met Dante then woke bruised from his attack. And the morning after Aaron and I ... I never did find all my clothing. Heat burns through me when I realise, that night was real. Aaron and I actually made love and it was perfect. So much so, I'd thought it a dream. We'd given ourselves to each other completely and I'd kept a part of him in return. As long as I care for the spark, Aaron will always be with me.

'I'll protect it,' I promise.

I wipe tears from my eyes but I can't help it, I'm just so happy. Hell, crying seems to be my super power anyway. I'm always doing it, it's just novel that it's for something positive for a change.

'Siren tears,' Eileiythia breathes. 'I wish you a long life thread, Daughter of Apollo.'

I'M warm and calm when I sit up in bed on the Guardian Isle. I'm in Aaron's room and the air smells like home. Sunlight floods through the ornate windows and I blush when I look down at the tunic dress I'm wearing. I keep waking in something different to what I fell asleep in and I want to know, who the hell keeps undressing me.

I stumble out of bed then jump back from the door handle when a shock of electricity snaps at my fingers.

Son of a mother!

I shake my stinging hand and scowl at the handle. The door opens a second later – Aaron's startled figure filling the frame.

A smile splits his face and he hugs me. 'You're awake!'

'Ow,' I yelp and shove him away, as more electricity snaps between us.

He stares at me wide-eyed then reaches for me again. Another bolt of stinging white cracks through the air and he jerks away, staring at me as I rub my stinging skin.

'What's happening?' he asks glaring at his hands.

I take a step towards him. 'I'm fine—'

He scrambles from my reach. 'What if I hurt you?'

'It's just a static shock,' I say reaching for him again. 'It didn't actually hurt, I was being a baby about it.'

He goes statue-still and I try to hide the rising panic in my stomach. I think this has something to do with carrying his spark and I'm worried I won't be able to touch him again. I take his hand and it stings like hell, a bright flash of white zapping between our bodies, before it dies and leaves a pleasant tingling behind.

Aaron blows out a breath and pulls me into a hug. 'Gods, I'm sorry. That's never happened before.'

I hug him back. 'People get static shocks all the time; it's nothing.'

His muscles relax under my questing fingers and I bite my lip. He's so hard all over, like marble made flesh and it makes me think of that night. The one I thought was a dream but was apparently real.

'I was starting to worry you were never going to wake up,' he growls, voice a deep, husky rasp.

'Is Joshua okay?' I ask not looking away from my task, even as I worry for my friend. Eileiythia told me he's okay though, so I'm not really worried.

'He's gone with Adonia to the temple of Aphrodite.'

I stop what I'm doing and meet his gaze. 'You let him leave the house?'

'I learned the hard way that you can't keep people locked away, even if it's for their protection,' he says.

'Is that supposed to be an apology?'

He heaves a sigh then pulls my lyre from his tunic and places it in my hand. 'I'm sorry, Inara. I thought keeping you confined would keep you safe. I got so caught up in trying not to lose you again, I didn't see how it was forcing us apart.'

'You kept secrets from me because you thought I was going to leave?'

'You left me back then, when you thought it would save me.'

'You didn't give me a choice, Aaron. I couldn't bear to watch you die.'

He rests his forehead against mine. 'I know, love... I know.' His arms tighten around me, his cinnamon scent a comfort all on its own.

I pull away, face burning and meet his gaze. 'Did I... visit you while we were apart?'

A look of deep pleasure fills his face. 'You did.'

Lava heat leaks into my stomach at his admission. 'Did I visit you *here*, the other night?'

He winces. 'It's been three weeks since you healed Joshua, Inara.'

'Three weeks! B-but I was only out for two after I brought you back to life. And Joshua wasn't dead; he isn't even demigod!'

He cups my jaw and husks, 'I remember you visiting me here, Inara.'

My panic fades behind a warm rush of shy desire. He smiles like he knows what I'm feeling and takes me to a set of drawers. He pulls out a pair of dark jeans and I wonder what he's trying to tell me until he passes them to me.

'These are mine,' I say.

'You left them here after your last visit.'

'No wonder I couldn't find them after I woke up,' I huff then realise what he's implying and blush. 'Aaron—'

He kisses me until my toes curl then rasps, 'I thought it was a dream. It was so ...'

'Perfect,' I say then bite my lip. 'I mean, it was perfect for me but I'd never –'

'Neither had I.'

'But, you're eighty-two and...'

'What?' he asks when I trail off, not wanting to sound offensive. It's a stupid thing to say or think.

'It doesn't matter.'

'What were you going to say?' he presses.

'It's just, you're so... I can't believe you've never – Aaron, you could get any girl you want. You should've heard the girls talking about you when we were split up during the Games. Do you even realise the effect you have on my gender? Any gender actually, since I've seen the way most people look at you.'

He shrugs like it's nothing. 'I never wanted the things I have with you, with anybody else. I love you, Inara. You're the only being I've ever loved this way and you make me feel things I didn't think possible.' He smiles. 'I'm glad you were my first and you'll be my last.'

'I feel like I don't deserve you.'

'Then the feeling is mutual,' he breathes and gifts me with more spicy kisses.

LOGAN AND TALIA are in the kitchen eating when we get downstairs. Talia rushes over and pulls me from Aaron before the door has chance to shut behind us. She shoves me into a chair and hands me a ceramic dish. I recognise the honey-soaked dessert and hum in pleasure.

'I made it just in case,' she says sitting a little too close in the chair beside me. Her brow furrows, silver eyes scrutinising me.

'What?' I ask around a mouthful of sweet, mouth-watering cake. I could eat this stuff all day, every day.

'You look different.'

I stop eating. 'Different?'

'Sort of... radiant,' she says.

I snort, 'I *am* the daughter of Apollo.'

'This is more,' she argues, tilting her head as if to get a better look at me. 'Maybe it's because you've been unconscious for so long and gone before that. I've missed you.'

I give her a hug. 'I've missed you, too.' I look around. 'Where's everybody else?'

'Adonia is with Joshua at the temple and Alexander is with Helen, in the Human Realm. Delia is with Dante and Milos. They're trying to find out which god is hunting you.'

'Milos?'

'He was sent by Poseidon to look for Dante,' Logan says.

I jerk to my feet. 'What!'

Aaron grabs my hand and tugs me back into my seat. 'It's okay, Milos and Dante are friends.'

'You can't scare me like that,' I huff.

'You care for Dante,' he says, an edge to his voice.

'He saved my life — What's not to like?'

'He can feel what you feel.'

I narrow my gaze at the accusation in his tone. 'It's just a Siren thing, like how I sense when danger is coming, or if someone is out of range for my voice to affect them.'

'You can sense that?' Logan asks, intrigued.

'And that's all I'm saying around you,' I scoff glaring his way.

'What did I do?' he asks innocently.

'I'm not passing you pointers on how to win a fight against Dante, Logan.'

'Princess, I'm hurt you'd think that about me.'

'I bet you've been itching to fight him since you learned of his existence,' I scoff.

His grin is wicked, those glowing coals in his dark gaze gleaming. 'It gets boring having only Aaron to fight with.'

'No, Logan.' He opens his mouth to argue and I hiss, '*No.*'

Siren song rakes its claws through my insides, wanting out. My hold on it after spending so much time with Dante is tenuous and I bite down hard on my lip as it sears a pathway up my throat. I'm furious that Logan has the power to annoy me this much and that anger fuels the icy part of me. I reach for my spoon, needing more cake to calm down and accidentally brush Talia's hand. A thread of electricity snaps between us, making her hiss and my spoon clatters against the table.

She laughs, 'I think Aaron is rubbing off on you.'

Aaron scrutinises me from across the table, so I force a smile and say, 'I shocked him earlier, too. Maybe I should invest in rubber shoes.'

Talia snorts and stuff more cake into my mouth. Aaron has that worried look on his face again and I'm worried that if he reacts this way to thinking he's given me a static shock, how will he react to finding out he's given me his spark?

25

I stand in the bedroom window, watching Inara and Dante on the edge of the cliff. He tucks a length of golden hair from her face as they talk and I fight the need to go down there and beat him. He takes every opportunity to touch her in front of me and I *will* make him pay, once I've figured out what Inara's hiding.

It has something to do with the electric shocks she's been giving since waking two weeks ago. They're getting stronger and more frequent and I'm terrified they're because of me. She doesn't seem in pain but she wouldn't tell me even if she was. She'd hide it, like she's hidden how painful it is to heal. I knew it caused her pain but she never made it seem unbearable. Watching Dante writhe in agony at just a fraction of what she feels though... I growl at her selflessness.

She gives Dante a shock as I watch and he rubs his arm, laughing. He's been using their half Siren heritage as reason to stay close to her. They share a connection I don't understand and he's using it to his advantage. He's always touching her and asking if she's okay. She follows him from the room sometimes looking concerned and when I ask, she says it's a Siren thing. When pressed, she admitted it hurts to keep her Siren voice locked inside and I've been thinking about it ever since. How much pain does she live with from suppressing what she is?

'*Anger activates it,*' she'd said, '*and because I can sense what Dante is feeling, his anger can activate it, too. He draws my Siren side out.*'

'*Then maybe Dante should leave,*' I'd said.

'*He has nowhere to go, Aaron! He has nobody ...*'

'*It was just a suggestion. I'm not kicking him out,*' I'd soothed at her horrified reaction.

I'd assured her Dante was welcome to stay, even though I'd wanted him gone. I don't know why she's so blind to what he's doing but then, Inara always sees the best in everyone. One false move though, and I'll beat him so badly not even Charon will recognise the remains.

'If you want me to do the honours,' Logan says stepping up beside me and nodding in Dante's direction. 'I'll happily hold him while you take out your frustrations.'

I sigh and meet his gaze. 'What news from the others?'

'The Human Realm is swarming with bounty hunters. Alexander has moved Helen for protection but there's no sign of Callista and no news of which god set her free.'

'And Dante?'

'Milos says Poseidon ordered the search to remain focused on the Human Realm, believing Dante will follow the rumours of Inara being sighted there.'

'He's assuming Dante is with Inara,' I say.

'Did she tell you where she went with Dante's key; why she was covered in blood when she appeared in the graveyard?'

'No, and I'm worried about her,' I say watching her through the glass. 'She's hiding something.'

'She's probably planning on sacrificing herself to save you again,' he says then shrugs when I glare at him. 'You know I'm right.'

'You don't have to be so blunt about it.'

'You know better than anyone that I'm not good at this, Aaron. I'm the son of Hades; it's my nature to be cold and lacking when it comes to … feelings.'

'You hide behind being the son of Hades because you're afraid to show people you care, Logan. Inara told me how you tried to stop her getting to Anthemusa and how you tried to save me.'

His jaw flexes as he glares out the window. 'It's too quiet out there,' he says dismissing the conversation but his digression only proves what I said is right.

'It's the calm before the storm,' I agree.

We turn at the sound of light tapping on the doorjamb to find Talia, dressed in armour. Her blonde hair is braided, silver eyes gleaming and expression tight.

'What is it?' Logan asks.

'I've come from the house in the valley,' she says.

'Are you crazy?' he snarls.

She shrugs, unconcerned. 'I left my favourite blade there,' she says, pulling the sword from its sheath. Her gaze tracks along the razor edge with a warrior's affection before fixing on me. 'There's something there you need to see.'

I look down at where Inara is sitting on the edge of the cliff, dangling her legs over the edge. I clench my fists at the sight of Dante's arm around her shoulders.

'I'll get Inara.'

Logan catches my arm. 'You don't seriously think you can bring her?'

'Look what happened the last time I left her. I won't lose her again.'

'It will explain where she went using Dante's key,' Talia says.

I sigh, convinced. 'We've got five minutes.'

I SIT on the edge of the bed, stunned. Scorched earth, broken arrows and an Ajax's spear proceeded the stinking remains of an Ajax. I don't know how Inara took down an Ajax alone or how she scorched the earth like that. I dial Alexander's number on the phone Helen insisted I get, needing answers.

'Aaron,' he answers before sounds of a scuffle come over the line.

Helen's voice replaces his. 'Aaron? What is it, is Inara okay?'

'She wants to see you and it's been pretty quiet here, so a quick visit would be safe enough,' I say.

'When can you come get me?'

I smirk. 'Put Alex back on.'

'I THINK I prefer travelling via Inara's key,' Helen rasps, stumbling forward.

Alexander catches her. 'Careful, love.'

'I'm okay,' she assures him then looks at me. 'Where is she?'

I point out the window and a deep frown sets her features. She follows my gaze and her eyes narrow on Inara and Dante's laughing forms.

'Who is that she's with?'

'Dante.'

She arches a perfectly tweezed eyebrow. 'You don't like him.'

'I don't,' I agree.

'Is that why I'm here, because you've got jealousy issues?'

'Inara can befriend whoever she wishes. You're here because I know she wants to see you and I thought it would be a nice surprise.'

She purses her lips at my answer then stalks from the room. Alexander smirks then follows her out. I go to the window to watch Helen stalk across the grass below. The girl stalks everywhere, taking no prisoners and putting everyone in their place. She's the weakest of the group but the one everyone is afraid to upset in case they suffer the consequences. I might not like her but her bravery is commendable.

She's halfway to the edge when Inara glances back. She rolls to her feet, pushing Dante's hands away and runs at Helen. They embrace for a long time and I calculate about five weeks since they've seen each other. I smile at Inara's happiness but it isn't the reason I asked Helen to come. She wants Inara to be safe as much as I do and if anyone can get her to confess the secret she's hiding, it's Helen.

26

Delia sits beside me on the sand. 'It's calmer today.'

I stare at the ocean and huff, 'I still feel his anger.'

'You're upset,' she says.

I shrug but she's right. Helen's monopolising Inara's time and Aaron seems way too smug about it. I think he invited Helen to keep me away from Inara but I'm actually worried about her. She's been sleeping so much lately, just randomly falling asleep in the middle of conversations. Yesterday she was telling me how hungry she was and the next moment she was curled up on the grass asleep. I should be up there keeping an eye on her but Helen seems to like me less than she likes Aaron. She goes out of her way to piss me off and Inara gets distracted by my bad mood, so I've come out of the way.

'What do you mean, you still feel it?' Delia asks.

I palm the black sand. 'The ocean is calmer but the tremors are getting worse.'

Her slender hand covers mine and pink infuses her creamy skin.

Her brown eyes turn deep and sparkly and the feeling I get when I touch Inara, tugs at my stomach.

'If I ask you to do something, will you?' she breathes.

'Yes.'

She edges closer. 'Will you – only if you want to … May I see your wings?'

Her face flushes crimson when I stare at her. 'Who told you I had wings?'

'Nobody told me, I *saw* it.'

'In a vision?'

Her red hair shimmers in the sunlight when she nods and that feeling in my stomach intensifies. I turn my hand under hers, taking hold of it and pull her to her feet.

'I'm sorry,' she says.

'What for?' I ask.

She frowns. 'I thought I'd upset you.'

Pain slices my spine as my wings unfurl, showering us with dark feathers. It's been too long since I've used my wings and I flex them outward before bending them around us. Delia's eyes are wide, studying the blue-black wall I've pulled around her. She hesitates as she reaches out.

'It's okay,' I breathe, terrified yet desperate for her to touch me.

Her mouth curves at the corners as her fingertips smooth across my feathers; pale hands stark against them. It feels so good and that delicious ache tugs through me for Delia, Oracle of Delphi and my oldest friend. My smile fades when I remember she's a temple priestess and virgin servant to her god. She'd never choose me over her life of devotion to Apollo.

'They feel like silk,' she says, eyes finding mine. 'Would you—'

'Yes,'

She smirks. 'You don't even know what I was going to ask.'

'The answer is still yes.'

'I want to go flying.'

I lock my arms around her waist. She's slender, taller than Inara but just as soft. She smells like orange blossom and the gold jewellery adorning her body jingles as we lift into the air. She squeals her delight and I grin.

Her arms tighten around me, eyes wide with wonder, as we climb into the sky. I take her around the headland, keeping close to the face of the cliff, out of sight. She unlocks her arms, holding them out and strumming the air with tapered fingers. It's the first time I've ever really heard her laugh and the sound is beautiful.

I alight on the sand where we started and Delia throws her arms around me. 'Thank you, Dante!'

She looks exhilarated, skin flushed and hair tangled around her face like fire. Something dances behind her chocolate eyes as she smiles up at me. She's so close, breath sweet across my face. The ache intensifies and it takes everything in me not to act on it.

I tuck a length of hair behind her ear as an excuse to touch her. 'You're welcome, Dee.'

I take a measured step back before I do something to ruin our friendship. Something like disappointment, flashes through her gaze but is gone before I can really analyse it. She pulls a basket from behind a cluster of nearby rocks and is smiling again when she turns back to me.

'I thought you might be hungry.'

'I'm definitely hungry,' I say. Just not for food.

27

INARA

'What?' I huff as Helen stares at me across the kitchen table. She's scared everyone off, so we're alone.

'Tell me what's going on,' she demands.

'You're going to have to be more specific.'

She moves to sit beside me. 'With this,' she says waving her arms in the air.

I put my fork down. 'You just gestured to all of me, Helen.'

'You're acting strange.'

'I'm not—'

'You've been stuffing your face every hour for the last three days, you keep falling asleep, you *look* different – and what's with the electric shocks you keep giving everybody?' she explodes.

'It's just static! And why does everyone keep telling me I look different? Nothing has changed, I'm exactly the same.'

Her eyes narrow into slits. 'You're lying.'

'Helen—'

'I swear to God, if you say one more word that isn't part of an explanation, I'll leave right now and never come back!'

I sigh. 'Aaron and I, we ... you know?'

She slaps her palms on the table. 'Oh. My. Various. Gods! Tell me everything.'

My skin turns hot. 'He gave me his spark.'

She snorts. 'Is that some kind of euphemism for sex?'

'No! Seriously, he passed some of his electrical energy to me when we ... you know?'

'Made love? Performed the horizontal mambo? Rocked the Casbah?'

I sigh, 'Yes.'

'So that's the reason you've been shocking everybody, and why you look so ...' She tilts her head to the side. 'It's like you're glowing. You've got this silvery shimmer around you.'

I look at my skin. 'I don't see it.'

'It's more obvious when I squint at you but trust me, it's there,' she says then smirks. 'So, have you done it since?'

'He doesn't seem to want to,' I admit, embarrassed and a little rejected. 'When I try to start anything, he deflects and it doesn't help that this thing he gave me is getting stronger.'

'Aaron's energy?'

I nod. 'At first I couldn't feel it but now ...'

'If you couldn't feel it, then how'd you know it was there? You might as well tell me, then I might forgive you for not telling me about you and Aaron doing it sooner.'

'I've been occupied,' I scoff.

'I told you about Alexander and me the morning after it happened. How long ago did you and Aaron do it?'

'When I thought Mila had killed him.'

Her face knots. 'How in the hell did you ... ?'

'I visited him. I thought it was a dream at the time.'

Her eyebrows reach for her hairline. 'This just keeps gets weirder and weirder, doesn't it? But that makes it nearly nine weeks ago, which is exactly my point. You're a sucky friend lately, Inara.'

'I thought you were dead, remember?'

'You've had plenty of time since then to tell me.'

'Just being around me has gotten you killed in the past and *this* is what you're claiming makes me a bad friend?' I scoff.

'I reserve the right to decide the terms of my friendships,' she answers.

'Fine, I'm sorry and I should've told you but I've been occupied. Zeus was the one who told me I was carrying the spark and I haven't gotten around to telling Aaron yet.'

'Hang on, you met Zeus, and he didn't—'

'Kill me?' I shake my head. 'Apparently carrying Aaron's spark has put me on his new-best-friend list.'

'Isn't this something Aaron should know about?'

'He should but I know he'll freak out, Helen. He's so protective and I don't want to give him something else to worry about. He's already trying to track my mother and figure out which god is hunting me.'

'He's already freaking out, Nara. He knows something's wrong.'

I bury my face in my hands and groan, 'He does, doesn't he?'

'He's not an idiot. If he's been watching what I have, he'd be crazy not to be worried. I mean, you know how much he loves me and he asked me to visit. If that doesn't tell you he's on to you, I don't know what will.'

I sigh, 'Okay, I'll tell him.'

'Good.'

'Thanks, Helen.'

She grins and cracks her knuckles. 'All part of the service.'

I STAND naked in front of the ornate mirror in the bathroom. Everybody keeps telling me how radiant I look but I just don't see it. I shrug and step into the pool of hot water in the middle of the room. The air crackles with electricity as I sink up to my shoulders and lay back.

I stare at the stone ceiling, muscles relaxing and listen to the hypnotic drumming of my heart. I frown and focus on a softer beating behind the sound of my own heart, like an echo but faster. A surge of electricity flutters through my core and I press a hand to my stomach at the calming sensation it brings.

My mind drifts to Aaron and I sigh. He hasn't touched me sincerely since I woke from healing Joshua. Even his kisses seem rushed, as if he's afraid to touch me for too long. I worry about how much more protective he'll get when I tell him I'm carrying his spark. What if he reverts to the way he was in the valley home? I don't know if I can deal with that kind of isolation again.

I step from the pool, pull on the cotton nightdress Helen brought me and tiptoe across the hallway. Aaron is downstairs and I'm too chicken to go tell him yet. I climb under the bedcovers and drag a pillow over my head to hide.

I wonder if there's a way to just give his spark back but flinch at the idea, a prickling shiver ripping down my spine. I don't want to give it back, even if I could. It belongs to me now and I care for it... love having it. I know it's crazy but I just do and I curl up on my side. I feel the spark as I drift to sleep; a combination of my blazing fire and Aaron's surging electricity, deep in my belly.

My eyes adjust to the darkness as I blink awake, wondering why Aaron isn't in bed with me. I start to panic, then make out the shape of him in the bed opposite. It's the second time this week I've woken to find him in that bed, away from me. Like I'm a leper. I push from the bed and stalk across the room but freeze when silver threads start snapping around me. Aaron stirs and I back away, scared if he sees me like this he'll never touch me again.

I creep to the door, light crackling around me as I touch the handle. I jerk back, hand stinging but the electricity doesn't dissipate this time. Tendrils of silver shiver over my skin, making me luminous in the dark room. It's hot and stinging but not really painful – yet.

'Erm, Aaron?' The light grows brighter and hotter and I squeal, 'Aaron!'

He shoots to his feet, sword appearing from nowhere. His eyes widen as they fix on me. 'Inara?'

'Tell me what to do!' I cry.

He shakes his head. 'I don't know what's happening. You're conducting lightning but I don't know where it's coming from, or how it isn't killing you.'

'Lightning?' Nobody mentioned anything about *lightning* when they told me I was carrying his bloody spark! After everything that's happened to me, lightning still sends fear gushing into my stomach and I gag.

He reaches for me but I shout, 'No, I might hurt you!'

He wraps his fingers around mine. 'Lightning can't hurt me, Goddess.'

Energy cracks between us when our hands connect. Aaron's skin lights up too, the electricity coursing from me into him. He pulls me close, expression awed as he looks down at me. Silver strings crackle between us, dancing over our skin.

'Does it hurt?' he asks.

'It's tingly but doesn't hurt.'

He cups my jaw, cerulean eyes burning brighter than I've ever seen. Touching him when we're both fizzing with lightning is ... *wow.*

'I don't know how this is happening,' he says.

'It's not you,' I whisper.

His fingers trace my face then my body and I might just explode. We watch the electricity dance, creating patterns where his fingers make contact with my skin and I moan in pleasure. He slips his hands around my waist, fingers tracing my spine before they tangle in my hair and his lips meet mine with a loud snap of white fire. I melt against him, his electric-burn scorching my flesh. He grips the hem of my nightdress and tugs it off. His gaze roams my body then he lifts me and carries me to bed.

I WAKE to Aaron tracing my curves. I blush at the memory of the previous night and lift my head from his chest.

He tucks a length of hair behind my ear and smiles. 'Morning.'

I climb his body and kiss him. A shivering current of electricity is exchanged between us and I'm breathless by the time I find the strength to pull away.

'Last night was amazing,' I say.

He smiles a new kind of smile and my heart stutters at the sight. 'Are you ready to tell me why you suddenly have the spark?' he asks.

I sit up and pull the sheet around me. 'When we were apart, I met your father—'

He jerks upright and snarls, 'What?'

I flinch. 'He—'

'No!' he snarls and scrambles from the bed, backing away from me like I've burned him.

I sit frozen, watching him yank on clothes, wondering what I've said to make him act this way. I get up and rest my hand on his arm.

'Aaron ...'

I slam onto the bed across the room before my brain can process what happened. Did he just ... Did Aaron just shove me? I stare at him in disbelief. He shoved me so hard it launched me across the room. I think he was aiming for me to land on the other bed but still...

'What the hell is wrong with you?' I yell.

'Don't touch me,' he snarls, his anger like knives against my flesh.

My Siren senses scream at me to *run* but I can't seem to move. 'I don't know what I—'

'I want you gone before I get back,' he snarls.

I flinch. 'What?'

He pins me with a venomous glare and rasps, 'Siren whore.'

I clamp a hand over my mouth as he glares at me with distain. A flash of silver delivers his key into his palm then he's gone in a bright glare of lightning. I sit frozen on the bed, unsure what just happened. Our conversation replays in my head but I can't understand why he'd react the way he just did. What did I do to make him call me a whore?

I scramble from the bed and pull on a clean tunic, feeling numb. I wipe my eyes and look around in a panic. Does he think I took the spark from him on purpose? What if he tries to take it back? Protectiveness rises through me, my throat burning at the thought. I need to be gone before he gets back because I won't let him take the spark from me.

28

I shove a temple priestess out of the way and stalk into the central chamber, black marble cool beneath my bare feet. Silver and violet silk line the walls; bowls of white fire framing the room. My chest is tight, ripped in two that Inara betrayed me. I gave her something I've given no other, and she ...

'Father!' I roar at the giant effigy in the middle of the room.

Lightning strikes the stone image of Zeus, bringing it to life and he says, 'Do my eyes deceive me? Has my heir summoned *me* for a change?'

'Of all the females you take, why'd you have to take her?' I growl lightning snapping around me, rage building in my chest. I pace the floor, trying to focus through the red haze.

'I don't understand what qualm—'

'Inara!' I roar. 'You know: blonde hair, green eyes – or did you forget her once you'd had your way with her?'

His laughter booms through the chamber. 'Did she tell you that, boy?'

I clench both fists, barely able to speak through my rage. 'She has the spark! You gave it to her while we were separated.'

My father laughs louder. 'You accuse me of that which you are guilty of?'

'You always have to – Wait what?'

'Did you actually listen to what she was saying, or did your opinion of me get in the way?' he asks.

I try to remember her exact words but all I can recall is the anger. I'd hated her more in that moment than last year when I'd tracked her with the intention of killing her. She'd broken my heart; crushed my soul.

'Explain,' I say.

The floor shakes as Zeus kneels, giant, stone hands resting either side of me, bringing us closer. 'You gave Inara the spark, Aaron.'

'Impossible! My spark is part of me, like my heart or my hand.'

'Your spark isn't part of your physical form. It's like your soul: connected to you but not corporeal,' my father corrects. 'You gave part of it to Inara the night she visited you, when you were separated; during your act of love making.'

'Don't tell me you were watching that,' I growl.

'I know many things without watching, Aaron.'

'It makes no sense,' I say frustrated.

'What's so difficult to understand? You passed your essence to her like I did with your mother. It's the way of life and now Inara is carrying part of you inside her, part of me. That's why I saved her from the Ajax in the valley; why she needs your protection more than ever.'

His words soak through my anger and I ask, 'What are you saying?'

He gets to his feet, his expression mirroring my frustration. 'Inara is carrying your child, Aaron.'

My mouth drops open. 'But we weren't ... she wasn't really there that night.'

'Inara is half god, too,' he chastises like I've forgotten my teachings on Demigod 101. 'Your connection is more than just flesh.'

I stare at him, mind swirling with too many questions. Overwhelming joy fills me as it starts to register, forcing me to my knees.

'She's carrying my child. I'm going to be a father.'

'You've made me proud, Aaron,' Zeus says.

Lightning cracks through the statue and my father is gone, leaving his effigy back in the centre of the room. I think it's the first time in my life he's told me he's proud of me but I couldn't care less in this moment.

I use my key to go home, teleporting directly back to my room. It's filled with Inara's scent; the bed sheets pulled back and some of her things missing. She's gone too and the image of her on the bed where I'd thrown her, looking at me like I'd driven a dagger through her chest, fills my mind. I told her to be gone before I got back, right before I called her... Gods, what have I done?

My feet slap the wooden floor as I race downstairs. Talia is sitting on the front doorstep, sharpening her favourite blade.

'What did you say to Inara?' she asks around the cleaning implement sticking from her mouth.

'Where is she?' I ask.

Talia takes the thing from between her lips. 'She rushed out ten minutes ago, without so much as a goodbye. What's wrong?'

I duck around Talia and out through the door. She calls after me but I ignore her. I have to find Inara.

29

Sharp sadness wakes me and I sit up, blinking in the sunlight as I gaze around the beach. I was sure I heard someone sobbing but there's no one here. I brush sand from my body as I get up then cringe as a thick wave of sorrow hits me. I look to the cliff-top in panic when it dawns on me what's happening. I feel it now, the distinct sensation of Inara's emotion and my wings unfurl.

I alight on the edge and run toward the house. She slips outside, dressed in armour and almost slams into me. Her eyes are puffy and red with tears and she looks over her shoulder when Talia calls her name from inside.

'Get me out of here,' she begs.

I pull her in and take off without hesitation, her strange new electricity stinging my skin. She buries her face against my chest, fingers gripping my breastplate and I frown. I take her along the coastline and alight on a small ledge sticking from the cliff-face. I put her down then watch as she gazes around the fissure.

'I come here sometimes,' I say feeling her question before she asks it.

She looks at me with sad eyes. 'Have you been sleeping outside again?'

'I like it, the sound of the ocean makes me less homesick,' I say. 'Tell me what happened to upset you, Angel?'

She arches an eyebrow. 'Angel?'

'Like the stone one in the graveyard,' I say. 'It reminds me of you.'

'Oh,' she says and looks at her hands.

'Well?' I prompt when she doesn't elaborate.

'Aaron and I had a fight.'

'About what?'

She shrugs but her expression is devastated. 'It doesn't matter.'

'If I take you back—'

'He doesn't want me,' she snarls.

I can't believe what I'm saying but I want to take her pain away. 'He loves you.'

'Not anymore,' she rasps, her pain crushing.

'You don't really believe that,' I argue.

'He just told me so,' she rasps.

I've seen the way Aaron looks at her, as if she's the centre of his universe. She has to be mistaken but she's trembling, clinging to me, tears splashing my armour. She startles when I draw away then watches me shed the metal from my body. Understanding fills her face and she pulls her armour off too. I wrap her back in my arms, her soft body moulding against mine.

'Aaron is a moron, Angel.'

'Everybody leaves me sooner or later. I know this and yet, I was still stupid enough to hope.'

'I'll never leave you, remember.'

'You shouldn't make promises you can't keep, Dante.'

I take her face in my hands and snarl, 'We belong together and I'll never leave you, Inara; NEVER. The Moirai weaved you into existence for me and I won't give you up.'

She frowns. 'The Moirai?'

'Clotho, Lachesis and Atropos: the spinners of destiny, the weavers and cutters of life threads.'

'You mean the Fates?'

'Yes.' I smile and comb my fingers through her silky hair. 'They weave the tapestry of life and entwined our threads together.'

She stares at me. 'Apollo told me once that we were a matching pair.'

She understands. 'It would be so easy,' I agree, 'so right.'

Her breath brushes my skin as she gazes up at me. I trace her face, relishing the soft burn of her energy as I stare at her lips. She stares back before shaking her head and backing away.

'This isn't right,' she says but her tone is unsure, expression torn. She wants me, like I want her, I just have to show her how it can be.

I catch her hand and pull her back in. She struggles but I hold her tight, her racing heart drumming against my chest as our bodies collide. She's so soft and I weave my fingers into her golden hair, holding her still.

'Dante, no.'

'I need to show you,' I rasp resting my forehead on hers.

Her voice turns husky, curious, 'Show me what?'

'How much we make sense.'

'We don't—'

Her plush lips turn rigid, reluctant when I kiss her. She tries to push me away, fingernails digging into my chest. Her delicious fire is intoxicating and I growl in delight. Our energies merge then, BAM... everything Siren switches on.

Instinct takes over and she stops resisting. She groans and a wave of her desire floods through me. It is unbridled, Siren desire; cold, primal and identical to mine. I grip her hips as she grips my hair and deepens the kiss. We're perfect together, my cool energy fusing with her delicious burn. We're fire and ice; two halves of the same whole – perfectly matched like I knew we would be.

A shower of golden feathers rain around us and my wings curve to meet hers. Everything about her draws me in and I never want to break this connection.

Her skin lights with sunshine, radiating through the small cavern and Inara jerks away. Her eyes are wide and dark as she presses shaking fingers to her swollen lips. She looks around dazed and breathless and I feel the same. Kissing her is beyond what I imagined and I need more.

'Angel,' I groan, reaching for her. My voice resonates like it wants her in its thrall.

She steps back. 'This is wrong.'

'You felt it too,' I argue. 'We match; we belong—'

'I love Aaron.'

Frigid Siren burn sears through me at her declaration, the ground shivering beneath my feet as I grab her wrist. She belongs to me and I will have her.

'You. Are. Mine,' I snarl down at her.

Her Siren energy connects with mine again and her expression ices over. I smile at her surrender before white fire flares between us and I slam into the jagged wall opposite. I smack against the ground and look up in time to watch her launch herself from the ledge. Time slows as her golden wings spread to catch the breeze, then she's gone.

I scramble to my feet, mind cleared by the electricity she just zapped me with. I lost all reason when my Siren side took over, destructive and volatile. She told me no but I didn't listen; didn't care. I throw myself from the ledge after her, needing to fix what I've done.

30

I can't risk returning to the house in the valley but I don't have anywhere else to go. Aaron doesn't want me and Dante... I press my fingers to my still-tingling lips as I emerge inside what used to be my bedroom. Siren fire sears through my veins, preventing any tears from forming. I snarl in frustration, vision hazy with the dark mist of my Siren state. My thoughts are cold and logical and I decide what just happened doesn't matter, since I'll never see Aaron or Dante again. They're dead to me now, so hold no more power over my life. I will fight my own battles and decide my own fate.

I squeeze through the bathroom doorway, fill the bath with water and rummage for clothes. I left my armour with Dante but the Artemis blade is still strapped to my thigh. I go through the motions, numb from what just happened. I've gone from life being pretty much perfect, to having nobody but myself to rely on. I've been expecting this day for a very long time but it still managed to surprise me. I'm stupid for letting my guard down again, for letting hope trick me into believing I could have more.

Water sloshes over the sides of the bath as I get in. I climb out as soon as my wings dissolve then get dressed in jeans, a top and ballet flats. I curse Talia and her delicious cake when I struggle to button my favourite jeans, since they were loose last time I wore them.

I stare at my reflection in the long mirror. I've grown used to being Inara, the god-sired Siren and this human guise no longer feels right. I've never really fit in anywhere though. Not with humans, not with other demigods and not on Anthemusa with the regular Sirens. The closest I've ever come is with Dante but he just screwed up our friendship.

I go back to my room and sit on the bed. Something hard sticks into my hip and I pull the rectangular object from between the sheets. Warmth fills my chest, finally penetrating the Siren burn frosting my insides. I gaze at the photograph of my family and snort at the outfit I'd been wearing. Helen was right that those shorts should've been burned. My smile fades, a tear finally dripping from my chin. I let them come, a little relieved that I can finally cry, and I hug the photograph as I curl up on the bed. I pull the covers over my head and hide from reality.

I WAKE to the sound of crying and draw my sword. I scrutinise the dark room as I follow the sound to the door and ease it open. A small, pale child looks up at me with startled eyes. I sheath my blade and smile at the little girl but she darts away down the hallway, fresh sobbing trailing behind her.

'Wait, I won't hurt you!'

I reach the bottom of the stairs in time to see her pass through the remains of a glass door. I flinch as I follow her outside, passing Hector's arrows sticking from the brickwork. I have to jog across the grass to catch up and when I do, she turns to smirk at me. The hairs on my nape stand tall and, as I watch, she dissipates like mist in sunshine.

The grass where she'd been standing, bursts into flames as the scent of brimstone fills the air. A dark, slender arm reaches from the flames, followed by its partner which is pale as milk. I back away as a tall female pulls herself from the fiery ground and stands to glare at me with blood-red eyes.

She is beautiful, with long, flowing hair to the backs of her knees, sharp features and curves for days. One half of her body is dark as shadow, while the other is white as bone, as if someone drew a line vertically down her centre. Her curves are muscular and the silver serpent winding her frame undulates as she moves.

The fire fades as if it never was and I look up as fresh fire rains from the sky instead. I duck the burning missiles that crash to the Earth around us, showering us in light. I cover my face against the heat, until heavy panting fills the air and I look around for the source.

Dense smoke clears to reveal a giant fox standing over the strange female. Its fur is luminous in the night, as if encrusted with jewels: beautiful but terrifying and I stare up at it in awe.

The female climbs onto its back and sits between its shoulders. 'So it's true, you carry the light of Zeus,' she sneers.

I match her glare. 'And you are?'

'Melinoe, daughter of Zeus and Persephone,' she says haughtily.

I frown, afraid of the answer but ask, 'Did Aaron send you?'

'I'm not here for my pathetic half-brother,' she scoffs.

'Then you're a bounty hunter.'

'I'm no bounty hunter, either,' she sneers like I've offended her even more.

'Then what do you want?' I huff bored of her theatrics. If she's going to kill me then she needs to get on with it.

'The game has changed, meaning you're no longer needed alive, Noisemaker.'

'Killing me has been the game all along,' I scoff.

She smirks. 'You know so little for someone who was such a commodity. Killing you will make Aaron suffer and I long to see it.'

'You're here to kill me because you hate Aaron?'

'I'm here because you cannot carry the light of Zeus and expect not to suffer the consequences,' she hisses. 'You cut your own thread the moment you conceived it and drew the wrath of a very vengeful god.'

'Vengeful?'

'You know nothing,' she snarls. 'It's a wonder so many have failed where I will succeed. You're a pawn; a bargaining chip in a battle that's been raging for eons. Conception of the spark changed the game and the god that seeks you has returned to wanting you dead, along with that *thing* growing in your belly.'

Something flutters inside, as if reacting to Melinoe's words. I palm my stomach and a surge of electricity shoots through me. She makes the spark sound like a physical thing, alive, as if it's…

'I'll enjoy cutting it from your corpse,' she says.

'You can try,' I snarl, voice resonating.

'Your voice cannot penetrate my retinue of souls,' she laughs as the translucent child appears at the feet of the fox-like beast. 'Like all of my ghostly entourage tonight, Adara was murdered by the Sirens of Anthemusa and I saved her soul. They recognise your pretty song as the last thing they heard before they died.'

Something reverberates through the earth, growing louder and louder, until I realise it's deep growling. It rips into a snarl, the fox's muzzle peeling back to reveal razor teeth. The girl smiles creepily before dissipating again and I lift my gaze back to Melinoe.

She pats the beast's head and says, 'Give the Siren a sporting chance, Teumessian; it will make it more exciting.' Her crimson gaze drops back to me. 'What are you waiting for, Noisemaker? Run while you can.'

I bolt into the darkness but it's futile. Aaron chose this valley so he could see if anything was coming towards the house and it works the same for getting out. Melinoe can see me for miles in any direction, hunting me down with her sparkly hell-fox. I left my damn key on the bed when I was distracted by that sobbing child and I realise now that she'd been the perfect bait.

The giant fox howls, making my skin prickle with fear as I scramble up the hill. My shoulders cramp, wings pressing to unfurl but that will be futile too. The beast Melinoe is riding fell from the sky and I don't doubt it can follow me up there.

It doesn't matter if I die but I can't let Melinoe destroy the spark. It's precious to me now and I promised to keep it safe. A soft current shivers through me, as if the spark understands what I'm feeling. It fills me with desperation and I push faster.

Heavy panting bears down on me before huge teeth sink into my back. The world becomes a swirl of stars and darkness, as I'm thrown through the air then slam against the dirt. A heavy paw crushes me into the earth and I pant against the grass, rasping to fill my lungs with air.

'I expected this to be more of a challenge,' Melinoe sighs.

I wriggle my hand free enough to slide it to my thigh. I free the Artemis blade but can't move the rest of my body. My right arm is the only thing not pinned, so I twist the blade upwards and blindly thrust. It thuds into something meaty and the beast howls, weight lifting. I gasp and roll onto my back but it pounces again.

'Sneaky,' Melinoe snarls.

Black spots crowd my vision as grief swells inside me. When I die, the spark will die with me and there's nothing I can do to stop it. Bright flashes blink in the encroaching darkness and I try to look around. I remember light like this the last time I was this close to death. It explodes around us and I blink at the familiar scene.

Confusion fills Melinoe's face before she and the fox are ripped away. I suck greedily at the air, bruised ribs protesting, and roll to stare up at Melinoe. She's looking away, towards the sound of snarling and I take the chance to escape. Nausea roils inside, my legs threatening to buckle, as I stagger back into the valley. If I can get back to the house to my key...

Melinoe grips my hair. 'Where do you think you're going?'

'Aaron won't care if you kill me! He doesn't love me anymore!'

She materialises a dagger from thin air and shrugs. 'Let's see what happens when I send him your head.'

White light snaps between us and she drops the dagger. I hug my torso, knowing instinctively that Aaron's spark created it, trying to protect us.

'I'm sorry,' I whisper hoping it will understand I did everything I could to save it.

'Stupid girl,' Melinoe hisses, retrieving the dagger from the grass. 'Zeus is my father and lightning cannot hurt me.'

Squealing pierces the night and I try to see what's happening. Melinoe grips me tighter, her crimson eyes callous as she raises the blade over my heart.

'Use your light!' Someone booms across the darkness. 'Daughter of Apollo; use your sunlight!'

My eyes widen at the command because I've only ever used my divine light for healing. Eileiythia's warning reverberates through my mind that using it will hurt the spark but if I don't, the spark will die anyway.

I grip Melinoe's wrist when she strikes, the dagger grazing my chest as I summon every ounce of strength I have left. Heat floods my broken body, fiery rage rolling up from my toes to my scalp. It wraps around the spark like a cocoon then bursts into the night, filling the valley with golden fire. The stars disappear as night turns to day and I scream in agony.

Melinoe screams too, shielding her face from my sunlight as the inky half of her bubbles and hisses under the rays. She yanks something from the silver coiling her body and flames rise around her. She slips beneath the ground and the translucent child appears to stare at me.

'I'm sorry,' I pant tears dripping from my chin. 'I'm sorry they killed you but I'm not one of them.'

My sunlight flickers then fades, cascading the valley back into night and a group of translucent figures appear around the child. They stare at me too, watching until the flames flare around them and when they die, the figures are gone.

I sob against the ground, body broken and unconsciousness pressing down on me. I have to protect the spark, so I fight the need to close my eyes. I hug my stomach and a feeling of love overwhelms me, as a tiny shiver of electricity echoes my emotion. An overwhelming thought, skirts the periphery of my mind. The way everyone speaks about the spark makes it sound like...

My spine prickles, the ground shaking as Teumessian bounds across the valley in my direction. I scramble onto my feet and stagger for the house but drop to the ground as razor jaws snap at my body. They skim my spine as I flatten against the earth. The Artemis blade is back where Melinoe tried to kill me, so I lift my arm to summon my bow. Teumessian growls, guttural snarl building as it tenses for the kill.

A giant man slams into the fox, wrestling it to the ground. His skin and hair glitter too, as if he's coated with precious gems. He's dressed in leather and metal, arm locked around the beast's throat, crushing the life from its body. He draws a blade from his belt and thrusts it into the fox's chest. A deafening howl rents the night as the man forces the fox onto its side.

'Get back where you belong,' he growls at it.

When he rips his blade free, glittering blood gushes from the wound. It pours onto the ground, flowing swiftly through the grass then starts to swirl. It forms a crimson whirlpool of light, draining the substance from the beast until it turns translucent. The whirlpool ribbons into the air and forms a vortex, spiralling into the sky and disappearing into space. A twinkle of bright stars appear in its wake and I stare in horrified fascination.

The giant man steps in my direction and I lift my bow, aiming for his chest. He halts and raises his palms in surrender.

'I mean you no harm.'

I nearly stumble under my quivering legs as I take a measured step back. 'I don't believe you.'

'I'm Orion. Poseidon is my father, Dante my half brother,' he says as if it will persuade me to lower my weapon.

'Melinoe and Aaron share a father but it didn't stop her from trying to kill me.'

He sighs, dropping his hands. 'Melinoe is jealous of Zeus's favour for Aaron over her. I've no reason to hate you, Inara. I'd never harm a niece of Artemis.'

'Artemis?'

Orion smiles and it lights his handsome face. He has the same sparkly, ocean-green eyes as Dante but his hair is blond.

'She's my best friend and hunting partner,' he says. 'You remind me of her.'

I lower my bow a little. 'You were the one who was shouting earlier, telling me to use my sunlight.'

'I wasn't allowed to intervene until Melinoe freed Teumessian from the stars.'

I look to the sky, understanding what I just witnessed. 'You sent him back.'

'And now I have to return too,' he says.

'Thank you for helping me.'

'You need to leave this place,' he warns, his body beginning to fade. 'Go back to the Guardian Isle.'

'That isn't an option,' I murmur as he drifts into the sky, his constellation appearing as he disappears.

I stumble back to the house, body aching with every step and collapse by the bed. I grip my lyre and force myself to my feet. Darkness creeps in around the edge of my vision but I can't stay here. I stagger through the doorway I've opened and look around.

My mind is a haze of pain and sorrow and I don't know where I've taken myself. The place seems familiar but I can't remember what I'd been thinking when I'd opened the doorway. I turn a slow circle on the tarmac and memories of the wreckage flood me; blood and glass, a burning lorry and a strange boy with icy eyes...

Screeching fills the air and I turn expecting another monster. I lift my hand to block the blinding glare as something slams into me. I roll over a polished surface and smack into something brittle. The thing jerks to a stop and I'm thrown back onto the tarmac.

Footsteps echo around me and a hysterical voice shouts, 'Ian, I think you killed her!'

Hands roll me onto my back and a male voice says, 'Can you hear me? Vicky, call an ambulance, she's still breathing!'

31

Delia appears in the temple doorway in response to my call. She's flustered; hair a tangle of red around porcelain shoulders.

'Aaron?'

'Is Inara here?'

'You can't find her?'

I've searched the whole island and the temple of Apollo was my last hope. I turn without another word and start running back to the house. Delia calls after me and I hear her following footsteps.

I burst through the front door and race to my room. Inara's scent is fading, meaning she hasn't returned. I grip my hair and pace. I did this. I failed her by letting my hatred of my father cloud my judgement. How could I ever accuse her of such a thing? I called her a vile name, not even giving her chance to finish what she was saying.

'Did you find her?' Logan asks from the doorway.

'I searched everywhere,' I say.

He steps inside. 'What aren't you telling me, Aaron?'

'She's... I have to find her, Logan.'

'Don't tell me then, but something happened to make her run like this.'

'She told me she met Zeus while we were apart,' I blurt. 'I thought he was the reason she was carrying the spark. I thought he and she had... And I called her ...'

'Idiot!' he growls and gets in my face. 'That girl sacrificed her life for you, Aaron and after bringing you back from the dead, no less. She gave everything and at the first test of honour, you accuse her of cheating on you with Zeus?'

'It's my first reaction whenever I hear anybody speak of my father! She'd been alone with him. He'd sought her out and not used the chance to kill her. I thought it was the reason she wouldn't talk about what happened when she used Dante's key. I didn't know I could give her my spark, I didn't... know,' I say scrubbing at my eyes.

Logan stares at me, looking disgusted at the sight of my tears. An awkward expression crosses his face, then he rests a hand on my shoulder.

'We'll find her and she'll forgive you,' he says.

'But where has she gone?'

'We both know there's someone else she is close to.'

I scowl because I don't think he's talking about Helen.

32

I climb from the doorway I've created, into the house where I first met Inara. Her scent hits me instantly and I smile that I knew she'd come to this place. I'm more tuned into the way she thinks than any of the others, which is why they're all still searching the Guardian Isle. I debate going back to fetch Aaron but I need to fix what I've done before I do anything else.

My eyes adjust to the darkness as I follow her scent. A small room upstairs is flooded with water, gold feathers sticking to the ceramic tile. I continue down the narrow hallway, then down a set of stairs. An Ajax spear juts from the tiled floor, glass crunching beneath my sandals as I step outside.

My hackles rise as the scent of blood and celestial energy hits me. My trident appears in a flash of blue light and I stalk across the grass to where Inara's scent is thickest. Her blade juts from the earth, coated in sticky blood that hasn't quite dried. Her energy burns my palms as I grip the hilt and rip it free. Something really bad must have happened for her to abandon her blade like this.

My spine prickles before the sound of soft footfall shuffles through the grass behind me. I spin to face the interloper, trident poised and stare at the creature before me. She's beautiful; wide, midnight eyes and a small straight nose that reminds me of Inara. Her mouth is cruel though, her jaw squarer and her hair a river of pitch.

Her lips curve as she holds her hand out for the Artemis blade. 'Give me that.'

Her resonating voice presses against my skin, sending a shiver of Siren burn through my chest and throat. I realise this is Inara's mother and it makes me think of my own mother, with the same midnight eyes and pearly skin. Something inside entices me to know this female but she's the reason Inara wakes crying at night.

'I think I'll keep it,' I say.

Her eyes go wide at my resonating voice and she snarls, 'What trickery is this?'

I rest the central tine of my trident under her chin. 'I don't think you're in a position to be asking questions.'

'You're demigod,' she says seeming unconcerned about the weapon at her throat. She looks down at my trident. 'And Poseidon is your father but tell me, which of us is your mother?'

'My parentage is not your concern,' I snarl.

'Aggressive,' she purrs. 'Your mother must be proud.'

'My mother is dead.'

Callista's eyes narrow. 'You kill your own?'

'Like you kill your male offspring,' I counter.

She strokes a finger down my chest, expression softening. 'If you return with me to Anthemusa you'll be the only male on an island of females. The others will fall over each other to get to you. You'd be their king; have anything or anyone you wanted.'

I slide the Artemis blade into my belt then slip an arm around Callista's waist. I trace slowly up her spine, trident still pressed to her chin. She watches with sultry eyes, biting her bottom lip the same way Inara does. I tangle my fingers in the silky hair at her nape and lean close. She whimpers under the violence of my grip and smirks.

'There's only one female I want and I'm about to give her one less thing to fear.'

'I see you've met my daughter and are willing to kill for her. Why, because you love her?' she sneers.

'What would you know of love?' I snarl.

'Siren women love just as passionately as any other – Just as I know Inara loves you.'

'She loves Aaron, not me.'

'The Son of Zeus?' she scoffs. 'Aaron isn't like us. He can never understand the connection our kind share. He'll *never* be able to make Inara truly happy, like you could.'

'She doesn't want me.'

'Inara doesn't know what's good for her,' Callista scoffs. 'She fights her Siren heritage because Aaron has convinced her it's wrong. If it's so wrong then neither of you would exist and until she realises the lie she's living, she'll never be happy.'

I stare at her feeling conflicted because everything she's saying makes sense. It goes against what I've been raised to believe but what if everything I've been taught is wrong? I've been locked away my entire life, believing it's for my safety but what if Callista is right? Have I been fed a lie to keep me in line? Can I never be happy if I don't accept the darker half of what I am?

I remember Inara's expression after I let my Siren energy take control. 'How can embracing the darkness make me happy? My Siren side is violent and merciless.'

'More violent than what you'll do to me?' she asks. 'Sirens may be cold and merciless, violent and cruel – but you enjoy it. Admit what Inara tries so hard to hide. Neither of you should be made to fear what's natural for our kind.'

'I'm not afraid,' I snarl.

She shoves my trident aside and presses against me, black eyes eclipsing my vision. I tighten my grip on her hair, forcing another whimper from her lips and she laughs.

'So very, very violent,' she praises. 'You'd be the perfect mate for my daughter.'

Wintry desire burns through me, webbing my insides with ice at her words. I sigh at the delicious sensation and my wings explode from my back in response.

Callista stares up at me with avarice and I growl, 'I don't need you to tell me Inara is mine.'

I tug her hair hard, making her cry out and let my trident vanish. Inflicting pain is more enjoyable when it's done with my bare hands.

I CLIMB from the pool of light into the graveyard to find Aaron and Logan waiting by the stone angel. I wipe Callista's black blood from my hands and bite back a snarl as I walk over to them. I can't believe they came here to look for her before the house in the valley. They really have no clue.

Aaron scrutinises my bloody clothing. 'What is that?'

'I finally met Inara's mother,' I answer.

Satisfaction fills me when Aaron and Logan's eyes widen. Even if I don't like them, I respect their skills. I've staved off fighting either because of Inara, but the itch to engage is strong and I know they feel the same way. Especially Logan. I see the respect echoed in their gazes now and hold myself back.

'Where is she now?'

'Dead,' I say.

'Do you know where Inara is?' Aaron asks.

'No.'

'She didn't tell you where she was going?' he presses.

'She was angry with me before she left,' I admit.

'Why?' Logan asks.

I look from him to Aaron and say, 'Because I kissed her.'

'What?' he snarls.

'I kissed her,' I repeat. 'She said you no longer loved her, so I showed her what it would be like with me.'

The early sunlight turns cold as Logan steps towards me. 'I'm going to enjoy this.'

I grin at the challenge, body primed from my encounter with Callista. I've never met a Siren other than Inara and the sensation was addictive. Callista was right about one thing: I shouldn't have to hide what I am. If people don't like it, that's their problem.

'No,' Aaron says stepping between us.

'Did you not hear what he just said?' Logan scoffs.

'Inara really said that?' Aaron asks me. 'That I don't love her?'

I've never seen him look so devastated, not even when Mila had him seconds from death. Soon he'll lose Inara forever when she realises like I have, she can't keep fighting what she is. With me she can be herself and it's only a matter of time before she comes to terms with the fact we belong together.

'She'll forgive you,' I say.

Aaron stares at me. 'Why are you telling me this?'

Because I want him to hope, so I can watch it die in his eyes when she realises she's mine. 'All I want is for her to be happy.'

He nods. 'Thank you.'

'Don't misunderstand me,' I warn. 'I won't hesitate to take her from you. She and I are designed to be together and she knows it. She just met you first.'

'If I hurt her again, I'll deserve to lose her,' he says.

'I'm going to vomit,' Logan scoffs and stalks away. 'When you two ladies have finished, you can find me by the gates, waiting to do what we came here to do – or has your new-found love for each other made you forget?'

I snort and follow Logan between the graves.

33

I cringe against the burn of sinew knitting; ribs popping back into place and the tang of chemical cleaner filling my lungs. I force my eyes open and blink against the light. I start to gag and sit up to pull a long plastic tube from my throat. It seems to go on forever, before dropping onto the bed. I stare at the white tube, similar to the one they put down Daniel's throat when he had his appendix out.

Objects in the room begin to register. Intermittent beeping drifts from a bed facing me, the occupant covered in a multitude of wires. I look down, realising I'm in the same condition. Needles protrude from the inside of both my elbows, pumping fluids into my body. Wires cling to my skin by tiny red and white tags.

I'm in a human hospital and I can't be here.

The machine to my left beeps faster as I yank the needles from my arms. I swing my legs off the bed and rip the white and red tags from my body. The beeping turns into a long, piercing wail and an alarm sounds. I try to focus through the woolly feeling in my head, the haze of drugs lifting, burning away with the increasing heat in my healing body. It's difficult to think and I can't find my clothes.

I stumble into an empty corridor, the sound of people running on linoleum loud in my muzzy brain. I feel their footsteps vibrating through the floor, their increasing proximity making my skin prickle. I head in the opposite direction, bare feet slapping linoleum and slip through a doorway. A team of medical staff rush by, going to the room where I woke up.

My heart pounds against my ribcage as I study my hiding place. There's a row of lockers and coat hooks. I pull on a set of blue scrubs, tuck my hair under the little hat and slip the mask over my face. My feet are still bare but there isn't time to hunt for shoes. I hesitate in the doorway at the amount of people that have appeared in the corridor, then step out.

'They've closed the road outside,' a nurse is saying. 'Whoever took her won't get far.'

'I'm worried for her,' another answers. 'She was in such a bad way when they brought her in. She won't last long off life-support.'

'They haven't even identified her yet, so I don't know who would want to abduct her from ICU,' the first nurse says.

'Maybe it was the people who hit her with their car.'

'They're still in the waiting area,' someone argues. 'What I don't understand is, who could get into ICU unnoticed?'

I find my feet and move towards the exit. I catch the door as a nurse taps in the security code to leave.

'Even if they find her in time, she'll probably lose the baby,' one of the nurses sighs.

I freeze halfway through the door and look back. They can't be talking about me like I'd assumed. I frown down at my stomach, not visible under the baggy scrubs. I'd know if I were pregnant, wouldn't I? Electricity zips through my core as if answering my unspoken question and I shove into the next corridor, mind going numb.

I pull the mask and hat off as I reach the main entrance. Everyone is searching for a girl in critical condition, so I go unnoticed as I walk out.

Tears burn my face as I bisect the carpark, a torrent of emotion threatening to break me. The first is terror, then excitement, joy and finally pain. I'm carrying Aaron's child and it all makes sense. It's what they meant about me carrying his spark and I feel stupid for not figuring it out sooner. All the hints were there but I was too caught up in the drama of my life.

But Aaron doesn't want me – Or maybe he just doesn't want me carrying his child. I'm alone in this and I hug my torso as I leave the hospital site. I don't need him to want anything from me anymore. I'll do it on my own and my best chance of survival is to hide.

I SURVEY the area again before slipping inside, never allowing complacency to set in even when I feel safe. I will never be safe and I say it aloud each morning as a reminder. Caution and vigilance are a small price to pay to stay alive.

I drop the bags of food on the little worktop then lift my face to the skylight. I want to take the boards off the windows and let the sunlight flood in but I won't risk it. Instead, I pull the single cupcake I stole from one of the bags and stick a little candle into the icing. I ease onto the makeshift bed in the middle of the floor and cross my legs. The wick grows hot between my fingertips, crackling with silver light, until a tiny flame appears. I watch it dance for a moment, then sigh and blow it out.

'Happy birthday, Inara,' I murmur. It's a birthday I didn't think I'd make it to and this isn't how I envisioned celebrating it.

I rest the cake on my stomach then lay back to watch the sky through the only unobscured window I have. I smile as I stroke my belly, the swell more noticeable when I lay like this. I have nothing and no one; alone on my eighteenth birthday; but I'm happy. It's been months since I've spoken to another soul but I haven't had to fight for my life either. It's peaceful and safe for my precious cargo; lonely but for the best.

I pull the thick blanket over my bump as I watch the brightening sky through the tiny skylight. It's getting colder each day and I'll have to move on again soon. My grandparents' beach hut has been sufficient through the summer months but I'll have to find somewhere warmer soon. My mind drifts to the Guardian Isle and its hot days; then, as always, I think of Aaron. I wince at the pain in my chest and scrub tears from my eyes. I hate that the ache for him has grown alongside the child in my belly. The disgust in his gaze the day he told me to leave haunts my thoughts. I should loathe him for how he treated me, not miss him with every fibre of my being.

My stomach rolls, as if I've driven over a dip in the road and I rub a soothing hand over my bump. 'I miss him, that's all.'

My stomach rolls again, electricity snapping around me; the baby's response to my sadness. Whatever mix of Aaron and I they'll be, they've definitely inherited my Siren ability to sense emotion. I sit up and hum. The soft sound sends shivering waves through the air and the foetus settles. Warm electricity tingles through me in response and I smile.

'I love you, too,' I say.

In moments like these, I'm glad I left. I don't feel like I need anyone or anything else, as long as I have the little spark growing inside me. I don't think of how terrifying the future will be once it's born. I just think of the love we already share and it's enough.

I eat my birthday cake then push to my feet. The sun is high, the beach busy with late tourists making the most of the warm September. I pack a rucksack and look around the hut. If I leave now I can break into the house with the secluded garden before the owners get back from work. I can take a shower and brush my teeth without them ever knowing I've been there. They have a quick-wash cycle on their washing machine too, so I can clean my clothes.

I force a slow pace as I stroll along the seafront. I hadn't realised how bad I'd become at playing human, until I'd noticed the stares.

Demigods move a little faster than humans do and it drew attention once my bump started showing.

Being five months pregnant is probably different for me than for a human woman too. I crave things and get tired easily but feel stronger than before, more resilient. I don't know if it's a Siren or a demigod thing but I'm grateful. I glance at the sun, wishing I could ask Apollo. The moment I call for him though, the other gods will know I'm alive.

It's better if everyone thinks I'm dead but I'm afraid I'm endangering my baby's life. I'm clueless about what to expect; not because of the pain but because of the process. I can't risk going to a human hospital and can't go to the Guardian Isle either. I'll be on my own and I'm terrified. I'm not human and any of my inherited abilities could manifest during labour. I constantly panic about what it means for my child. They'll be a mix of human, Siren and the divine and I pray we'll be able to blend in.

I think back to Aaron's last words to me and no matter how many times I replay it, I can't understand what I'd said to upset him. Did he know I was carrying his child? Is it why he called me a whore? Did he think I'd tricked him into it?

I rub my eyes at the memory and chew my lip to hold back tears. Aaron hates our child and an insidious voice whispers it's because they'll be part Siren. He was okay dating a Siren but didn't want to procreate with one. The thought makes me angry and I huff when my bracelets ignite in response. I take a calming breath and remind myself that I'll never see him again. Even if I do, I'll protect our child from him.

34

AARON

Logan opens a fiery doorway with his key and the stench of ash and brimstone fill the air, even as the temperature drops ten degrees. Shadow reaches from the darkness beyond; cold and silent.

'Is this the only way?' I ask, the hairs on my nape rising.

'You can always pay Charon to ferry you in but he doesn't make return journeys,' Logan answers.

I huff and drop through the flaming doorway, scouring the inhospitable gloom when I land. There isn't any sky, just swirling mist overhead and it makes me feel trapped. Logan lands beside me then turns, as if expecting someone. I turn too and there's a female a few metres away. She has no mouth, pasty skin and walks away the moment we make eye contact. She's heading for a sheer rock face and I wonder what she's doing, until an opening appears in the rock.

Logan shrugs when I look his way for answers. 'Don't ask me.'

'Shouldn't you know how these things work? You looked like you expected her to be here.'

'I think we're supposed to follow her. She's an invitation and you can't get in without her.'

As if listening, the girl half turns and glares at us. She doesn't speak, just fixes us with an annoyed stare when we don't follow.

'I think you're right,' I say.

This is the third time I've been to Hades. The first was while fighting with Logan as children. Hades had just gifted Logan his key and Logan wouldn't let me near it. I only wanted to look but he'd refused and we'd ended up in a tangle of limbs on the floor. Logan hadn't meant to open the doorway, it just happened and we'd fallen through.

Then there was the time I died on Anthemusa and Inara brought me back. I feel now like I did then: the hairs on my nape standing tall, waiting for attack. There are things lurking in the darkness here, things that eat flesh and thirst for blood.

Logan starts whistling a merry tune, seemingly unaffected by the rolling gloom and dank air.

'Seriously?' I scoff.

'Spending copious amounts of time here as a child numbs you to it,' he says. 'Besides, it isn't all bad. The Elysian Fields and Isle of the Blessed are beautiful. It's because we're so close to Tartarus that it's so _'

'Tartarus!'

'I didn't choose where the Moirai live, Aaron. An audience with them isn't supposed to be easy.'

I think of Inara. The last three months have been worse than any kind of torture Tartarus can offer. I've searched for her everywhere. She left her armour on the Guardian Isle and Dante found her blade in the valley. I followed a report Helen saw in the Human Realm about a girl being abducted from Intensive Care, but by the time I got there the trail was dead.

She just...vanished, like the way Mila did when Logan killed her... I shove the thought away because Inara can't be dead. My heart would feel it if she were, wouldn't it? The fear that she's gone tries to choke me. She hasn't visited me in her sleep and the gods have lost her from their radar. Word has spread that she's gone but I refuse to accept it.

We follow the mouthless girl through a jagged opening in the rock, her dark robes rustling against the ground. The air grows damper and colder the deeper we get and we seem to travel for hours, until the narrow passage opens into a large chamber. Three females in white are waiting there, the walls of the cavern lined with the tapestry they are weaving. Woven, multicoloured threads form a brilliant ribbon of light around us and I stare at the spectacle.

The females look neither young nor old, as if frozen in the moment between adolescence and adulthood. Their eyes are completely white and unstaring, yet still track our progress when we enter the room. I recognise them from the symbols tattooed on their necks: shears, a measuring rod and a spinning-wheel.

The girl bows to them then leaves as silently as she arrived. She steps directly into the rock wall and disappears, like the black surface absorbs her.

Clotho, the Fate with the spinning-wheel symbol, studies me with her colourless eyes. 'Ask your question, Son of Zeus.'

I lick my dry lips, glance at Logan then say, 'I seek Inara, Daughter of Apollo.'

Clotho plucks a brightly shining thread from the air. 'The Siren girl; I remember spinning her thread.'

I stare at the vibrant gold between Clotho's fingers, my relief a physical thing. 'She's alive.'

'Her time has grown immeasurable on her current path,' Lachesis says and I pull my eyes from Inara's life thread to look at her. The measuring rod symbol glitters on her neck in the soft light from the thread and I swallow.

'She's so much closer to my blades when your threads are entwined,' Atropos tells me, sliding her ancient fingers along the edge of her life-ending shears.

I frown at her admission and ask, 'Would her thread be safer if I left her alone?'

'Your destinies are already one, Son of Zeus; life threads woven in an inseparable union,' Clotho says and plucks another thread from the air.

A shiver rips down my spine when I recognise the silver light of my own thread. Clotho lifts her arms wide, my thread in her left hand and Inara's in her right, until they became taut and I can see they're woven together.

'You see now,' Lachesis says. 'You are joined together and your destinies are forever entwined.'

I swallow, wanting to ask my next question but fearful of the answer.

'Ask,' Atropos says as if knowing my mind.

It makes sense, since she knows of things that are to be. Logan is watching me though. I haven't told him yet, haven't told anybody – but I need to know.

'Is Inara still carrying... is she still... ?' I stop, throat dry with the fear that something bad has happened to our unborn child.

Clotho plucks another thread from the air, a mixture of silver and gold and radiant with life. Gods... I reach for it but hesitate. Clotho nods and places the thread in my upturned palm. It stings with electricity, yet burns with sunlight. Then she takes it back and all three threads vanish. I stare at my palm and wipe a tear.

'What was that?' Logan asks.

I look at my brother and know I can't hide it from him any longer. I wanted to find Inara first, so we could tell people together. That's the way these things are supposed to work. I didn't want this moment to be anything but joyful.

'Inara is carrying my child, Logan.'

His eyes shoot wide with shock.

'You'll find the Daughter of Apollo in the Human Realm,' Atropos says scrutinising the tapestry as if words are written there. 'She's in a place where Thalassa meets Gaea.'

I frown; Thalassa and Gaea are ancient immortals from the very beginning of time. I try to remember my teachings. Thalassa was goddess of the surface of the ocean and Gaea was the Earth...

'She's by the ocean?'

Atropos nods and holds out her hand. 'This will take you there.'

She drops a small, gold sphere into my palm when I hold my hand out and I say, 'What do I do with it?'

'Eat it,' Lachesis orders.

Atropos snatches hold of my wrist when I move to put the sphere in my mouth. 'Payment is required for such a gift.'

'What kind of payment?' I ask.

'Blood payment.'

I flinch. 'You want my blood?'

The Fates look at me greedily. 'It's been a long time since we tasted the wine of the living.'

'But if I die, I'll be unable to leave the Underworld.'

'Bloodletting shouldn't cut your thread, boy,' Atropos says.

'Bloodletting?'

'We don't require all of it,' Clotho says like that makes it all better.

Logan steps between me and the Fates. 'Take my blood as payment.'

'Son of Hades for the Son of Zeus?' Lachesis hums and Atropos releases me.

'Logan, no.'

'Inara and your child will need you, Aaron.' He turns back to the Fates before I can respond and asks, 'Do you accept?'

They wrap ageless hands around his and say in unison. 'A deal is made. Take the orb, Aaron for you cannot break your brother's bargain.'

'Logan,' I rasp.

He meets my gaze. 'The payment is made and you cannot change it. Don't waste my blood or the orb, Aaron.'

The little gold sphere is sweet and delicious, dissolving on my tongue before sliding like honey down my throat. Lightning crackles around me, fierce bolts of white more powerful than I've ever generated. I've only experienced power like this in the presence of my father.

'The Ambrosia Orb has increased your divinity, Son of Zeus,' Atropos says. 'Now you can use your link with Inara to find her.'

'Ambrosia?'

'Your new-found immortality is limited,' she cautions, ignoring my shock.

'Immortality?' I rasp.

'As with the Daughter of Apollo, you may still be killed by the hand of another. True immortality is only gained by those deemed worthy: beings of proven purity and valour. Only they may be granted entrance to Olympus.' Atropos says.

'What in Hades have you given me?' I say.

'What are you waiting for?' Logan growls. 'Find her, Aaron – before somebody else does!'

I meet his gaze. Logan is giving me everything, again; sacrificing himself to give me what I want.

'Thank you,' I breathe.

He smiles. 'I expect a mention in your child's Naming Ceremony.'

I nod feeling oddly emotional, then close my eyes and think of Inara. Instantly, I sense her through the connection we formed when she brought me back to life. Her heat fills my veins, intoxicating my being and I sigh in relief. Just feeling her burn after so long is everything and I let her fill me up.

When I open my eyes, I'm somewhere new. I hear the sound of waves crashing and the air is filled with Inara's sweet scent. But she isn't here. I turn a slow circle, scrutinising every detail of the tiny space. There's food on a counter and a makeshift bed in the middle of the floor. I frown at the ruffled blankets, wondering if she's been living like this for the last three months.

I push the door open and look out. Waves and an ivory beach stretch before me. It's busy with humans, splashing in the water and building castles on the sand. I glance at my armour-clad body and release a frustrated growl. I'm stuck in here until nightfall, until I can acquire clothing that will blend in. I let the door bang shut and consider going to the Guardian Isle to get clothes but I can't afford to leave this place until I find Inara, not even for a second.

35

The clothes are warm from the dryer as I pull them on and sigh happily. I tie my hair into a knot at my nape and tuck the rest of my clothes into the rucksack. My jeans sit just below my bump and I pull my top down to cover it. It springs back up, exposing a slice of flesh and I make a mental note to procure bigger tops. I glance at my profile in the mirror and smirk. From the back it doesn't look like I'm pregnant but from the side you can't miss it.

I retrace my steps, making sure there's no evidence of my being in the house then climb from the window, down to the garden. I glance around until I'm sure I haven't been spotted then take a steady stroll back to the beach.

I stop along the promenade to sit on a bench. It's rare that I allow myself the luxury of sitting out in the open to enjoy the sunshine – but today is my birthday. Cake, clean clothes and sunshine – what more can a girl want? Compared to some days in the last few months, it's downright five stars.

I watch two small children play on the sand. Their laughter drifts on the air and I find myself laughing too. Maybe one day I can be like the woman on the sand, watching her children play. I stroke a hand over my belly, wondering what my child's laughter will sound like.

Something glints in the sunlight and I look down at the silver cup on the bench beside me. Fragrant steam billows from the gold liquid inside and I freeze with dread. Eileiythia picks up the cup and sits on the bench in its place.

She tucks a curtain of dark curls behind her ear, milky eyes panning to me. 'I've spent much time trying to locate you, Inara.'

She offers the cup but I stare at it like it's filled with snakes. 'I just want to be left alone.'

'I understand,' she says then smiles. 'I see you've been taking excellent care of the spark.' She inches the cup of ambrosia tea in my direction. 'It's good for the baby.'

So now she's calling it a baby? Bloody figures.

I huff and take the cup. Eileiythia sits back and looks out to sea as I drain the sweet, delicious liquid. Gold light explodes across my skin like last time and I glance around at the passing people.

'I've raised the veil for my visit, so they can't see us,' Eileiythia says.

I suddenly understand why nobody is staring at the goddess on the bench and hand her the empty cup. 'Thank you.'

She takes the cup then palms my swollen stomach. 'Very good care indeed,' she hums happily then sits back and says, 'It's pretty here.'

'Not that I don't appreciate your visit but how did you find me?' I ask.

'I've been running a psychic sweep since you disappeared and today you just appeared.'

'If I show up on your radar, does that mean...?'

'Somebody has located you,' she says, 'somebody who doesn't know how to disguise the trail left when moving between the ethers of the universe, like with my veil. When I leave, I suggest you move on if you don't want to be found.'

I hug my stomach in sheer terror. The light is dissipating from my skin and when it does, Eileiythia will be gone, taking the protection of her veil with her.

I stand as soon as the light completely fades. 'I'm sorry, I can't stay.'

'I understand,' she says then is gone in a flash of pearly light.

I hurry along the promenade, holding my bump as if I can protect it from anyone that might find us. An electric flutter shivers through my core from the precious cargo I carry. I want to stop and whisper calming words to my child but I no longer have that luxury. I have to collect the rest of my things and get the hell out of here. I glance at the afternoon sun, wondering if calling my father will increase the risk of being found. I shake my head and hurry on, knowing that would be stupid. The more people that believe me still dead, the better. I don't want reports of my sudden appearance getting around and a fresh set of hunters baying after me.

I glance around before opening the door to the beach hut. Aaron's scent hits me before I register him standing there. My rucksack hits the floor as he stares back. His pretty eyes widen then track down to my swollen stomach. He reaches for me and I freak, kicking the fallen rucksack at him and slamming the door in his face. He calls after me but I'm already running.

Tears stain my face as I run and people stare, a few asking if I need help but I don't stop. I hear the hut door slam against its frame and glance back when Aaron shouts my name. He's running now too, silver armour glittering in the September sunshine.

I rip my gaze away and turn onto the steps leading from the beach. I hit the bottom step as Aaron reaches the top. Heat wells in my palm as I summon my key for the first time in months. I've abstained from using it for fear it might attract unwanted attention but that ship just sailed. I dive through the gate of the house I broke into earlier, silent waves rippling around me as a doorway opens.

I emerge on familiar tarmac and hurry to the side of the road. I rest my hands on my knees, trying to catch my breath and curse myself for dropping my rucksack. I wipe my eyes and look around the site of the accident. The stretch of road is in the middle of nowhere, surrounded by fields on all sides. I look down at my key, not wanting to risk using it again but unsure where to go from here.

I'm only walking for a few minutes when a car pulls up beside me. 'Need a lift?' the human asks.

I glance at the child strapped into the child-seat in the back and wonder when I started referring to people as 'humans'. I breathe deep through my nose to check for scents before deeming them safe.

'Thanks,' I say and slide into the front passenger seat.

The woman looks at my bump in concern. 'It's dangerous to be wandering country roads in your condition.'

'I'm just out for an afternoon walk and wandered a little far,' I lie.

She doesn't look convinced and asks, 'Where can I drop you?'

I wonder what my grandparents will say if they see me like this and ask, 'Do you know the Sycamore Estate?'

She frowns. 'You walked all the way from there? It's at least eight miles.'

'If it's too far –'

'No, it's fine. I'm just surprised.'

I shrug like it's nothing and look out the window.

36

I catch a glimpse of Inara as the doorway shuts behind her. I growl in frustration and kick a hole in the fence lining the garden. I'd been so close and she'd been so afraid of me. My anger evaporates because I can't blame her for not wanting to see me, not after what I did the last time we were together. If she just gives me the chance to explain, to apologise... I shake my head because she's changed so much. I hadn't expected to be so overwhelmed by seeing her that way; belly swollen with our child and radiant in a way that's more than her connection to the sun god. She's never looked more beautiful.

I close my eyes and think of her warm essence. There she is, like a beacon in the darkness, filling my veins with that tantalising fire. I breathe it deep and open my eyes.

The scene is instantly familiar: that long, deserted road where I'd watched her clamber from a mangled car. I'd been so sure I'd finally get my chance to kill her and now all I want is to wrap her in my arms and never let go. It's what I should've been doing from day one, what I'd promised I'd always do but have failed too many times to count.

I shelter my gaze from the sun when something glints on the horizon. I realise it's an approaching car and move to hide in one of the fields. I narrow my gaze when the car stops less than half a mile ahead, the passenger door swinging open. Somebody gets out but I can't see around the open door. The driver's door opens and a tall female gets out. She stares back the way she came, calling to someone. I watch her walk around to the passenger door and slam it shut, before getting back into the car and driving on.

Golden hair comes into view from behind the car, framing a figure I'd know anywhere. Inara is running away and has put at least another half a mile between us. I set off after her, ignoring the woman in the car when she slams on the brakes to watch me pass, her mouth a little *o* of surprise as she takes in my battle-armour.

Inara is fast but I'm faster and the power I've gained since the Fates gave me Ambrosia is immense. My leather sandals slap the tarmac, breaths fast and hot as I close the gap between us. She glances back with a quarter of a mile to go, a flash of golden light bursting from her left wrist.

'No!' I shout.

I can't let her use her key again. If I can just get to her, apologise... The atmosphere wrinkles ahead, a doorway tearing a hole through space.

'Inara!' She looks back, emerald eyes wide as she runs inside. 'No!'

I slow to a stop at the place she disappeared. I pinch the bridge of my nose then fill my lungs with oxygen and concentrate on finding her again. This time I'm not going to lose her. I make the connection and her sweet essence fills me once more.

37

I trip over a tree root and land on the grass, unsure how Aaron keeps finding me. I look wildly around as I push to my feet, wondering what that poor woman must've thought. I'd thrown myself from her car after screaming for her to stop and then Aaron had chased me. He's faster than I remember and I rub my eyes, mentally and physically exhausted. I can't keep this up much longer and I look up into the tree before I climb. Green leaves rustle around me, instead of the burning orange colour they'd been when I'd hidden from Diana here so long ago.

I climb higher this time, immersing myself in the thicket of leaves as my spine prickles. Surely it can't be Aaron again. Even if he used his key, he can't have guessed my location already. It's like he has a tracker on me or something.

I consider summoning my bow but he steps into view below and I freeze. My fingernails dig into the sappy branch, heart racing. He scrutinises the canopy, then drops his gaze and moves on. I'm shaking from more than fear and feel like my heart will beat through my ribcage any second.

I wait in the tree for hours, until the sun slips below the horizon and the temperature drops. My body aches from hours of not moving, stomach cramping as my cargo reacts to my fear. Stars begin to glitter from between the leaves and frost forms on the branches around me. I bite my lip and look down, knowing I need to find somewhere warmer. I scrutinise the ground for a long time then climb down, joints popping in the silence of the surrounding fields.

I land with a soft thud and smooth a hand over my stomach. 'It's okay.'

An electric shiver flutters through me in response, before prickling spikes down my spine. My bow flashes into my right hand, a silver arrow appearing as I draw on the bowstring and spin to face the threat. The shimmering barb is inches from Aaron's throat as he stares at me with wide eyes.

'Don't move,' I snarl.

His eyes are neon fire in the dark. 'Goddess –'

'I'm not your "Goddess",' I sneer. 'I'm the Siren whore you ordered to leave your home, remember.'

His spicy scent teases my senses and every cell in my body aches for him. I bite my lip so hard I taste blood and my hands start to shake. I'll kill him if he gives me no choice and I'm terrified that's about to happen. Nobody will take the spark from me, not even him.

My stomach cramps, electricity snapping around me and I glance between my bump and Aaron. The spark never moves this much, so something must be wrong. Maybe I ran too much or spent too long in the tree... Aaron inches closer, expression a mix of awe and worry.

'I said don't move!' I hiss.

Pain grips my abdomen and I swallow back a whimper. Not for me because I'm no stranger to pain but for my child. Something is very wrong and I need to end this.

I draw the bowstring a little further and aim the barb at the dip in Aaron's throat. 'What do you want?'

'To apologise for what I did to you – What I said. I'd thought ... I love you, Inara.' His gaze drops to my stomach. 'Both of you.'

It's too perfect. 'I don't believe you.'

He frowns like he expected a different response. 'You can trust me.'

'You don't deserve my trust,' I scoff.

He sighs, 'You're right, I don't but I want –.'

'I don't care what you want anymore,' I snarl.

Something occurs to me and I blanche. Aaron is who Eileiythia was referring to. He's the reason I'm now appearing on the divine radar after months of careful hiding.

'We were fine before you came looking!' I growl. 'Nothing has tried to kill me in months, then you show up and draw attention to the fact I'm still alive.'

He stares at me confused. 'What are you talking about?'

'Whatever you did to find me alerted the entire cosmos of my continued existence, Aaron! They're going to come after me again and I'm not exactly going to fit into my armour right now.'

He pales. 'They just told me I'd find you. If I'd known ...'

'Who told you?' I hiss.

'The Moirai,' he says. 'They told me we were destined to be together, that our threads are woven as one.'

He isn't here because he wants to be then. 'You're here because the Moirai told you it will happen,' I say in understanding.

Something withers in my chest and I let the bowstring slacken, arrow vanishing. I should be relieved he isn't here to kill me but I just feel sick. No matter what he's done, I still love him and a part of me breaks all over again that he doesn't love me back. I thought that part of me broke three months ago but apparently I still have pieces to shatter.

Electric pain webs through me and I groan, clutching my stomach. The spark doesn't like my heartbreak and it's much stronger than the last time I felt this way.

'Don't,' I hiss when Aaron reaches for me.

'Let me help you,' he begs.

'Help me by telling everyone you've killed me,' I pant. 'You owe me that much.'

I turn away but he growls and clasps my arm. I try to pull away but he grips tighter and yanks me back.

'Let go,' I snarl, voice reverberating with Siren rage.

'I'm still immune to your voice,' he says, flaunting the evidence of my love for him.

I get in his face, furious at his audacity and growl, 'Release me.'

'I won't!' he growls back. 'I love you and can't ever let you go. Gods, I told myself I'd leave you be if you rejected me but...' He draws his sword and presses the hilt into my palm, pushing the tip under his breastplate. 'Kill me now because I will not – cannot – live without you, Inara.'

His sword thuds to the dirt between us. 'No!'

'If you don't love me anymore then what does it matter?'

'You already know I still love you,' I scoff. 'For God's sake, you're the one who didn't want me, Aaron! I can't just let you... I won't let you...' I struggle against his grip on my arm. 'Get off me!'

'I'm sorry I hurt you,' he rasps, tone desperate.

He tucks a length of hair behind my ear and I glare at the ground, struggling to hold onto my anger. The gentle touch brings back visceral memories and it's breaking my resolve. I should hate him for what he did but I just can't. He's my weakness and I loathe that I'm this way around him.

'You have to forgive me,' he breathes. When I shake my head, he puts a finger under my chin and forces me to meet his gaze. 'Forgive me, Inara.'

I'm lost at his pleading, unable to take a deep breath. The pain eases from my abdomen, as if the physical contact with Aaron soothed our unborn child. Is this what the spark wants, to be near its father? I shake my head in wonder and Aaron lets go. He stares at me with an agonised expression then sighs and closes his eyes.

'I'll always love you,' he tells me. His body flickers with white light and he starts to fade.

'Wait!' I hiss.

His eyes snap open, burning pools of blue fire. He solidifies again and I wonder how he nearly left without even using his key.

'You were just going to leave without hearing my answer?' I scoff.

'But, I thought –'

'You thought wrong,' I snap.

He stares at me then rasps, 'Please say it.'

I lick my dry lips. 'I...' I look away, huff then meet his gaze. 'I forgive you.'

'Again,' he says.

I slap him hard across the face. 'I've chosen to forgive you but you called me a whore, Aaron and I want to know why.'

He rubs his cheek looking uncomfortable. 'When you told me you'd met my father I assumed...'

'What?' I press when he hesitates.

His throat dips. 'You had the spark and Zeus has a thing for beauty. I thought he'd been the one to pass it to you.'

I shove him away in disgust. 'I can't believe you'd think that about me. After everything we've been through –'

'It's a reflex where my father is concerned! You're important to me and Zeus has a habit of taking the things that matter most, Inara. I don't trust him with you.'

'You should've trusted *me*,' I snarl, outraged.

'I do trust you,' he says taking my hands in his. 'Let me take you home and I'll show you ...'

I jerk free. 'I'm not going anywhere with you.'

'Inara ...'

'Nothing you can say will change my mind! You can't just –'

He grips my nape and crushes his lips to mine. I shove him off but he catches me and yanks me back. The sweet crackle of his lightning and his spicy taste on my tongue, slice through my barriers like he's taking a hammer to them.

My angry snarl tapers into a whimper and I grip his hair. Lightning snaps around us, arcing between our bodies, as he kisses me senseless. He rips his lips away when we're both breathless and presses a tingling hand to my swollen belly. I shiver under the powerful current webbing beneath his splayed hand and his gaze softens. He kneels and presses an ear to my bump.

'I hear our child's heart beating,' he rasps.

The last of my anger fizzles out and I say, 'I think they missed you.'

He stares up at me. 'Really?'

I nod. 'So did I.'

He stands and cups my jaw. 'I swear I'll never hurt either of you again, Inara.'

'You need to prove it,' I say. 'Forgiving you is one thing but the trust... It won't be so easy.'

'I'll earn it back.'

I scour his expression then sigh, 'Take us home then.'

THE GUARDIAN ISLE still feels like home, even after months away. Aaron snags my hand when I step towards the bedroom door, expression nervous.

'There's something I need to do first,' he says.

He sits me on the bed and I watch warily as he rummages through a drawer. I stroke my stomach at the near-constant shivering of the spark; its content akin to an electric hum. Aaron turns back and kneels at my feet. He rests a hand on my stomach then presses something into my palm. I gaze down at the three emeralds embedded into a dainty, ornate ring.

'I had it made from the butterfly pendent,' he says.

'I went back to fetch it from the graveyard after Zeus saved me from an Ajax,' I say. 'He was the one who told me to go back for it.'

I watch the realisation that his dad was the reason we found each other back then, dawn across his face. Shock replaces the realisation, then confusion and finally guilt.

He sighs, 'These emeralds brought you back to me once and I never want you to take them off again.'

'It's beautiful,' I say then frown when he just stares at me expectantly. 'I don't know what else you want me to say, Aaron.'

He takes it from me and pushes it onto the third finger of my left hand. 'Say yes.'

I stare at him in shock and blurt, 'Is this because I'm pregnant? If it is, I don't think –'

'It's because the last few months have been the worst of my existence,' he says. 'I can't live without you and I want you bound to me in every way possible.'

I stare down at the jewelled band on my finger, knowing I should tell him to go to hell. He's watching me though, eyes bright pools of hope. This morning I woke with nothing and nobody and now Aaron is asking me to marry him. I'll belong to him and the notion is archaic, but he'll belong to me, too. It feels like winning and I nod. He drags me into his arms and kisses me fiercely.

'Happy birthday,' he breathes against my lips.

I wipe a tear from his cheek then pull him back in for another birthday kiss.

38

DANTE

Familiar warmth floods my body and I snap my focus in the direction of Aaron's home. Inara is here; close enough that I feel her. I turn my attention back to Delia and she's watching me with concern.

'I have to go,' I say and push to my feet.

She gets up and wipes dirt from her hands. 'What is it?'

She reaches for my hand but I step from her reach. If she accidentally uses her psychic abilities on me, she might detect the rush of Siren ice stinging my flesh. I can't control it anymore – haven't been able to since kissing Inara and I can't risk Delia finding out.

I flinch at her hurt expression. She's my best friend and I don't want to hurt her, so I swallow the burn from my throat until I can safely speak.

'I'm sorry, Dee ...' I wince and swallow against the acid of holding it back. It hasn't been this difficult for a long time.

'Dante,' she says taking my hand while I'm distracted.

Apollo's sacred garden falls away; the flowers we've been tending replaced by black rock and white sand. I look around the strange place. Sultry air presses against my skin, as a perfumed breeze swirls around us. I feel the strongest urge to go inland, as if there's something I need to see.

Inara steps onto the sand and I stare at her swollen belly, her flowing dress draping over it. Golden hair dances in the breeze as she pads down to the ocean. She's crying and I step in her direction.

Something snags my hand and I turn back to meet Delia's fear-filled gaze. I cup her jaw and call her name when she continues to stare at Inara.

Finally, her gaze meets mine. 'This is Anthemusa,' she rasps.

I look around with new appreciation before my gaze tracks back to Inara. I stare at her stomach again and cold pleasure fills my flesh. If I find her first, she'll never know Aaron is desperate to find her and that could be my child in her belly.

Delia recoils from me, the vision crumbling around us. 'W-what was that?'

'What?'

'I felt something from you, something...icy.'

'It was my first time seeing Anthemusa,' I say smoothly and wonder when I became so good at lying.

'That coldness is your Siren energy?'

'I can't help what I am, Delia.'

'I didn't mean–'

'None of you ever mean it but you all still manage to express your disgust in some way.'

'Who?' she questions earnestly.

'Aaron, Logan, Adonia, Talia and let me not forget Alexander and his human female,' I huff, annoyed that she's acting so blind to it. 'You and Joshua are the only ones who treat me kindly but he went home and you ... Gods, even Milos is afraid of me and I've known him all my life.'

'Dante—'

'Don't bother,' I growl and stalk from the garden.

Inara's scent hits me as soon as I step inside Aaron's house: sunshine and Siren. I follow the sweet fragrance to the kitchen and stop in the doorway when I see her. She's sitting alone at the table, hair in a low knot at her nape. A few strands have come loose, falling across her face and I smile.

Those emerald eyes grow wide when she notices me, then a bright smile lights her face. Relief floods me that she isn't angry like I'd feared.

'Dante,' she breathes, pushing to her feet.

My smile fades, gaze fixing on her swollen belly. It isn't as big as in the vision but it's there and rage rolls through me. She's carrying someone else's offspring; probably Aaron's and the thought of him being inside her – his seed leeching from her body... Inara halts halfway across the kitchen as she experiences the venom of my emotion. My hands curl into fists and I glare at her. She's supposed to be mine and seeing her this way feels like betrayal.

I turn and run and she calls after me. I'm out of the door, wings unfurling before she has chance to finish my name. I throw myself from the cliff, Siren rage searing my insides. How can she do this to me – to her kind? We belong together but she doesn't care that it's tearing me apart.

I spiral down to the beach and summon my key. Luminous water rises around my ankles and I think of the house in the valley, done with waiting for Inara to see things my way.

39

I stare at where Dante just disappeared over the cliff then crouch on the front step to retrieve one of his ebony feathers. His cool energy stings my fingertips and I frown, heart still racing from the crushing weight of his emotion. I haven't felt cold rage like it since Anthemusa and I need to know what happened to him since I left. I step outside to follow but stop, afraid.

Delia appears from around the corner, red hair tangled around her shoulders. She stops in front of me, then cries out and throws her arms around me.

'You're alive!' She pulls away and looks down at my belly. 'And ... Oh!'

'I've missed you,' I say pulling her back into a hug.

'I've missed you, too,' she rasps.

I wipe her tears with my sleeve and ask, 'What happened to Dante?'

'He was here?'

I nod. 'He saw I'm pregnant, got angry and left.'

'It must be because of the vision,' she says.

'What vision?' Aaron asks from behind me.

I turn to see his drawn expression. 'Did you find Logan?'

He nods. 'The Fates barely spared his life.'

'You went to see the Moirai?' Delia chastises. 'How could you be so stupid, Aaron?'

'Nobody believed Inara was still alive and I had to find her.'

'If you want to blame anyone, blame me,' I say. 'I'm the reason Logan almost lost his life, *again*. I'm always the reason things like this happen.'

I lace my fingers with Aaron's. I feel so guilty because Logan almost died so Aaron could find me. After all this time, neither of them believed I was dead and I want to see him; thank him.

Aaron squeezes my hand and asks, 'What's going on?'

'Dante and I shared a vision,' Delia says. 'Inara was pregnant in it.'

'Why would he be angry when he saw me if he already knew I was pregnant?' I ask.

'He was angry? Are you okay, did he hurt you?' Aaron growls.

'She was on Anthemusa in the vision,' Delia says. 'He probably saw you were pregnant and is afraid the vision will come true.'

My grip tightens on Aaron and I shake my head, voice trapped behind the lump of fear in my throat. I can't go back there, I won't. The spark reacts to my fear and I rub a soothing hand over my bump.

'I won't let Callista have my baby,' I snarl.

Silver threads snap around me, the spark growing more distressed. I pull my hand from Aaron's and clutch my stomach. Pain grips my abdomen but I can't control my fear. If the baby is a girl she'll be trapped on Anthemusa for life and groomed to be a monster. If it's a boy, they'll... I shake my head and force back bile, unable to even think it.

'Take deep breaths,' Aaron says coming to stand in front of me.

'You don't know what they do to their children, Aaron.'

'Callista's dead, Inara. Dante killed her while you were away.'

'W-what?'

'He found her while searching for you and killed her,' he says. 'You know what Delia sees is only a possibility. It doesn't mean it will come true.'

Aaron drops to his knees, lightning snapping around him as he splays his hands over my stomach. 'Be calm,' he croons.

Calming electricity rolls through me and the lump comes back to my throat. Warm tendrils of love, reach to where Aaron's hands rest on my belly and he stares up at me in wonder.

'Can you feel it?' I whisper. 'Our baby loves you.'

'You can really feel that?' he rasps.

I nod. 'The spark senses what I feel and reacts. It felt my fear just now and got scared.'

He strokes his hands over my belly. 'What does it feel now; is it okay?'

'You calmed it down. It knows you're there, Aaron.'

He whispers something against my bump and another flutter of warmth shivers through me.

'Okay,' Delia says breaking into the moment. 'My visions aren't certain but we shouldn't take unnecessary risks. If anyone discovers you're still alive, they'll hunt you again.'

Aaron gets to his feet and herds me inside. 'Delia's right. I need to keep you safe.'

I pull against his hold. 'This isn't going to be another house arrest is it? You remember how well that worked out last time, Aaron.'

'You can't risk going out for at least a few days, Inara. Surely you understand?'

'I do,' I sigh. I spent more than a few days at a time, cooped up in the beach hut, so I don't know why I'm making such a fuss. At least this time I have people to talk to.

Aaron kisses my forehead. 'Thank you.'

Talia bursts through the front door, skin shining with sweat. She bends to catch her breath, then glances at me.

Her silver eyes widen. 'Inara ... I – I'm sorry, I'm happy to see you but Logan ...'

'Upstairs,' Aaron says.

She runs past us and I move to follow but Aaron catches my hand. 'Give them some time,' he says.

'I can help,' I argue.

'Not in your condition.'

I remember Eileiythia's warning about hurting the spark. 'Maybe if I just ...'

'Logan is stronger than anyone I know, Inara. He'll be furious if you risk our child's life to save him some pain,' Aaron says.

I hate that he's right. Logan is infuriating but he's fiercely protective, loyal and cares deeply for those he loves. He paints himself as the antihero because it's what people expect from a Son of Hades. But he gives so much for so little in return and I wish I could repay him for it.

I WATCH the churning ocean from the bedroom window and chew my lip. It's been a whole week and Dante still hasn't come back. Siren burn grates at my insides and I growl because he knows what this will be doing to me. I abandoned him the same way though; fled after he confessed his feelings for me. He thought I existed to be with him and that's so messed up I can't even begin to pick it apart. Something about him has changed since I've been away and I'm worried.

I remember how it felt to kiss him; easy and right but so very, very wrong. His kiss set the darkness inside me aflame, filling my flesh with wintry fire. It consumed me, smothered me in primal desires I didn't know I was capable of feeling. It was terrifying and alluring and I'm scared to ever feel that way again. I do love Dante, just not the way he wants and I hope one day he'll understand.

'Shouldn't you be getting ready?' Logan asks from the doorway.

'Logan!'

I hurry over and throw my arms around him. 'You're awake, and ... Wait, what are you doing out of bed? Does Talia know you're walking around?'

'Whoa,' he laughs, grinning down at me. 'I didn't realise you'd be so fat. Are you really only six months?'

'What's wrong with being fat?' I huff.

He holds his hands up in defence. 'You look radiant.'

I purse my lips. 'Thank you.'

He smirks. 'Uncle Logan has a nice ring to it.'

'Being an uncle implies you're responsible, which I know you aren't,' I scoff. 'How could you let the Moirai do that to you?'

'You're welcome,' he laughs then, 'Shouldn't you be wearing something more suitable for this thing?'

I glance at where Delia laid out new robes. 'I've never been to the temple of Zeus.'

'You're nervous?'

I shrug. 'What if he says no?'

'Apollo won't refuse your marriage to the Son of Zeus, Princess, especially when you're carrying Aaron's child.'

'But what if he's angry with me, for not telling him?'

'You mean like Apollo didn't tell you he's your father for the first seventeen years of your life?'

'How come *he* gets to choose who I marry?' I say. 'What if I never transitioned and still lived in the Human Realm with my human family? Would he have insisted a human male ask for permission to marry me? It's so ... archaic, like I'm up for sale to the highest bidder.'

'Get dressed, Princess. You and Aaron love each other and that's all that matters. The Engysis ceremony is just a formality. It changes nothing, not really.'

'Then what's the point? Aaron already asked me and I said yes. In my eyes, we're already engaged. I don't need Apollo to make my decisions for me.'

'These are the traditions Aaron was raised with. He believes in them and the longer you keep him waiting, the more he'll worry you've changed your mind.'

'Why aren't you dressed yet?' Delia huffs as she walks in.

Logan smirks. 'Inara's having second thoughts; she's thinking of marrying me instead.'

I slap him. 'Get out.'

'Don't you want me to help you into your new robes?'

'Out, Logan,' Delia scoffs pushing him into the hallway.

I hear his laughter even after Delia shuts the door. She turns and gives me a *look*.

'Okay, okay.' I surrender, picking the dress up from the bed. 'We're only going to ask permission, it's not like it's the actual day.'

'No it isn't,' she agrees. 'You'll be bathed and dressed by me in Apollo's temple on *the* day, so you'll have no choice but to be on time.'

The smile falls from my face. 'Wonderful.'

She grins. 'It is, isn't it?'

40

The old temple priestess bustles into the main chamber, white firelight reflecting from her silver robes. She can barely contain her smile as she leans in to speak to me.

'The Daughter of Apollo is here,' she says.

I let out a relieved breath. 'Thank you, Leda.'

She leaves then comes back, followed by Inara and Delia. Inara gazes around at the silver and purple décor, abusing her bottom lip as she nervously grips Delia's hand. Her hair is curled and she's adorned in white and gold. She smiles when she sees me and my heart stutters within my chest.

She reaches for me as we come together in front of the statue of Zeus but Delia shakes her head and whispers in her ear. Inara drops her hand, looking apologetic. I want to kiss her so bad it hurts and it takes everything I have to hold back.

With a smile of encouragement, I turn to the statue of Zeus and shout, 'Father!'

Delia whispers in Inara's ear again and she steps forward, calling for Apollo. She shoots me a secret smile, her cheeks blushing pink as she steps level with me again.

Leda drops to her knees and presses her forehead to the marble as a bolt of lightning strikes the ground. I roll my eyes at my father's youthful appearance. We look the same age – something Zeus never does when we meet alone. It's for Inara's benefit and a staunch reminder of how much my father likes to be popular with the ladies.

Apollo flashes into the room amid a warm wave of sunlight. There's something furious in his emerald gaze when it sweeps to me. Panic grips my stomach at his glare and my jaw tightens to the point of snapping. Everything is backwards. I should've asked for permission and married Inara before we made love but I'd thought it was a dream. At least, when I'd passed her the spark I had and it's why I hadn't used protection.

'Who requests the right of Engysis with my daughter?' he asks starting the ceremony.

I step forward and offer my hand. 'I do.'

'You violated my daughter, Son of Zeus without my permission and now your seed grows in her belly.'

Inara flinches in my peripheral vision but I keep my gaze on Apollo. 'I don't see our union as a violation. We came together because we love each other and I will love her even if you deny our marriage. I want to make things right for her and prove I'm worthy of her love, though.'

His eyes narrow and the moment grows tight. He reaches for my hand and I wince at the intense heat of his grip, wondering if I'll still have a hand by the time he lets go.

'You have my permission,' he smirks. 'You had it all along but I needed to make sure you had the right intentions.'

'The right intentions?'

He looks at Inara. 'My daughter wouldn't want you to marry her just because she's pregnant. I wanted her to hear you say it.'

She smirks. 'Thanks, Dad.'

Delia's eyes go wide at the informal address and I stare too. I've never witnessed this relationship between Inara and Apollo; never actually seen them together, except from afar. The concept of such a bond is foreign to me; to be friends with your divine parent after they abandon you at birth because they aren't supposed to interfere. I realise Zeus is watching me. He smiles as I meet his gaze, his eternal eyes full of knowledge, as if he can feel the jealousy uncurling in my stomach.

Apollo places his hand on Inara's to complete the ceremony. 'I give permission for Aaron, Son of Zeus to take the oath of Engysis with my daughter. May your days be long and filled with sunshine.'

I lace my fingers with Inara's and she smiles, looking at me like she's won a prize. The snaking jealousy melts from my gut and I breathe easier. It's done, I have permission and soon we'll be bound in mind, body and soul. Apollo and Zeus start discussing details but all I can focus on is Inara. She looks so beautiful: creamy skin, bejewelled eyes and silky, golden hair. Soon she'll be all mine forever and I cannot wait.

41

DANTE

Inara's pretty eyes widen when I step into the room. It's suddenly silent; Aaron, Logan and Talia staring at me with hostility. Inara stands and I force my gaze to stay on her face when her belly comes into view. She's gotten much bigger in the three weeks I've been gone and more fragile looking. Disgust oozes through me as I try not to think about part of Aaron growing inside her; polluting her perfection.

I force a smile when I feel her hesitation and say, 'I'm sorry I freaked out last time.'

'I understand, Dante. Delia told us about the vision you shared.'

I raise an eyebrow in confusion, not sure what she thinks she understands. Her concern washes through my flesh like a tropical wave and triggers my Siren burn. It sears through me and she presses a hand to her throat in response.

I hide a smile at the evidence of our connection and give her an apologetic look. I turn and hurry from the house, counting the seconds as I stroll across the grass towards the edge of the cliff. Footfall sounds behind me and my smile widens as my wings unfurl. She's so predictable, still so caring, but I can fix that.

'Dante!'

Her resonating voice presses against my skin and I bite back a groan. Her Siren song is the only one that calls to me this way.

I pull moisture from the air and rub my eyes with it before turning to face her. 'I didn't mean ... I just can't control myself around you since that day, Inara.'

She takes my hand, her searing energy prickling my skin. 'Where have you been? I was worried sick.'

'I didn't think you'd want me around anymore.'

'Why would you think that?'

'I don't fit in here; don't belong.'

'You belong with me,' she scoffs.

Cold pleasure, rips through me at her words but I'm careful not to let it seep past the barrier I've created. It's taken three weeks to perfect my control but once she realises she loves me, I'll let her back in.

'Will you walk with me on the beach?' I ask.

She glances at the house. 'I'd better tell Aaron –'

'Just for a few minutes,' I beg. 'I want to apologise in private and Aaron doesn't like me enough to leave you alone with me much longer.'

Her smile is relieved. 'Okay.'

I pick her up and drop from the cliff. She rests her head against my shoulder, hugging me tight. She fits against me perfectly – but then we were designed to be together; made for each other. Everything is going to be fine.

My wings spread, catching the thermals as I glide us down and alight on the sand. I sit her on one of the smoother black rocks and she gazes up at me, golden mane swirling around her shoulders in the breeze. I smile and allow the barrier to fall. It crashes beneath the crushing weight of my Siren energy and Inara blanches.

'W-what did you do?' she rasps.

'He set himself free,' Callista purrs emerging from behind a group of tall rocks to my left.

Inara's fear slams into me, eyes wide as she twists in her mother's direction. 'But...you're dead.'

'And miss the birth of my grandchild? I've spent a lot of time searching for you, Daughter.'

'What do you want?' Inara snarls.

Her rage sends a delicious shiver through me, causing intoxicating prickles to pepper my skin. She's so perfect like this; so full of Siren burn.

'What I've wanted for the last eighteen years, Inara – *You*. Except now I'm gaining an added bonus,' Callista says smirking at her belly.

Inara throws herself at Callista and claws at her face, wilder than I've ever seen. 'I won't let you have my baby!'

I yank her away and twist her arms behind her back when she fights me. She whimpers in pain as they reach dislocation and delight oozes through me at the sound. I want her to hurt, like I did when she abandoned me here with the male who threw her away — The male she's gone crawling back to at the first sniff of an apology. It's pathetic and I won't let her lower herself to such a level any longer. She will embrace what she is and it will lead to her embracing me.

Callista's eyes shine midnight fire as she stands, dabbing a bleeding claw-mark on her cheek. 'That's it,' she preens stroking Inara's face like a proud parent. 'Let the rage connect you to what comes naturally. Let it open you up to what you really are.'

'Why are you doing this?' Inara screams at me.

I glare down at her in disbelief. 'Because you should be with me, not Aaron! I'm doing what needs to be done to restore the balance to what it should have been.' I soften my tone. 'You'll understand once you see.'

'See what?' she sneers. 'Do you really think this is going to make me want to be with you? Siren connection or not, I will never want you the way you crave, Dante.'

I growl in her face but light flares around us before I can answer. Hera appears in its wake, draped in rich garments and a crown woven within her red-brown curls. I clasp my hand over Inara's mouth and spin us to face the goddess. Inara stiffens at the sight of her and struggles anew.

'You've done well,' Hera praises. 'Tell me what bounty you want and I shall provide.'

'I want Inara,' I say.

She whimpers when I tighten my hold, halting her struggles. I bend to lick her face, letting my Siren energy drench her flesh. She tries to resist, back arching as the ice creeps through her middle. Soon she'll be mine and I'll have an entire island of Sirens to stop Aaron from reaching her. She'll hate me at first but eventually she'll see it my way and relent. She *will* learn to love me.

'She doesn't seems to like your suggestion,' Hera chuckles. 'I'll grant your request, so you may take the girl with you to Anthemusa. And you,' she addresses Callista. 'You've served me well too, Siren.'

'I want the child.'

'The child needs to die,' Hera argues. 'Choose something else.'

'I didn't say I want it alive,' Callista says.

Hera's face lights with amusement. 'So the rumours are true. Very well, Zeus will be furious when he finds out.'

Inara's elbow jams into my ribs and she wriggles free. 'You'd kill my baby because you're mad with Zeus?'

'If you'd kept your legs together I'd have only needed you,' Hera sneers.

'Why? Why are you doing all of this?'

'You were supposed to be my bargaining chip to lure Aaron. He's the one I want dead: Zeus's little pride and joy, pushed into existence by that human whore.' She smirks. 'Things are working out so much better now, though. Aaron will suffer the rest of his days, knowing his child was murdered and his female was given to another and trapped on Anthemusa. What's the saying mortals use: a fate worse than death?'

'You won't just get away with murdering people Zeus cares about,' Inara growls. 'He'll figure it out.'

'I got away with murdering Aaron's mother and I think Zeus actu-

ally had feelings for her,' she scoffs. 'Humans are so easy to manipulate and she made it all the way to the Flowery Isle by herself. It was
fun watching little Aaron's face as he watched his mother drown. It
tortured him for years.'

'How does it feel?' Inara snarls.

Hera frowns. 'How does what feel?'

'To know you're the worst kind of monster?'

'You're the Siren – you tell me,' Hera sneers.

'I didn't choose what I am and I fight it every day but you – you
choose to be this evil and for what: jealousy over your husband's
infidelity?'

A dagger flashes into Hera's hand as she turns to Callista, 'You'll
make your daughter watch while you kill her child, then we'll see
who she thinks is the worst kind of monster.'

Inara's terror hits me, piercing the thick wall of Siren ice coating
my insides. I want Aaron's child out of her but it never occurred to me
how that would happen, until now. Or that Callista would... I shake
my head against the frigid haze frosting my thoughts and suddenly
wonder what I'm doing. I didn't kill Callista that day because she'd
offered me what I craved most but this was never part of the bargain.
I envy Aaron but I don't want to watch his child murdered – Inara's
child, because it's a part of her too.

Her fear bleeds through the wintry rage, tangling my insides and
gripping tight. It spears the ice, shattering its hold on me and I blink
dark mist from my vision. Inara's emotions slam into me full force:
sorrow, pain and crushing despair. I try to pull a wall up between us
but her thoughts connect with mine and I flinch.

'*Don't let them kill my baby. Take me – take me and spare my child.
Don't let them, I can't bear it. All that love... Oh god, she's going to cut it
from me and make me watch ...*'

'No!' I snarl, shoving Inara behind me.

Her surprise prickles through me as I summon my trident and
aim it at Hera.

'What are you doing?' Callista hisses. 'We're so close and Inara
will be your prize.'

'Move out of the way, boy,' Hera snarls.

'This isn't right,' I growl. 'I won't let you kill her child.'

'You think you can stop me? Get out of the way or die with her.' I lift my trident in response and Hera sighs, 'Have it your way.'

I brace myself for death, the force of her divine energy slamming into me as she stalks my way. I've felt energy like this from my father and know I don't stand a chance.

'I'm sorry, Angel,' I shout over my shoulder, needing Inara to know I didn't want any of this. I still want her but not this — never this.

Hera grips my trident like it's nothing more than a toy. She pulls me towards her and I stagger against her immeasurable strength. I feel like laughing because this is the stupidest thing I've ever done. The only thing I regret right now though, is Inara not standing a chance once I'm gone. It's my fault she's here and I don't deserve her forgiveness.

I ready myself to fight for as long as I can to protect her but Hera freezes before the fight even starts. Her eyes are narrowed, hands locked around the trident and I wonder what's happening, until I hear it. It presses against my skin like audible silk and I groan at the sound.

Inara's song resonates through the warm air, sinking beneath my skin and plucking the strings of my soul. It's the most beautiful thing I've ever heard and I stare at her, transfixed. She's ethereal and fierce; gold wings arcing behind her and defiance painting her face.

Callista tackles her and jams a blade into her chest. Inara starts choking, her song cut off by the blood spraying from her mouth and nose. I start singing in her stead to keep Hera from waking but it means I have to stay close enough for it to work. I glance at Hera to make sure she's within my thrall and by the time I look back, Callista has dragged Inara from reach. I try pulling Hera closer to their fight but she won't budge. It's as if she's hewn from rock and I growl in frustration.

I yank my trident from her grip, aim and throw it as hard as I can, roaring Callista's name so she turns to me and widens my target. Her expression is a mask of violence, until a fleshy thud announces the razor tines of my trident burying themselves in her torso. Her eyes blow wide as she stares up at the shaft angling towards the sky.

Inara slumps to the sand when her mother's grip loosens. Callista falls to her knees, a smile curling her lips as she says something to her daughter. The sound doesn't carry over the crash of the waves and it's then, I realise I've stopped singing. I spin back to Hera but she's gone.

I turn a circle on the empty beach before turning back to the ocean and curse. Inara and Callista are gone too, my trident half buried in the surf. Inara described once how Sirens dissolve into black mist when they die. I retrieve my weapon, gaze scouring the beach. Inara isn't like them. She won't just disappear if she dies. She can't!

I spot the indentations of her footprints in the sand and blow out a relieved breath. I track her around the headland but her footprints vanish where rock litters the beach, down into the water. I turn a panicked circle, knowing she's here because I'm close enough to feel it. She's in agony: pulsating, crushing pain, and I think... It feels like she's dying. I pluck a golden feather from the black sand, panic threatening to choke me. I call her name and feel a spike of terror from her in response.

'Inara, please, I only want to help.'

42

INARA

Dante's voice echoes around the rocks again, sounding as terrified as I feel. But Dante's a liar and I'd be a fool to trust him ever again. I press a hand to the wound in my chest, as another gurgling mix of air and blood bubbles out. I sink lower into the ground, tears staining my face that I'm going to die and so is my baby.

Unbearable pain pulls at me from the inside and a scream rips free. I push against the jagged rock at my back, wings arcing around me, as I press my heels into the sand. I claw the rocks either side of me and gasp for breaths that will not come.

Dante splashes through the surf to where I'm hiding and I gasp, 'Stay. Away.'

He ignores me, moving closer, so I lift my right arm and my bow materialises. I pull on the string and he freezes, eyes fixed on the glittering barb of my arrow.

He holds his hands up. 'I want to help.'

'Liar,' I gasp, more blood bubbling from my chest as I aim for his heart.

Blood gushes into my mouth, chest convulsing as I try to fill my remaining lung with air. I fight it, knowing I just have to stay alive. I slam against the rock at my back when another wave of pain grips me, digging my heels deeper into the sand. My bow disappears as I lose focus and then Dante's hands on me.

'Get. Off!' I pant.

His sparkly green eyes eclipse my vision as he bends over me, his concern drenching my flesh. I used to think his eyes were beautiful but I hate them now; hate him. He's the reason I'm here and my baby might die. More pain hits me and I can't voice the scream for lack of air.

He takes my hands. 'I think the baby is coming, Angel.'

I stare at him, hatred momentarily forgotten. 'No – Not due for another two ...'

Blinding pain prevents me from finishing. Something crunches and Dante swears, before electricity starts snapping around me. He jerks his hands away when it cracks against his skin and I notice his misshapen fingers. The crunching sound makes sudden sense but he still reaches for me again. More lightning pops against his skin and he jerks away, hissing in pain.

'I can't touch you,' he says.

I scream; lightning surging through my flesh as pain pulses through my core. Why is he just standing there, looking at me like he's the one dying?

'Get Aaron!' I scream, digging my fingers and toes into the sand. It solidifies as lightning blasts it into glass. Dante's still standing there, staring at me like an idiot. 'Need. Aaron. Dante! Please, what...are you waiting for?'

He finally scrambles to his feet, sand and air spraying me when his wings beat down to take off. I feel the snap of my own wings, trapped between my writhing body and the rock at my back. I bite down hard on my lip then crawl into the water and collapse on the sand. I curl into a foetal position and let the waves crash around me.

A few feathers wash past as my wings disintegrate in the surf then I sit up and clutch my stomach.

I sob through more agonising pain, recognising the contractions for what they are now. I'm not supposed to give birth for another two months and I'm in no state to after Callista's attack. I feel the spark's distress through the building agony and try in vain to sooth it.

Lightning snaps around me, shivering threads of silver skipping over my skin. It crackles over the water, glowing brighter with each pulse of pain. Blood pumps thickly from my chest as I pant through the contractions, wondering where the hell Aaron is and what's taking so long.

I'm facing the beach, the ocean rolling in around me. I press my palms into the sand and arch my back to search the sky for Dante. I lift my knees at the next contraction and push down with my heels. My insides feel like they're being yanked out and I whine in agony. Another shudder of distress rolls through me and I rub my bump.

'S'okay,' I pant but scream when fresh pain zips down my spine.

I've heard human women speak of childbirth but they never described it as being like this. Lightning sizzles through the air, as if in answer to my thoughts. I'm not human; I know nothing of what this is supposed to be like. I pant around the hissing hole in my chest, the pain there nothing compared to the cramping in my stomach. More blood fills my mouth and I wipe it away with the back of my hand. All I have to do is stay alive long enough for my baby to live.

43

Dante squeezes through the kitchen doorway, face pale against a backdrop of ebony wings. He looks startled: ocean-green eyes wide and skin smeared with crimson. His gaze fixes on me as he ignores Logan's surprise over his wings and works his mouth like he wants to say something.

Dread fills me and I stand up. 'Where is she?'

'I tried to help but can't get past the lightning,' he says, voice shaky and a step from resonating.

I grip his shoulders and growl, 'Tell me where she is, Dante.'

His eyes focus and he grabs my wrist, pulling me from the house. I run with him towards the edge of the cliff and he drops back, sliding his arms around my chest and throws us from the edge. The ground disappears beneath us in a sheer drop to the sand.

'Sorry,' he pants. 'There's no time and she needs you.'

We bank around the headland, gliding closer to the ground before alighting where the rocks appear to roll into the ocean. I turn when Dante releases me, about to ask where Inara is when a scream pierces the air. My muscles tighten at the sound and I start running, weaving toward the most agonising sound I've ever heard.

I stop at the water's edge, horrified. Inara is in the water, legs bent at the knee and arms buried to the elbow. Her once-white dress is now bright crimson and blood smears the bottom half of her face, staining her hair and shoulders. She screams again, body tensing, then slumps and starts coughing. Her eyes snap open as I splash through the surf.

'*Gods,*' I breathe, dropping to my knees beside her.

My eyes are drawn to the well of blood hissing on her chest. It drips from her mouth as she struggles to breathe and I guess that one of her lungs is punctured. Lightning snaps between us in arcs of white fire, intensified by the water.

She shakes her head when I move to lift her from the water. 'S-save – save... our baby.'

'I'll get you back to the house and everything will be okay,' I tell her.

'No,' she starts to say then throws her head back and screams. A massive surge of electricity pulses through the water. The sand shivers with the current then she slumps and gasps for breath. 'It's... time,' she pants. 'It's coming now.'

'But... it's too soon.'

'Aaron!' she screams, another bolt charging the water.

I scramble behind her, putting a leg either side of her hips and pull her close, so she can rest her back against my chest. I smooth wet hair from her face and rest my hands on her stomach. Lightning blasts my palms, her body convulsing against mine. I conduct the bolt and the atmosphere and water become less charged. I channel the current through my body so Inara doesn't have to channel it through hers. She's immune to a point but wasn't born to withstand bolts like this.

I kiss her temple. 'You can do this, Goddess. I know you can do this.'

Her ragged breathing fills the air and I try not to think about the gaping hole in her chest. I can't help wonder how she got it, though. Dante's blood-smeared skin flashes through my mind but I push it away. I don't have time to think about things like that yet.

'I can't,' she sobs. 'Too hard... don't think...'

'I'm here with you,' I say then wince when her body tenses and she screams again.

The water grows warm around my feet and turns dark red. The bottom half of her dress turns red too, before the next wave crashes around us and washes it away. Panic fills me because she's losing too much blood.

'Dante, get over here and take my place.'

He hesitates on the sand and I growl. He claims to love her but won't take a little lightning sting? If Inara didn't need me, I'd throttle him.

'I'm conducting the bolts,' I yell.

He steps into the water and Inara freaks. 'Keep...him away...from me!'

I stare down at her. 'Love, I need him to hold you while I –'

'H-hold myself,' she rasps. 'Don't w-want him...near.'

I glance between them. What in Hades did he do to make her hate him so much? I eye the bloody hole in her chest again. If I lose either of the precious lives I'm holding, I'll kill him.

'Aaron!' Logan shouts, running from between the rocks and splashing into the surf. He drops to his knees at Inara's side and swears.

'How –'

'She's in labour, Logan.'

His eyes widen. 'What?'

Lightning surges through my palms from Inara and she screams again. The bolts are getting closer together and she just needs to hang in there. Her scream dies in a fit of coughing, blood spraying the lower half of her face. Her head lolls against my chest, eyes rolling back.

'No!' I clasp her face. 'No, love,' I say shaking her.

She moans; eyelids fluttering as she focuses on me. 'Aaron,' she murmurs, 'save ...' Another bolt cuts her short and her body arches.

Something moves beneath my palms, her stomach dipping.

'Logan, take my place.'

He cradles her the same way I did, while I scramble to her front. I kneel between her thighs as warmth gushes around my knees. Her next scream slices my heart, then her body flops.

'No!' I growl leaning over her. 'Goddess, don't do this.'

My tears splash her face as I try to shake her awake again. Why isn't it working? I can't let this happen. I can't lose her.

'Come on, love,' I beg and press a hand to her chest.

There's no answering thud from her heart but I won't give up. Her body jerks when I blast a massive dose of lightning through her. She doesn't respond.

This time. Please let this work.

I let another bolt build in my palm but her eyes snap open before I can pass it to her.

She looks down. 'It's coming,' she pants as if nothing happened.

I scramble back onto my knees and dip my hands beneath the water. Logan snarls as lightning pulses from her, snapping across the surface of the ocean and fizzing the air. I feel the spark, suddenly in my hands and hold my breath. She screams again and a warm, soft weight fills my palms. My heartbeat eclipses all sound as I feel the tiny child moving in my hands. I lift it from the water and stare at the perfect thing I helped create. A startled cry fills the air and I smile.

'My baby,' Inara wheezes.

I look at her: broken, bloody and dishevelled but I've never loved her more. I wonder how it's even possible to love her more than I did before, when I'd loved her with every fibre of my being. I place our child in her outstretched hands and she curls it against her.

Tears and seawater roll down her exhausted face. 'Hello,' she rasps. The child goes quiet at the sound of her voice and tiny tendrils of lightning crackle around baby and mother. She smiles, still panting for breath. 'I love you, too,' she whispers then looks at me, face filled with pain. 'You need...to take...him now, Aaron.'

Him.

Fresh elation fills me; I have a son? I'm so happy I didn't even think to check. I wipe a tear from my face, then frown when her words register. Fear creeps in as I study her pasty skin. Her still-laboured breathing seems shallower – raspier.

'I love you,' she wheezes.

I shake my head. 'Don't you dare.'

She kisses the top of our son's head and offers him to me. 'Cut the...umbilical cord.'

I draw a dagger from my belt and cut the cord, before taking the baby from her shaking hands and passing him to Logan. Talia sloshes through the surf, holding a clean blanket. She takes the baby from Logan and wraps him up. Inara winces when our son starts crying, her gaze tracking Talia's every move.

'So...beautiful,' she rasps, tears streaking her face. Her gaze pans to me. 'Tell him...about me.'

I pull her from between Logan's legs, into my arms. 'I won't let you do this,' I growl. 'You need to stay with me, with our son. I can't... I can't do this without you, Goddess.'

She cups my face with a trembling hand. 'You'll...be a wonderful...father. Tell...him...I love...him and remember...I'll always...love you.'

I blink through my tears. 'Please don't leave me.'

Her breaths come short and sharp. 'I, would, stay, if, I could,' she gasps.

Her hand slips from my face, body convulsing. Her eyelids close and she goes still.

'No,' I breathe, shaking her. 'No!'

I press my hand to her chest again and blast her with lighting. Her body remains limp and unmoving in my arms.

Wake up! I have to make her wake up!

Logan's hand grips my shoulder. 'Aaron,' he says in an unfamiliar tone.

'No,' I snarl, shaking him off.

'She's gone,' he rasps. 'Let her rest.'

I glare at him then look at the beach. 'Where is he? Where's Dante?'

'He left,' Talia says rocking the bundle in her arms.

'I'll kill him,' I roar then shield my eyes from a bright flash of light.

Apollo drops to his knees in the water and rasps, 'Give her to me.'

I grip her tighter, frightened to let what I have left of her go but he's already pulling her from me. Intense heat brushes my skin as Apollo's arms wrap around her lifeless form. I hug my torso, heart splintering in my chest.

'Move,' he says but I stare up at him, too broken to comply. He looks up from his daughter and says, 'Time is slipping away. You need to move.'

Logan pulls me from the water while I stare at her lifeless form in Apollo's arms. I feel hollow, as if someone ripped my heart away. She's gone, my life, my heart... everything.

A wail breaks through the haze of pain and I look at the wrapped bundle in Talia's arms. She's shifting from foot to foot, swaying the child in an attempt to calm him. Her silver eyes meet mine when I reach for my child and she hands him over. I cradle him in my arms, so tiny and perfect. He's still creased from being curled inside the womb but he looks like me.

'My son,' I breathe.

He stops crying at the sound of my voice and opens his eyes. The air leaves me in a startled breath when I see they are two pools of emerald fire. Elation spirals through the crushing grief that I have a part of her, looking back at me.

I smooth a dark curl from his face. He stares at me with wide green eyes, then yawns and falls to sleep. I focus on his soft breathing and burning heat. He's like her in that way too and my heart aches. I feel so close to drowning and the tiny baby in my arms is the only thing keeping me afloat.

Gold light and a wave of heat pull my eyes from my son. Apollo is no longer visible behind a blinding veil of sunlight. I step towards the water but shield my gaze from a blazing flare that floods the beach. I blink when it fades and splash into the surf, turning a circle. Logan and Talia stand dazed on the beach and Inara's body is gone. Apollo has taken her.

No.

I glare at the sun and roar, 'Apollo!'

The child in my arms starts crying again, his lightning licking my skin. I cradle him against me, speaking in a soothing voice, while my heart crumples in my chest.

44

I crawl up the riverbank, clawing at the thick mud for purchase. It oozes between my toes and fingers, as I scramble to the top and look back at the river. Frigid air clings to my skin as I stare down at my blood-drenched dress. It's smeared in mud and slime and things from the riverbed. I have a dim recollection of pain and the nagging sensation that I've lost something important. My chest tightens at the sensation and I bite back a sob.

I stare across the murky water, at the dim light swinging from the bow of the boat. It slides through the water like a leviathan; a dark and looming shadow in the gloom. Ghostly figures litter the deck, staring with unseeing eyes as the terrifying skeletal creature ferries them across the river. Sobbing carries to where I'm standing as the boat passes. The skeletal figure at the helm tracks me with its eyeless gaze, like it knows I want on that boat. It isn't the scariest thing in this place but I've learned not to provoke unless necessary.

I turn to the endless dis beyond the river; darkness and gloom as far as I can see. It hurts to look at it and I hug my stomach for comfort. I look down for what feels like the millionth time, unnerved by the recurring feeling that something is missing. I still can't grasp the memory of what and panic threatens to choke me. I don't know what it is that I've forgotten but my chest wells with sorrow at the loss. I've searched for this unknown treasure for as long as I can remember, but there's no end to this hell.

I palm my stomach, unbearable sadness forcing me onto my knees in the mud. Bone-deep despair floods my chest and I curl in on myself, withering under the torment of my existence. There's nothing before this anguish and nothing but more of the same to come. I feel hollow and brittle and I'm desperate for an end to this relentless torture.

I look up when light floods the abyss, wondering if I'm dreaming. I know the word but don't quite remember what dreaming is. Only nightmares exist in the abyss and I wonder if this will turn into one too. The light draws closer, growing brighter and hotter – reaching for me. It's probably a trick but I can't bring myself to run anymore. My freezing extremities tingle in the blazing heat, as a man appears from inside the light.

I gaze up at him when he offers his hand, recognising his face but can't remember where from. He smiles, golden hair and green eyes shining. He isn't like the other beings in this place, that slither in the darkness, shying from the light. I don't fear him like I fear them and I take his offered hand. Burning fingers encase my mud-slicked skin, helping me to stand. He scoops me into his arms when I stagger and I press close to his glorious heat, terrified he'll disappear.

'I've spent a long time looking for you, Sunbeam,' he says, voice thick with emotion.

Is Sunbeam my name? I open my mouth to ask but, though I understand his words, the memory of how to reply is gone. I sigh and close my mouth, frustrated. Whoever he is, I've missed him. I don't have any memories of him but... I *know* him. I *know* lots of things without understanding why, like the way my spine prickles when danger approaches. Or that something terrible happened that I can't remember.

His kind eyes grow soft and he stroke my muddy hair. 'Don't worry, Sunbeam. I'm here to take you home.'

END OF PART *Two*

45

SNEAK PREVIEW

SNEAK PREVIEW

SIREN FIRE
The Siren Series Book Three

ARON

COALS ignite along the bottom edge of the walls, casting indigo light into the space as I follow Logan into the room. Despite the dark flames, the room remains near freezing and I can't imagine anyone wanting to spend time here. It's no wonder Logan hated coming here as a child.

We reach an ebony throne on a raised dais at the front, the piece of furniture somehow sinister in the dismal space. I look around feeling watched but we're surrounded by shadow. Even the ceiling is a vast expanse of darkness, like outside the palace; no stars just endless night.

A growl sounds from a shadow-drenched corner before a solid mass detaches from the darkness and steps into the dim light of the coals. I back away as the three-headed beast stalks us. It snarls, an enormous muzzle peeling back to reveal razor teeth. Hot breath billows into the frigid air, making the creature seem to steam as its crimson gaze tracks our every move.

'Cerberus, heel,' Logan growls.

I tear my gaze from Cerberus to stare at my brother. Even in the heat of battle, his voice never held the icy quality it does down here. It's a side to him I've never witnessed; the side that's at home in the Underworld and fits in with how others perceive him. It's a perception he's happy to hide behind but I've come to know better. Once you get past Logan's icy demeanour, there's a great warmth to behold. It's a fire in winter, seeping to your bones if you're lucky enough to be allowed near it. I never would've even glimpsed it if it weren't for Inara.

The hound drops obediently onto its haunches and lowers its central head when Logan approaches, allowing him to scratch its face. It releases a low whine and flops onto the floor, lifting its left head to stare at me.

'Come fuss Cerberus before he decides to use you as a chew toy,' Logan tells me.

Cerberus releases another whine, lolling onto the floor when I scratch behind one of its ears. I grin, thinking he isn't so bad once you get past the teeth and claws.

I stumble when he leaps from the floor to sit facing the throne and Logan drawls, 'Father.'

He pets the hell beast as if Hades hasn't just graced us with his presence then sighs and turns to the ebony throne. The dark-eyed god watches us from a lounging position on that sinister chair, features so like Logan's it's like seeing double.

'Logan,' he says before his lightless gaze pans to me. The corner of his mouth twitches with a smirk. 'Welcome back, Aaron.'

Right, that time I died.

Hades disappears in a swirl of dark smoke and materialises before me, brandishing a dish brimming with...fruit? 'Pomegranate?' he offers holding the dish beneath my nose. The aroma is sweet and enticing, curling around my senses and making my mouth water.

Logan bats the dish from Hades' hand when I reach to accept his offer. It clatters against the floor, scattering sticky fruit across the marble and I frown in disappointment before shaking the hazy thought from my head. I don't even like pomegranate, so can't understand why I feel so upset.

'I've already warned Aaron about partaking in your little *treats*, Father.'

The memory of Logan's warning comes back in stark detail. Before we got here, he reminded me of his father's love of entrapment through the use of imbued fruit. He warned me not to accept anything to eat and drink from his father and I almost failed at the first hurdle.

The smile bleeds from Hades' lips and the temperature turns arctic. 'I have quarrel with the Son of Zeus, yet you bring him *here* to plead for his lover's life,' Hades growls making every hair on my body stand tall.

'I have no quarrel with you,' I say.

His dark gaze lasers on me. 'I don't take kindly to those who steal souls from me, *Nephew*.'

'I'm not here to steal Inara from you,' I say. 'I came to ask if you'd give her back.'

'*Inara* stole *your* soul from me,' he scoffs.

He's angry that I cheated death and with Inara for helping me do it? This isn't good. My chance of getting her back is diminishing by the second.

'Will you take my soul in place of hers?' I ask. We'll still be parted but at least our child will have his mother. Inara will live and be free from this place, back under the sun where she belongs.

'You dare request a favour in return for something I should already own?' he sneers. 'I can be cruel and unpitying but I'm fair, Aaron. I help create the balance this universe relies upon, even if it brings grief to those still living. I want what was stolen from me; I *want* your soul.'

A feminine snort proceeds the woman that steps from the shadows. She's so beautiful, she's almost painful to look at – elegant and lush and difficult to look away from. She has flawless mocha skin, hazel eyes and curves you'd want to study with a map. Those hazel eyes sparkle behind thick lashes as she steps up to Hades, her floral scent infusing the frigid air like spring in midwinter.

'Fair?' she scoffs, her cupids-bow mouth curling. A trail of flowers bloom over the marble in her wake as she glides up to Hades, dying almost as soon as they've opened. 'You call forcing me into marrying you fair?'

This is the queen of the Underworld?

She smiles fondly at Logan. 'Good to see you again, Lo-Lo.'

Lo-Lo?

'Persephone,' he greets with a conspiratorial grin.

'Aaron's soul belongs to me,' Hades fumes then glares at me. 'I hope you bid farewell to the light boy because we don't get much of that here.'

Persephone inserts herself between Hades and me, her movements seductive. She curls around him and nuzzles his ear. She licks up his neck and makes a purring sound that makes me feel the need to turn away. His onyx gaze darkens in response and she whispers something to him.

He glances between us then makes a sound between anger and frustration. 'Get out of my domain, Son of Zeus!'

Logan steps between me and his father. 'Would you deny me if I accepted your offer, Father?'

'You know the answer to that,' Hades says, his tone razor-sharp.

I glance between them, wondering what Logan is talking about?

'Give me Inara, Daughter of Apollo – Alive and re-fleshed and I'll accept your terms,' Logan says.

Hades' demeanour turns furious and my mind screams at me to run. 'I cannot *give* what I do not have.'

The temperature drops impossibly colder and the shadows leech at the small amount of light left in the room. Ice crusts over the marble and my breath fogs out in front of me.

Logan blanches. 'She isn't here?'

'Inara Thompson is not in the Underworld,' Hades growls.

His words are a knife to my heart and the last thing I expected. She wasn't like the monsters on Anthemusa; she had a soul and this is where souls go when the body dies. I held her body after she died and she didn't disappear like other Sirens do, so she has to be here – has to be somewhere I can reach.

Logan grips my arm. 'It's time to go, Aaron.'

He drags me from the throne room when I don't move to follow and I rasp, 'She isn't here, Logan.'

'I know,' he says like he can't believe it either.

'I can't live without her.'

He slams me against the passageway wall. 'Daniel already lost his mother; don't let him lose his father too. You know as well as I what that's like, Aaron.'

I try to recollect my parentless childhood but all I can think about is Inara. Hades is Lord of the Dead. He knows the location of every soul that crosses the threshold from life to death but doesn't know where Inara is. The only explanation is that she doesn't have a soul and the concept is unbearable. Even if Hades had refused to give her back I'd taken solace in knowing she'd be here, on the other side of the river, one day. But she isn't anywhere. I'll never see her again, hold her...

Inara is gone.

'I didn't think she was like them,' I rasp. 'I was so sure she had a soul; sure I'd felt it.'

'Inara was nothing like those things on Anthemusa, Aaron,' Logan says. 'She was sunshine; pure and bright and you have to be here to tell Daniel about her, like she wanted.'

When I nod, Logan relaxes his grip. He leads me along the

passageway, the silence profound. It's suffocating, like the finality of Inara's death and I have to break it.

'What did you offer your father in exchange for her?' I ask.

He glances my way then admits, 'Me.'

I frown. 'What do you mean?'

'It doesn't matter because it didn't work,' he says.

What the heck does Hades want Logan for? Protectiveness for my brother rises through me and I silently vow to get the answer out of Logan. Then I will protect him, the way he's always protecting me. I will be the brother he deserves.

'Persephone did that to make Hades release me, didn't she?' I say.

'The only thing my father wants more than maintaining his precious balance, is Persephone.'

'Does she really hate him that much?'

'No, yes... She hates him as much as she loves him, Aaron. He tricked her into marrying him but she also wanted to get away from her controlling mother.'

'Demeter is controlling?'

'Persephone is very beautiful, very intelligent and very manipulative,' he says. 'History paints her as the victim but who's to say she isn't the one who tricked my father? He's obsessed with her, as you just witnessed – enough to give up his quest for your soul. He had you in his domain and, without Persephone, you wouldn't be leaving with me right now.'

'Your father lets her manipulate him?'

Logan smirks. 'For the right reward.'

I make a face and change the subject, 'You and Persephone are close?'

His expression turns uncomfortable. 'What makes you think that?'

'She called you Lo-Lo.'

'Do you think I enjoyed visiting this place as a child? The only way my father got me to come here was by tricking me in the same way he tricked Persephone. After he abducted her, he fed her pomegranate seeds, so she'd have to return each year and spend time in his realm. Persephone still spends half the year on Earth fulfilling her duties with her mother and half in the Underworld with Hades. She always made sure she was here for my visits, though. Her presence was... invaluable, when I was a child.'

I remember Logan leaving for four weeks every winter when we were children but never understood where he went. All I knew was Logan hated leaving more than he'd hated me.

'Logan –'

'I don't want your pity, Aaron. Besides, this place isn't so bad once you get to know it.'

'Are you trying to be funny?'

He shrugs. 'I made the best of a bad situation.'

'How can you make the best of anything here?'

Logan summons his key. 'Thanatos is a good drinking partner and, like I said, the Isle of the Blessed is a beautiful place.'

'You go drinking with Thanatos, the Demon of Death?'

A shaft of light blinds us when Logan's key opens a doorway back to Earth. He grabs my arm and pulls me through.

46

AUTHOR'S NOTE

I f you've made it this far, thank you for reading and please consider leaving a review.

A massive shout out to all the amazing people in my life who enable me to write my stories. Publishing my work is daunting because it's sharing a little piece of my soul with you and that's scary. I feel very honoured that you'd spend your time reading my works and I appreciate every single one of you.

I hope you enjoyed the second book in the *Siren Series*. Sorry for the cliffhanger ending but I promise you'll find out what happens in the third and final book of this series (unless I write a spin off at some point).

Thank you for being so patient with me through the rewrites. I've got so many new stories to share, so watch this space. Book three is in progress and will be out later this year, so watch out for that too.

Another massive thank you for taking the time to read my books. I love you all and you're the reason I keep writing.

ABOUT THE AUTHOR

Hannah lives in Derbyshire, England. When she isn't reading or writing, she likes to walk in the Peak District, act like she knows what she's doing in life and hang out with her husband and son. She also loves coffee, chocolate and just eating in general.

Her passion for writing sparked through her love of reading as a child. She'd spend hours imagining fantastical places and adventures. Her desire for escapism only grew once she discovered the grim reality of adulting (boo hiss).

Hannah writes young adult paranormal, contemporary romance, fantasy, romantasy and science fiction. She is currently an Indie Author for her novels of which she has had to scale a very large learning curve — Several actually. She dabbles in short stories, copywriting and is also known for writing serials.

Hannah would love to hear from you. If you have questions about any of her books, interviews, book signings, etc, please use the email address or visit her on the socials listed below.

Email: hannahwestauthor@gmail.com
www.hannahwestauthor.co.uk

www.ingramcontent.com/pod-product-compliance
Lightning Source LLC
Chambersburg PA
CBHW061954170626
46813CB00006B/2641